I0602394

LUST FORGED
BOOK 8 OF THE GIFTING

LUST FORGED

The Gifting Series #8

Ex-socialite Leona wants nothing more than to enhance the mechanics within sex-cybs, not to mention improve their performances with their 'lovers.' It's a job where she's safe in an all-woman factory on Callisto, and far from her matchmaking mama. When the chief engineer is incapacitated, Leona's required to gift—her term would be pimp—sex-cyborgs to prospective clients. On an Etterian battleship, surrounded by gorgeous males, she tries not to think of sex when it's her work, especially with the Sub-Commander Aaro whose neon-blue eyes are the stuff of her erotic dreams.

As a diplomatic favor, Aaro must abandon his task to guard Earth, and perhaps find his *Dar Eth* or soulmate, all to protect cargo en route to many worlds, including the dangerous and unpredictable Yithia. Princess Oriana is most concerned for the two human female engineers determined to ensure the deliveries are successful. A simple enough mission until one human enters Aaro's cargo bay, dropping him to his knees.

But revealing to independent Leona that she's now trapped in a marriage isn't something Aaro can bring himself to do. He violates all he stands for, every ounce of honor by not telling her the truth. All in the hope she will choose to love him.

Also by Sevannah Storm

The Blood of Legends Series

The Huntress

The Healer

*

The Gifting Series

Soul Forged

Fate Forged

Sun Forged

War Forged

Star Forged

Shadow Forged

Earth Forged

Lust Forged

*

Standalones

Xiaxan Fox

Ire of Silver

The Shikari

Sol Survivor

*

Plump Playwright Series

Plump Jane

Seducing Amelia

Loving Finley

Keeping Tessa

Kissing Navy

*

COMING SOON

Inkoded

Fire Forged

The Crucible of the Eternal

Chapter One

The yowl of a panther marked the passing of another hour. Leona nursed her champagne, tempted to throw it back like a shot of tequila. Her black gown squeezed the air out of her lungs, and her heels pinched, yet here she smiled, bobbing her head at people she was supposed to know. Or care about.

Her mom, adorned in a silver-sequined gown, glided from guest to guest, her long nails trailing muscular arms. The more she flirted, the more tokens the gala event generated for those poor astro-hopper children. Leona grimaced. The spitting image of her mom, except for the eyes, she 'benefited' from her mother's more lecherous advances. The same men would accost Leona when possible. Like mother, like daughter, right?

"Leelee," Mom sang.

Leona winced and threw back her champagne before swapping the empty glass for a fresh flute.

"Mingle." Mom sidled beside her and faced the room. A cloud of rose-heavy perfume slapped Leona in the face. She sucked in a breath then held it, though, that was futile when she needed oxygen to live.

"Why? The same people attend these parties, Mom." *So boring.*

"Bradley's here."

Leona stilled and glared at her mom. "So?"

"He asked after you." Mom shook her wrist to drape her diamond tennis bracelet better as well as to catch the eye of any envious observers.

No matter how many times Leona rejected Bradley, he ignored her, proving how much her opinion mattered. Of course, with Mom on his side, Leona had two yapping dogs at her heels.

Leona cupped her mouth and pretended to whisper, "Oh? Did you tell him I had a vaginal infection just last week?"

A soft squeal strangled Mom, and she spun on Leona. "You never—"

"Discuss personal biological matters in public." Leona intoned in her best impression of Mom's high-cultured accent. "What about semen? Is that off the table?"

Mom gurgled, her face flushing coral.

"You have to know what that is, Mom. You of all people have exchanged bodily fluids, or will you finally put me out of my misery and tell me I'm adopted?"

With a death grip on Leona's forearm, Mom twirled, checking to see if anyone eavesdropped.

"That is enough. You will play nice, Leelee, or everything you take for granted will be snatched from under you."

Leona sighed. That threat again. "I won't marry Bradley to keep my apartment, Mom. And I sure as hell won't let him near Dad's investments."

"We shall see." She huffed off, sparing Leona from another second breathing in her cloying perfume.

Only tokens and social standing had mattered to Mom. Foisting Bradley onto Leona made sense from that perspective, though what she'd learned, the poor man was in dire straits financially. Mom must want to barter Leona's inheritance for his status. Regardless, she wanted no part of it.

Avoiding small talk and lecherous hands, she weaved through the crowds mingling to the background jungle sounds. She much preferred a thunderstorm to the constant chatter of birds and startling roars of predators. Classical music was abolished along with all forms of music too far back to remember. Something to do with a music vid causing mass epilepsy among young women. Though, humans being rebellious, the industry had moved underground for the most part. And governments being corrupt, the chance to cancel movies had been too tempting to resist. Which left the written word as the only means to while away time. Unfortunately, paperbacks after the eBook takeover were rare.

Stepping onto the balcony, she scanned it, searching for a quiet spot to pass the time. It had only been an hour, and despite it not being respectable to leave so soon, she was tempted.

The dome shimmered above the city skyline. The air tasted like stale sweat but was preferable to her mom's perfume. A cool breeze toyed with a curl draped artfully down her cheek. She leaned her elbows on the balustrade, peering across the crowded city. Cars zoomed up high or below, depending on their technology, and holograms curved around buildings, advertising the latest trends. Beyond that, distant stars glimmered, winking at her in enticement.

Facing the crowds, Leona studied them. The lighting added a golden glow to their joyful faces. No one was *that* happy. In the end, it was all false. Lies, politics, and greed awaited her pointless life. She had a degree in engineering, not that it made a difference to her mother's plans for her.

John Wright strolled past the gaping doors, a sex-cyb on his arm. Despite his graying temples and the thickening of his belly, his cheeks flushed with health. His bombastic laughter drowned out the jungle noises as he ushered his latest cyborg product around the room.

Owner and creator of Cyborg Enterprises, or Cyb Ent, wealthier than all the guests combined, he kissed cheeks, fondled asses, and made lewd comments. She shivered. Not that he had ever approached her. Still, she'd avoid him when possible.

A short brunette in silver appeared in her line of sight—Mom gliding toward her, and on her arm was the debonair Bradley Wentworth the Third.

Leona grimaced, wishing she could roll her eyes, flip them both the finger, and escape off-world. Instead, she straightened, squared her shoulders, and pasted on a polite smile. All those wasted years at finishing school kicked in, and she reverted to the perfect debutante. To do what she wanted, be who she wished to be, was a closely guarded dream. But if Mom said one word about Leona and Bradley doing anything together, even sharing a limo, she'd lose her shit.

"Bradley, how lovely to see you." She kissed each cheek, choking on his cologne.

With a delicate hand to her mouth, she cleared her throat. A husky voice would be construed as an invitation.

Suave, perfectly combed dark hair and hazel eyes, he cut a fine figure in his tailored tuxedo. Still, he made her skin crawl with his lingering gazes and not-so-subtle advances. Not to mention, how many times he'd cornered her for a quick fondle.

"Beautiful as ever, Leona." He flashed a smile, gracing her mom with it too. She giggled as if she was young enough to date him.

"I thought a June wedding would be lovely." Mom squeezed Leona's arm.

"Oh? For whom?" Leona fluttered her eyelashes in 'wild delight.'

"Why, you two, of course."

Leona dropped this useless charade. "No, that's never going to happen."

Mom sliced glances between her and Bradley while digging her nails into Leona's arm. "Don't be silly, Leelee, we discussed this."

Leona tugged her arm free and offered the sweetest smile. "No." Facing Bradley, she patted him on his upper arm. "You're a womanizer, think too highly of yourself, have no idea how to build wealth, and besides, you haven't proposed."

He opened his mouth to speak.

She held up her palm. "If you do, it's a thousand versions of no."

Mom dragged Leona aside. "Have you lost your mind?" she hissed, her cheeks red. It wasn't a good color on her. "I have never been so ashamed—"

"No, I won't marry a bully, lech, and spendthrift, Mom."

She gaped. "But—"

"So he comes from a prestigious family and has the connections to boost your standing. It's not enough for me. I'm not you. I don't care about any of this." She swept out a hand. "When will you realize that?"

Mom threw up her arms. "You're so like your father."

"Let me handle this, Elise." Bradley crowded Leona. "Leelee, please, stop this nonsense."

She glared. "I fucking hate being called Leelee, I don't care enough about you to marry you, and we have nothing in common, Bradley. I am done talking about this." She pointed at him. "Find someone who will fawn over you, because it won't be me." She turned her finger to her mom. "You, stop trying to live my life for me. No more controlling my every move."

"It's that damn university that ruined her." Mom flashed Bradley an apologetic smile. "She'll come around."

With a scream of sheer frustration, Leona abandoned all hope of an amicable parting. "Goodbye."

Mom whined, "Leelee, where do you think you're going?"

Bradley caught Mom's arm and held her back.

"Away from you. Don't try to find me." Leona strode off, whipping her skirt in agitation.

Mom called after her, and Leona muttered a curse, flipping her the finger. The crowd parted, gasping and tittering. It was the final straw, the impetus she needed. Kicking off her shoes, she ran, unraveling her tight coiffure, and tossing hairpins along the way.

She was done, free, and running. The first would be to get a job, somewhere so far her mother couldn't find her. Tokens weren't an issue thanks to Dad's investments. He'd divorced Mom for a woman much nicer, bought a yacht, and hadn't survived a tropical storm. Not that Leona begrudged him what little happiness he'd found.

With a wave, she hailed a cab and climbed in. Not once did she look back. She grinned, excitement sweeping through her like bubbly champagne.

The sky had never looked more beautiful. The city glowed with bright pinks, reds, and oranges from the many billboards. Her smile refused to fade. With a swipe of her wrist across the paypad, she leaped from the cab when it stopped outside her apartment building. Throwing things into a bag, she chose only what she might need. Okay, maybe one evening dress, but no heels, just boots, jeans, T-shirts, and the shifting digital photo-frame of her father.

She yanked the dress over her head and let it pool on the floor. With a giggle, she kicked it, uncaring that it was precious silk. Pulling on leggings, a baggy T-shirt with her university emblem, and sneakers, she was ready to walk away from her life. Mom would cut off her funds, but Dad had been sneaky, leaving a separate account with a tidy sum for Leona. She'd learned long ago that only the public image mattered. Knowing her mom, she planned to bamboozle Leona into staying, obeying, and birthing babies with Mom's ideal man.

Leona sat on the bed, the bag at her feet.

Activating her phone on her palm, she dialed her old professor, then pinned her hand to her cheek and her fingers across her ear. Now, for the next step in her impromptu escape plan.

"Well, a blast from the past." Dale Ellison laughed.

"Hi, Professor. I need your help." She winced. Talk about abandoning all niceties.

"Oh?" He paused. "What have you done, Leona?"

She squared her shoulders and said, "I'm running away from home."

"A little late, but hey, who am I to judge. So, how can I help?"

She drew a pattern on her knee with a manicured fingernail, silently praying he could help her. "A job not on Earth. Preferably on the outskirts of the universe."

"Ah, now that's something doable. Here I worried you'd ask me for a kidney. Sore out of those, my dear." He coughed. "I do know of some vacancies at Cyb Ent."

She slumped, then stiffened her shoulders. Sacrifices had to be made for her own good. "Will I have to deal with John Wright?"

"I doubt it. I have other contacts. I'll drop them all a message. They'll call you."

Shit, now she had to wait? Where? Maybe getting on a shuttle and leaving Earth might be wise. She could think of it as a vacation. "Thanks, Professor. If I can escape Earth before my mom descends—"

"You're avoiding your troubles, Leona."

She huffed. "You don't know my mother. She trains bulldogs, she's that tenacious."

"I met her once, so you have my sympathy. I believe, if my memory serves me well, she squeezed my ass."

Heat burned Leona's cheeks, and she swallowed the lump forming in her throat. *Yup, that sounds like Mom.* "I'm sorry."

Dale chuckled. "I shouldn't complain. It's been a while since a beautiful woman propositioned me."

Leona snorted and clapped a hand across her mouth. "Thanks for the assistance, Professor."

She stared at her palm, a giggle slipping free. Grabbing her bag, she jogged out of her apartment to hail another cab. Destination: the spaceport.

Chapter Two

Lunar Base orbiting the moon
One year later

LEONA NURSED A COFFEE, the real kind. Fake cream topped it, but the beans were from Ganymede, and the coffee flavor wasn't an imitation. It was the one thing she splurged on, dipping into the funds her father had left her. She hummed after another sip. He'd approve. She studied her nails lined with grease. He'd approve of that too.

Licking the sweetened cream off her lips, she gazed through the café's windows to the bustling port below. A flickering dome protected the people while ships of all sizes docked. A speedster zipped behind an ice hauler plodding along. Like bobbing heads of flamingos, mechanical platforms dipped and rose around the crafts they refueled or repaired. Beyond was the endless expanse of space. It felt surreal to sip coffee with stars engulfing her view. A far cry from balconies at extravagant parties on Earth. She wouldn't change this for a second of her old life, except perhaps for more time with her father.

Flicking hair out of her eyes, she admired the play of sunlight and artificial beams off the ships: speedsters, haulers, researchers, salvagers, and hers, a luxury cruiser.

Professor Ellison had come through for her, landing her an engineering post on a trillionaire's ship. She could count on one hand how many times she'd met her 'boss.' For the most part, they ferried dignitaries, politicians, and celebrities to the outskirts of the galaxy—a trip to see the Milky Way up close.

Despite visiting Lunar Base often, she wasn't here long enough for anyone in high society to recognize her. And on board the cruiser, the captain, Dunny, dealt with their guests, leaving her to ensure the ship ran smoothly. Not the piloting part. Navigating through asteroid belts or a crowded docking seemed a little hazardous. Although, truth be known, having such power under her control did sound intriguing.

Overall, her job was perfect, making her a moving target for anyone Mom would hire to find her.

She choked on a sip of coffee when a massive battleship slid into view. It had to be a substantial distance from the docks, but at this angle, it dominated. People stared. As did she.

Sleek and gray, it caught any light and shimmered. Who the hell owned such a ship? She didn't doubt its lethal capabilities, not with seven gigantic canons mounted to the bow, port, starboard, and stern. The fuel for this thing, she imagined, could power the Lunar Station for a year. Her fingers twitched at the thought of inspecting their engines.

A bay door opened and out shot a smaller ship like a flattened drop of mercury. It docked below without fanfare. There was no waiting time, nothing to hinder the new arrivals. The men striding out in military garb as black as night made her grin: Etterians. She should have known. Sure, she'd heard of this new species but never had the privilege of seeing them in real life. Images on her Optical Data Implant or O.D.I. embedded in her left wrist, couldn't compare to reality. Not that she was close enough to note the details. From this distance, they were tall, about six-foot-ish, broad-shouldered, bulging biceps, and barrel-chested with thick braids trailing them. They formed an impressive example of manhood.

"Gorgeous, right?" Melissa sank into the chair opposite Leona.

"Yes," she rasped, cleared her throat, then chuckled. "I've never seen a more beautiful ship."

"Oh, Leona, you're hopeless." Mel shoved her dark hair off her shoulder to plaster her face to the glass. "Do you think I could walk up to one and proposition him?"

Her garbled words summoned a flood of scenarios. Leona almost pitied the man she approached.

She faced Leona while bouncing in her seat. "Do you think Dunny would delay departure for an hour or ten?" She wiggled her eyebrows. As the luxury cruiser *Riptide's* hostess, why not?

Leona snapped her gaze to where the *Riptide* was docked. It looked so tiny compared to the Etterian's smaller ship. In canary yellow with blue stripes, the diamond-shaped cruiser was a child's plaything. She gasped.

Jumping to her feet, she splayed her fingers on the table and narrowly missed knocking over her cup. "What the hell?" The *Riptide* had powered up. It bolted.

A ping zinged up her arm. Activating her O.D.I., she read the message. Her ears hummed while she blinked as if in slow motion.

"Fired? How dare he." She grimaced at the bitter bile coating her tongue and hurriedly sipped her coffee. The timing was too perfect like Dunny had something to hide from the Etterians? Or was he just antsy with a battleship on the horizon?

"What?" Mel dragged her gaze from the Etterians striding down the causeway. Even from this distance, their bronze skin shimmered. A human ambassador scurried alongside them.

"*Riptide*'s gone, babe. We've been fired."

Mel gaped. "But... What about my stuff? All my clothes?" She activated her O.D.I. "That fucker. When I get my hands on him..."

"Still, he's going to have to pack my things, and him touching my underwear coils my stomach." Leona rested a hand on her belly as if doing so eradicated the images of Dunny's fat fingers clutching her favorite bra.

"Now what?" Mel slumped. "This is goodbye?"

"I'm afraid so, Mel." Leona grimaced. "I like this as much as you do." She tapped her requirements into her O.D.I and browsed the job market, check-marking the interesting ones.

Mel shrugged. "Well, I was thinking of taking a vacay to the ice pools of Europa."

Leona hesitated, hovering a finger over the green tick on a job at Cyb Ent. Could she work for John Wright? She doubted she'd meet him or that he'd remember her from her former life. "Oh, too cold for me, babe. Try Hawaii Island." She hit the green tick and pinched her lips. Jobless, she couldn't be choosy, and the job mentioned relocating to a moon around Jupiter.

"Too expensive after that eruption destroyed half the island."

Leona glanced at Mel. Yeah, that had been bad and unexpected. The minimal plume hadn't affected Earth's atmosphere for long, but the lava flows had wiped out most of the resorts and homes.

"Besides, I could do with a sugar daddy for a while, and maybe the parties at the Blue Eden on Europa would be just the right place to find such a man...or woman." Mel grinned, leaped out of her chair, and paused. "Better buy clothes for the trip." She chewed on her bottom lip. "Oh, and I need to find a ship headed that way. Duh. I'll check in when I'm settled." A quick kiss to Leona's cheek and she was gone, leaving Leona to stare at her empty cup.

She should've known things were going too well. It had been over a year since she'd abandoned Earth, her mom, and Bradley. Hell, she hadn't thought of them in months.

Mel was right, though. A few items of clothing would be needed, no matter what path the future took. Leona swiped her wrist over the paypad and left the café. Weaving through the busy causeways, she aimed for the elevator while considering her options. Upstairs on the Grand level were better but pricier shops. Still, investing in decent undergarments meant they lasted longer. What were the chances she would run into anyone she knew? Zero. She chuckled. Earth belonged to the upper echelon of society. Most thought space travel beneath them except for short vacations to gaze upon a nebula or black hole or to attend an unavoidable event. Though, she doubted they'd travel to the moon. The trip would be such an inconvenience, y'know.

Stepping out of the elevator onto crisp beige flooring, subtle lighting, clean walls, and expensive displays didn't spare her from spying a familiar man in the crowd. She blinked, at first unable to place his scruffy beard and hair. Then she cringed and spun on her heel. *Can my day get any worse?*

The elevator doors had closed, trapping her. *Apparently, yes.* She punched the button, summoning the next one, and prayed Bradley hadn't seen her. *What are the effing odds?*

"About damn time I found you, Leelee." He gripped her arm, digging his nails into her skin.

"I hate Leelee." She yanked but to no avail. "How did you find me?" Scowling at him, she tugged again.

He scoffed and tightened his grip, sending pins and needles to her fingertips. "Like I don't have spies? They let me know every time the *Riptide* was scheduled to dock here. I hopped onto the first shuttle every time but couldn't catch you."

Shit. "For a year?" She shuddered. "Go away, Bradley. Find some other heiress."

"My father approved this match, otherwise I wouldn't bother with a snobby bitch like you. You're coming with me. You've sent me on a merry chase, and I've had enough."

Despite the numbness of her arm, she faced him, shoving her face into his. She'd never seen him this unkempt, but the reason behind his state didn't matter enough for her to ask. "Leave me alone, or so help me, I'll donate all my tokens to a charity. I don't want anything to do with you or my mother. Why can't you accept that?"

"You don't know *what* you want." He sneered. "You are un-equipped to go it alone, demeaning yourself and whoring your way across the galaxy."

The elevator pinged.

His focus flew to the occupants in the elevator. At last, he released her. "Come with me or else, Leelee."

Rubbing her arm, she shook her head. "Goodbye, Bradley." She stepped backward into the elevator, her gaze fixed on him. If he followed, she'd scream. That would bring security to her aid and buy her a chance to escape.

When the doors closed on his face, she slumped. Relief flooded her, but the hairs on the nape of her neck remained sensitive. Until she was far from Earth and its moon, she wasn't safe. She wouldn't put it past him to kidnap her. Had Mom made a deal with Bradley Senior? Sold Leona to the highest bidder?

"Silly idiot. Or else? Who speaks like that?" she muttered. Finding a job was imperative and now urgent. She punched her O.D.I, and scanned the jobs she'd applied for. Nothing yet. "Shit. Shit. Shit."

The elevator climbed to the corporate and ambassadorial offices on the upper levels. She had time to choose the next destination. No way would she return to Grand, but she did need clothes. After that encounter, she longed for a stiff drink. She raised her chin and stared at the elevator buttons. Safety was in a crowd. The Sky Lounge, its lettering highlighted in gold, seemed the best option. Might as well go to the top, find a dark booth, and order online.

When the elevator stopped, an arm reached over her head and held the door open.

"Thank you," she said and met the man's gaze. All thoughts slammed out of her head. Dark blue eyes, riveting against bronzed skin, blinked at her. Filling the elevator were Etterian men, their gazes on her.

"You are welcome, milady."

Heat scorched her cheeks when she realized they waited for her to exit. She did so on rubbery knees. Holy shit, they were *gorgeous*. Mel had been right about that. The use of 'milady' fluttered butterflies in her chest. How Arthurian, as if she was nobility and precious. Eager to save face, she veered toward the Sky Lounge, following the signage. The men trailed her, escorted by a gibbering ambassador.

When she strolled into the bar, the hostess ran a gaze over Leona's oil-stained cargo pants and tight tank. She'd forgotten she wasn't dressed for the upper echelon. That was to be expected when she'd only been granted a short leave. The promise of a coffee had canceled her usual concern over her attire.

"A table, preferably by the window." She met the woman's hard gaze while using her classiest finishing-school accent.

"We are fully booked," the hostess snapped.

"Join us," an Etterian offered.

The hostess flicked her glare at the men behind Leona then paled.

Squaring her shoulders and plastering on a smile, Leona faced the men. "I couldn't possibly intrude—"

"Please."

At the man's intense gaze, she relented. "Thank you."

The ambassador, in his embroidered cloak, dark leggings, and slippers, scurried ahead. Before Leona could follow, two Etterians led the way, another ushered her in front of him, and the rest fell into line. They surrounded her with a wall of muscle like she was royalty. The patrons watched them pass. This day was *so* not going her way.

When they reached a table, they waited for her to slide in first. She hurried to do so, then rested her elbows on the edge of the glass table, staring at the many armor-cladded sets of legs visible beneath. Chunky black boots adorned their feet.

"Your drink preference?" The ambassador arched a brow, his lips pursed.

"Cognac."

He scowled but placed her order. "Sirs?" He scanned the men crowding the booth.

"What would you suggest?" The Etterian who'd invited her met her gaze.

"Depends on what type of day you've had." Hell, she might even order a second cognac.

He grinned, forming a dimple in his left cheek. "A good one."

"Ah, then perhaps a soda, a fruit juice, or a cocktail."

His eyelashes fluttered, drawing attention to their absurd length. "A fruit juice seems safest."

She scanned his broad shoulders and doubted he ever worried about safety. "Mango is my favorite, though a good orange juice, freshly squeezed, is amazing."

"Very well, we shall try those, Ambassador Hyatt."

The man beamed and nodded at the waitress.

"Your cognac implies what sort of day for you?" another man asked.

"The best until my colleague and I were fired. Just as you arrived. Captain's guilty conscience, perhaps?" She dipped her chin at the truth in her jest. What had Dunny done? There were rumors he'd been smuggling something, but she'd never paid it much attention. "Then running into my mother's idea of the perfect husband for me. Now coffee is too weak for how frustrated I am." She stared out the window at the same view as earlier, only higher up.

"I am Supreme Commander Nerx." He gestured to his men. "Sub-Commander Matir, Medic Aldur, Data Officer Ziot, and Pilot Edon."

"A pleasure to meet you all. I'm Leona Williams." She settled her attention on the oldest of the men, Aldur. He must have been in his early fifties if she judged the lines marring his features. No gray peppered his tight braid. Still, each man around the table had been smacked with the handsome stick.

"This is Ambassador Hyatt. He is accompanying us while we await permission to land on Earth."

"How do you do, Ambassador." She bowed her head.

A ping shot up her arm, and she smiled in apology. A scan confirmed a job offer at a Cyb Ent factory on Callisto. She grimaced but accepted it. The tokens were good and the package better than on *Riptide*. Instructions followed, including her passage on the first transporter heading for Callisto. She had a few hours until its departure.

Despite what she'd heard of Cyb Ent, their security was top-notch. Except, of course, for their sex center on the surface. Bradley wouldn't be able to find her in the bowels of Callisto. Nor would he make it past the center. Perhaps working for John Wright wouldn't be so bad, after all.

"Here you are," Bradley's voice sliced through her moment of jubilance.

She didn't respond. Instead, she tapped on her O.D.I. to log a harassment complaint, adding her father's old friend and retired judge to the message. Every Christmas, he checked in with her, keeping abreast of her life. It was at his insistence she contact him should this situation not resolve itself. He knew full well what her mother and Bradley were capable of

"Come now, Leelee." The fool stood in the passage and gestured as if he expected her to leap over the table to grasp his hand.

She stared at him.

His face flushed the color of a young beet. His gaze darted around the table. "Don't make me call your mother."

Under the vigilance of the Etterians, Leona was torn between a sense of security and embarrassment. What must they think of her? Disobedient? A bad daughter?

"Please, call my mother, and I shall explain...again, how I don't want to marry you. If you're after Dad's tokens, she's spent it all, including my trust fund. Quit being her lapdog, Bradley."

His cheeks trembled. A twitch formed below his left eye.

"Excuse me." A waitress squeezed between him and the table to slide across glasses of fruit juice. She placed Leona's cognac with a little more reverence, as expected.

"Leelee—"

"The lady has spoken," Nerx said, his voice firm, his words clipped. "I suggest you abandon this path you have chosen."

Bradley bristled. "I don't know who you are, but this is a private matter."

She swallowed hard, considering leaving with him to avoid a scene. But her legs wouldn't work. Every part of her didn't want to be alone with him.

Five Etterians rose, looming over Bradley, who had to lean back to maintain eye contact. As much as Leona wanted to see the shit kicked out of him, the way the ambassador hopped from one foot to the other had her envisioning a diplomatic incident playing out.

"It's best you leave." She matched Nerx's tone. "You've had my answer. It hasn't changed and never will."

"You say that now," he snapped, his gaze shifting between the men.

"Security, please remove this man." The ambassador gestured to Bradley.

With her gaze willing him to leave, she missed security's arrival. Two beefy men in blue uniforms gripped Bradley by the arms and dragged him out of the Sky Lounge.

Leona grimaced, left to handle the aftermath. Her cheeks burned, and yet, she couldn't deny the warmth of relief pooling in her belly. "I'm sorry, Ambassador Hyatt, my mother—" She pressed her lips together. No explanation could excuse Bradley's behavior. "Thank you." She tried to meet the gazes of the Etterians, hoping to convey her sincerity. One by one, they settled in their seats.

The tension eased from her shoulders. She drew the cognac closer and cupped it, waiting impatiently for the heat from her palms to warm the brandy. The men grumbled and mumbled, nodding as if they understood each other. She sipped from the snifter, savoring the smoky flavor as it burned its way from her tongue to her belly. Yes, this was what she'd needed.

A ping from her O.D.I. confirmed Dad's friend, the ex-judge, had filed a restraining order against Bradley *and* her mother. The latter was a surprise but so welcome. She grinned and lifted the drink to the Etterians and Hyatt. "To new beginnings."

Hyatt swirled his whisky before throwing it back. She hid a grimace at what her presence had put the poor man through. The Etterians mimicked the raising of their glasses, with frowns marring their brows.

"It's a toast," she said.

Their eyelashes fluttered again before they lifted their drinks.

She opened her mouth to ask, but Aldur tilted his mango juice at her. "To new acquaintances, milady."

"Permission has been granted," Nerx said and placed an empty glass on the table.

As one, the men rose. Leona hurried to do the same, throwing back the cognac like it was water. "Sorry, Dad," she whispered. Without thinking, she swiped her wrist over the paypad and grimaced. Right, that mistake would be expensive.

The ambassador gaped, but she nodded at him as if paying a fortune for freshly squeezed juice and decades-old cognac was the norm for her. It used to be. She glanced at the Etterians. So worth it. Had she been alone with Bradley, who knew what he might have tried.

"May we escort you to your destination?" Nerx asked, his scowl darkening his eyes.

"No, thank you. I need to purchase a few things before boarding a transporter." She shoved her hand out. "Thank you, again."

He shook her hand, as did the others. They stroked her knuckles or held her hand longer that was necessary like it was the first time they'd touched a woman. After saving her ass, they could hold her hand for as long as they wanted to. Then with a smile in place, she marched down the passage and slipped into the closing elevator doors.

Chapter Three

Adjusting the new backpack over her shoulder, Leona waited at dock 'D46,' her gaze fixed on the transporter before her. Frequent sweeps of the crowds confirmed no Bradley stormed toward her. Boarders had formed a queue, and like a law-abiding citizen, she slotted into place. The ship looked to be in good condition with a recent paint job. A few scrapes and dents showed through the crisp white. Those were expected with a ship class this antique. Still, the old girl had been well-cared for. ShipCo was a reputable transportation company that had started as a courier service and had decades ago extended to personnel carriers. Their logo blazed across many docked ships, from haulers to speedsters.

The hatch opened, and a man in a crisp white uniform stepped onto the ramp. "I'm Liaison Officer Fedorov." He raised a tablet. "Cyb Ent employees Williams and O'Sullivan?"

"Here," a woman huffed, staggering under a mountain of luggage.

A waterfall of silver-blonde hair cascaded over her face. Tight jeans and a black tank hugged a curvaceous figure. Ballet slippers made her feet look tiny. Leona grimaced and glanced at her mid-calf black boots into which she'd tucked her cargo pantlegs. Nothing feminine there, but then again, she hadn't been fired in her casual clothes.

"I'm Williams," she called, slipping out of the queue.

"This way." Fedorov gestured.

Stuck behind O'Sullivan, Leona could do nothing but watch as the poor woman tried to squeeze her luggage through the narrow door. There was no help Leona could offer without worsening the situation.

"So sorry," the woman whispered.

"No problem." Leona smiled despite the impatience that tapped her foot on the metallic and demagnetized causeway. She studied the people going about their business, half-expecting Bradley to emerge. She wanted on the ship and off the moon, A.S.A.P.

Fedorov waited patiently, not once giving a hand. After O'Sullivan thumped and massaged the last bag through, Leona followed. She veered around the sweating woman and paused in front of the officer.

"Cyb Ent have secured V.I.P. seating for their employees." He sighed. "That would be you. This way..." A pulse ticked at the base of his jaw. "Please."

This time, Leona stayed on his six, letting O'Sullivan labor behind her. They marched through three large rooms housing rows of seats—each one semi-enclosed with a safety bar raised—toward the cockpit and along a short passage.

He stopped outside a lockered alcove. "Stow your luggage here." He pointed to the ceiling and the hatch through which a ladder disappeared. "Your seats are on top for the best view."

O'Sullivan groaned while she trudged behind Leona. "Damnit, I'm too unfit for this bullshit," she muttered.

Leona's lips twitched, but she reined in the smile threatening to slip free. "Thank you, sir." She removed her backpack, slid it into an open locker, and snapped the door shut with her thumb on the biometrics.

A grunting O'Sullivan kicked her luggage to fit the narrow lockers. Up the ladder Leona climbed, trailing Fedorov. The view, framed by thick seals, showed parts of the Lunar Base and Earth in the distance. Six seats faced the curved glass. Leona chuckled at her good fortune, having expected to endure an uncomfortable chair and an irritating neighbor for the duration of the flight. Each V.I.P. chair was luxury: padded, semi-cocooned, with cryopen dispensers. *Nice.*

She chose the center of the row and lowered herself into the seat's plush confines.

"The auto-servo will serve you any beverage or meal of your choice." Fedorov cast a glance at O'Sullivan, who crawled through the hatch before peeling herself off the floor. "Have a pleasant flight." He disappeared down the hatch, leaving them alone.

The woman collapsed into the seat beside Leona. A sheen of sweat dewed her cheeks and forehead. Strands of hair stuck to her skin. "Hi, I'm Sophia."

"Leona."

"I thought I would miss my flight." Sophia hitched a thumb at her luggage. "Had to move out on short notice." Her lips curled in disdain. "Found out my fiancé had a few just-in-case women on the side." She grimaced and raised a shiny gaze to the ceiling. "Storage bays on Lunar are expensive as hell. Cyb Ent came to the rescue."

"Same."

Sophia fake-gaped. "You dated Simon too?"

"I got fired this morning, applied at Cyb Ent, and here I am," Leona said.

Sophia sighed. "Sorry, sounds like you had a shitty day."

"It started with the best intentions." Leona pressed a button on her armrest. A door opened, and an auto-servo in a tuxedo jacket rolled toward her on track-guided wheels. Behind it was deep closet forming a narrow galley. "A Ganymede coffee, please."

"Oh, yes, that sounds amazing." Sophia clapped, her dark green eyes twinkling.

"As ordered," the machine droned and wheeled backward.

"So, what's your life story?" Leona asked, her gaze fixed on the ships and cranes through the glass.

"Nothing much. Lost my folks at an early age, which made me the surrogate mom to my younger sister, Thea." Sophia ran her palms along her armrests. "She'll follow once I'm settled. I left her on Earth to finish high school."

"Alone?" Leona gaped.

"Yes, for a few months." Sophia cast her gaze downward. "We have to eat, which means I need to work where I can find it."

"True." Leona stiffened. She was in the same boat. Paying for the juice and cognac, though a faux pas, might have major consequences. "I suppose it's tough for her, watching you head into the unknown."

Sophia shrugged while picking at a loose thread on her jeans. "She thinks I have Simon. Thea's independent, has her own ideas on how she wants to live, to survive. She has these dreams of studying further." Sophia winced. "I can't afford to send her anywhere."

Leona couldn't relate. Even in death, Dad had ensured she had whatever she needed or wanted. Getting into her preferred university was a given, and the cost negligible. "Doesn't Cyb Ent have an education program?"

"They do if Thea works for them for three years after graduating." Sophia slumped. "She doesn't want to make that sacrifice."

"Three years can be a long time for the young."

Sophia giggled. "Decades long. You?"

Leona hesitated. Mentioning being born with a golden spoon in her mouth might not go down well. She couldn't lie either. "My mother's trying to force me to marry an ass. I'm on the run, and underground on Callisto seemed the best place to hide."

"Holy shit." Sophia cupped her mouth.

"Yup, he showed up on Lunar today. Etterians saved me."

"No." Sophia gaped. "I'd heard they were on the station. Are they as gorgeous as in the digi-mags?"

Leona laughed. "Yup, even Medic Aldur in his fifties was sexy as hell."

"It's a pity I didn't see them." Sophia clasped her hands to her chest. "I could do with a soulmate."

Leona hummed. "Yes, that's right. They believe in that nonsense."

Sophia gasped. "You don't?"

"Nope. Two people destined to be each other's forever?" Leona unclenched her fingers. "I might be a little jaded. Mom and Dad... Their divorce was...bitter. Then Dad died on a cruise with his mistress."

Tears filled Sophia's eyes. "Oh, I'm so sorry."

Whoa. Leona studied Sophia's genuine reaction for a moment then hurried to say, "It happened a while ago, but I like to believe he was, at last, happy."

Sophia accepted the coffee the auto-servo offered her. Leona did the same. She cradled the cup and inhaled the pure goodness. Starting and ending the day like this was heaven, regardless of what had happened.

"What did you apply for?" Sophia asked between sips.

Leona glanced at her. "Engineer." Though what she'd do, she didn't know.

"Same, but I don't have any experience. I'm coming into this job a newbie." Sophia scrunched her nose.

Leona smiled. "I'm sure they'll have something perfect for you. Experience comes with time and practice."

"True." Sophia downed her coffee and handed the cup to the auto-servo. "I had a shitty night. Do you mind if I nap?"

"No, not at all. Need a cryopen to sleep?" On instinct, Leona raised her hand to swipe the paypad. She resisted lowering her arm when she realized Sophia might not be able to afford a pen.

Sophia paled. "No, I'm good."

"Suit yourself." Leona raised her coffee, inhaled, then took a sip while Sophia clipped the safety bar in place.

From her O.D.I., Leona texted an old friend of Dad's, asking him to look into Thea O'Sullivan and whether she would be a candidate for a scholarship. That was all Leona could do for now. Dad had invested in a few educational funds across various industries. Perhaps one of them might suit Thea's goals.

Leona ordered a bowl of steamed dumplings, having not eaten since breakfast.

While she ate, she glanced at a sleeping Sophia who was worried about experience. Leona'd been headhunted by cruisers and haulers, but *Riptide* had been cushy. Maybe her opportunities were due to her degree. How had Sophia gotten into engineering? Where had she studied? Cyb Ent wouldn't hire just anyone, Leona was sure.

She settled back when a voice announced their imminent departure. In a few hours, her second attempt at a new life would begin. One where she worked for the most lecherous man in the galaxy. So horny, he'd invented sex machines. Still, they were incredible, or so she'd discovered. Some of his schematics he'd made open source and were used for course material. She knew the intricate workings of a sex-cyb, so, in a way, she was ideal to work for Cyb Ent. It was quite ingenious, come to think of it. Allow the universities and colleges to train your future workforce. Nowhere had anyone ever implied that John Wright wasn't brilliant.

For the first time, she considered what her job might entail. Hopefully, she got to work with sex-cybs and not on their factory line. Building cybs like a jigsaw puzzle didn't appeal to her. If she could be allowed to help perfect the sex-cyb's movements and mannerisms... That it had to do with sex, well, she'd had a few lovers during her studies, but making their reactions more human was breaking technology. Sure, artificial intelligence had been the core focus for centuries, but to give sex-cybs A.I. would be inhumane, turning them into sex slaves. It was safer to consider them luxury sex toys than a machine with emotions, thoughts, and hopes.

Night sounds played on the speakers, hushed to not disturb, and perhaps induce sleep in those unable to afford cryopens. Using a pen for such a short journey was a waste of tokens. Leona adjusted the chair's embedded heater, sighing when warmth seeped into her muscles.

As the stars sped past with Mars the size of a marble, her eyelids drooped.

LEONA AWOKE TO SOPHIA leaning over her. "What? Have we arrived?"

"Yup." Sophia gestured to the glass. A dome separated them from the arid wasteland of Callisto.

Leona pushed herself up and took the time to stretch. She peered at the platform on which the transporter had landed. A rectangular opening led underground. Two women stood in front of it. One wore black overalls, the other flaunted a crisp white designer suit. Circling them were four women in red military garb. The colors had to mean something.

"It's us they're waiting for. The tourists have been ushered into the sex center."

"Oh," Leona gasped and bolted for the hatch. With her backpack slung over a shoulder, she helped Sophia wrestle her luggage free. Once the mountain had been piled on the provided trolley, they strode toward the women.

One was tall, broad-shouldered, and muscular, with long brown hair in a tight braid. She held her shoulders back, almost military in stance. "Sophia O'Sullivan?"

"That's me." Sophia did a finger wave.

"Tina Olson." She grinned. "Welcome. Come with me, and I'll get you settled."

Sophia cast a glance at Leona, hesitated, then trailed Tina. They paused on a flat surface then slowly descended out of sight.

"Leona, I am Cary Bacharach. Welcome to Callisto and Cyb Ent. Mr. Wright will see you now."

Leona smothered a squeak. This was...unexpected. Not once had she considered he'd be planetside.

Cary didn't wait, spun on a heel, then stepped onto the platform. Leona hurried to do the same. She spread her legs as if she was on her father's yacht. The lift lowered, smooth as butter. Holographic railings appeared. Levels whizzed past the lower they traveled, flickering scenes of offices, drafting rooms, canteens, training rooms, and vast factories. The only one with passages and doors had to be the barracks. The temperature cooled, and the air became thin but remained breathable. She shivered, wishing she'd bought a jacket. Four sets of clothes were all she'd managed to fit into the backpack. When she was settled, she'd place an order.

Her darting thoughts served as a distraction. Why would Wright want to see her? She clasped her hands in front of her, squeezing and releasing her fingers to calm her nerves.

The platform hummed as it slowed to a stop. Cary stepped onto the plush carpet of an office. *Wooden* bookshelves lined the walls and were stacked with paperbacks, hardcovers, and bric-a-brac. A solid walnut desk sat to one side.

"This is my office. Beyond is Mr. Wright's." Cary marched across to the paneled door and entered, turning to wait for Leona.

"Ms. Williams?" John Wright rose from behind his larger desk and crossed a Persian rug to clasp her hand, urging her farther into his office.

Her upbringing kicked in, and she summoned a veil of politeness. He was known to be a lech, but the urge to flee didn't grip her. She would, however, continue to be on guard.

"Ganymede coffee, please, Cary." He settled his brown gaze on Leona. "That is your preferred beverage?"

Leona nodded, her tongue tied.

"Excellent." He released her and gestured for her to sit in one of his plush *leather* highback chairs.

She hesitated. *Holy shit, wood and leather?* He was wealthy, but this extravagance? Where did one find either in this day and age? Mom didn't even live in this level of luxury. Aware he waited, she still didn't budge. He'd made no lewd comment, hadn't ogled her like she'd seen him do at parties... In fact, he came across as a friend with powerful resources.

"Let me cut to the chase, Leona. Your extrication from your mother's clutches was a splendid display of independence. Rigel would have been proud."

Leona sank into a chair, trying not to gape at him. "Of course, you knew my father."

"I've been waiting for you to apply at Cyb Ent since Ellison called me." John chose a chair beside her. "You weren't the smartest in your class, but problem-solving during cybs studies has kept my eye on you."

She blinked. "Why wait?"

"You have to *want* to work here. Cyb Ent has a certain..." He grimaced. "Shall we say, distasteful reputation? Stands to reason when we're all about sex." He ran his fingers through his gray-laced blond hair. With a dismissive hand, he gestured to his khaki slacks and plain white button-up shirt. "This is more me, but one must play a part. The clientele expects it." He twisted the dull platinum band on his ring finger. "You might not believe this, but I have never...tested my products. My late wife, Yvonne, was my everything." He cast his gaze downward. "I know how the universe perceives me. Let them think what they will." He raised his chin when Cary entered, carrying a tray.

"So, you knew I was using my grandmother's maiden name?" Leona accepted the offered cup and saucer, the delicious aroma of coffee teasing her nose.

"Yes, and the Wentworths knows this too. Best to change it again." John smiled at Cary as he too helped himself to a cup. "I have my best people on it. To Earth, you don't work here."

Leona sipped her coffee, her gaze on the man. "Thank you, Mr. Wright, but why help me?"

"Rigel would have done the same for my daughter, God rest her soul."

That's right. His wife and daughter had died in an assassination attempt.

"I'm sorry for your loss, and yes, Dad would have." Leona finished her coffee and slid the cup and saucer onto his desk, careful not to scuff the wood. "What do you expect from me?"

"What do you want to do?"

She froze. What a delightful opportunity. She grabbed at it with both hands while excitement zinged through her body. "To perfect the sexual experience. I know the cyb's mechanics, as ingenious as they are. What would make the experience more pleasurable is if the cybs perform better, more naturally. I imagine Maloidians and algri would require different approaches. Not to mention..." She blushed, not wanting to imagine Nerx in such a light. "Etterians."

John clapped his hands once. "Then that is what you'll do. Your choice of assistant, of course. We're about upskilling and empowering our employees."

"I've only met Sophia O'Sullivan. I'll assess the other engineers and inform you of my decision, Mr. Wright."

"Call me John when we're alone or around Cary." He pressed a button on his desk. "Babe, send in Chief Sugar." He grimaced, revealing his opinion of the woman. "You'll report to me, but for appearance's sake, Chief Sugar is your superior."

Leona bowed her head. "Odd name."

"She'll explain the hierarchy. I play my role well, Leona. It's kept me revered or hated, not to mention sane. Cyb Ent has over forty-two thousand employees." He slumped for a second before straightening. "Too many people depend on me for survival."

"Right away, Big Daddy," Cary said through the intercom.

Big Daddy, Leona mouthed.

John winked at her.

The door opened to the tall blonde who'd swept Sophia away. "You called, Big Daddy?"

"Chief Sugar, this is Leona, a recent hire as an engineer. See her settled, and take special care of her."

"Will do." Tina ran a long perusal over Leona when she pushed out of the leather chair. Tina's lips pursed, her cheeks flushed, and the admiration in her eyes said she liked the look of Leona.

Oh, so that's how the cookie crumbles. Leona wasn't interested in anything romantic if Tina was thinking along those lines. After they shook hands, Leona nodded at John, then trailed Tina onto the platform.

"Welcome to Callisto. Babe gave me a heads-up that you're destined for my division. I've placed you and Sophia next to each other since you arrived together."

"Thank you." Leona frowned. "Babe?"

Tina sighed. "Big Daddy, A.K.A. Mr. Wright, doesn't want to take the time to learn our names. Depending on where you work, you're given a uniform color and a 'rank.' Sugar to all the mechanics and engineers in black overalls. Candy to the catering staff in blue leggings and jackets. Dusty to the cleaners in brown overalls. Barb to the security officers in red armor. Babe to the managers in white suits. Boo to the nurses in green surgical gear, and Sunny to the hostesses in bright yellow."

Leona swallowed a chuckle. "You've got to be kidding."

"Afraid not. You can learn names if you choose, especially when you work with the same colleagues, but it's best to start with the ranks to get used to them. We're stuck on this moon, buried underground with no one for company except women." Tina's grin took on that of Red Riding Hood's wolf. "We don't damage the merchandise, so Cyb Ent only employs women. Every few weeks, there's a weekend trip to the closest station for a little action. We call those slut runs. If you're into that sort of thing, the schedule is posted in the canteen. We don't mix with the other colors."

The platform stopped four levels above John's office. Passages trailed off in four directions, doors lined both sides in what Leona had assumed were the barracks. Every fourth or fifth door stood open. The odor of onions permeated the air.

"You're in the east wing. Bathrooms are shared." Tina pointed at an open door. "Besides the main station's canteen, each barracks has their own. You keep walking until you reach the end of the passage. Us engineers stick together. West is the medical staff and security. South is catering and cleaners. North is managers and hostesses."

"It seems so organized." Leona glanced at the other passages, hoping to hide a wince. *What it looks like is a cult.*

"It works, I suppose," Tina said.

Cyb Ent has forty-two thousand employees? "Does that mean Callisto isn't the only manufacturing plant?" Leona asked.

Tina shrugged. "Pick a moon or planet humans have set foot on."

"Earth's moon?" At Tina's nod, Leona gritted her teeth. Like cargo, she'd been shipped to Callisto because John was here. He'd said he'd been keeping his eye on her. Surely not since Dad died?

Tina waved a wrist over a keypad, and the door with black lettering '#57' opened. "This is you. Security has allocated access via your O.D.I. Toss in your things and follow. I'll take you to the canteen to meet those eating dinner."

Leona stepped inside the five-by-five-meter cube that would be her home for the foreseeable future. A metal table sat on one side, a double bed nestled in the corner, and a closet with an aerator occupied the right wall; a personal built-in dry cleaner made life so much easier.

She dumped the backpack on the bed and faced Tina. "Why are the bathrooms shared?"

"Has to do with the age of the facility. As one of the first, piping the water and sewage was clumped together. The newer bases are better designed."

"Who maintains everything?" In the passage, Leona waited until her door slid shut.

"We do." Tina tapped her chest. "Us engineers and mechanics."

"Hence the black overalls?"

"Yup, grease and dirt made our purple uniforms black, so Cyb Ent changed them." Tina strolled along the passage, hesitating until Leona fell in line. "You've been issued one set of overalls plus steel-tipped boots. Need more, those are at your expense."

"I suppose only one is needed when aerators launder our clothing overnight."

As they walked, the hum of voices grew louder. Leona breached the canteen, crowded with at least forty women, all in various states of dress. They wore their black overalls, but for the most part, they were undone and hung over their asses. Colored tanks, sweaters, or just a sports bra covered their top halves. Thick chunky boots were the norm.

"Many Chief Sugars are managing our teams. Get used to being called 'Sugar.'" Tina raised her arms and addressed the crowd. "Fresh meat."

As one, they slapped the table amid cries of welcome and greetings. Sophia sat to one side, her eyes wide. She waved and gestured to Leona to join her.

"Thanks, Tina…Chief Sugar," Leona said, rising on her tiptoes to see what was on the menu.

"I'll send through your schedule," Tina said. "Go eat."

As soon as Leona sank onto the bench, Sophia leaned in to whisper, "Stick with me. I've had four propositions already and received about a dozen texts." She tapped her forearm below her O.D.I. "Not that I mind, of course. It's just, after Simon…" She winced.

Leona grinned. "You're gorgeous, what's not to like?"

"Stop it," Sophia gasped, her cheeks flushing pink. "I'm too scared to choose a team, especially if one of my…admirers is there. I'd be walking into 'awkward.'" She shivered. "I can handle being hit on but not every damn day."

"Maybe they'll get the hint?" Leona scanned the buffet. She'd eaten, sure, but the aromas were making her mouth water. Thankfully, nothing stank of onion.

"Look at this," Sophia hissed, shoving her activated O.D.I. in Leona's face. A few of the same numbers had repeatedly messaged her.

Leona sighed. "How much do you know about sex-cybs?"

"Nothing. I was hired to maintain infrastructure. How many dark corners are in the bowels of this station? Shit." Sophia slumped, her mouth turning downward. "I just got here, Leona. I can't…leave. I *need* this job." She wiped a tear off her cheek. "I knew this was too good to be true."

"Well, I suppose I could ask for you to be my assistant." Leona hesitated, then tapped on her O.D.I. to submit her choice. "Done. Now can I eat?"

Chapter Four

Orbiting Earth
Etterian battleship, Valiant
Year of 12254, October

Aaro twirled the Maloidian daggers and charged, deflecting Supreme Commander Oyaz's greatsword with each strike. Sweat tickled his neck where it dripped. A fleeting glance highlighted the males watching their supreme commander battle his new sub-commander. Every morning before Aaro's first *giyua* juice, Oyaz tested his mettle on the common's sparring mat.

As the sub-commander, Aaro had to cater to Oyaz's idiosyncrasies. From what he'd heard about Xan, Oyaz's former supreme commander, sparring was a daily event fraught with violence and laughter. This day, Oyaz was about to abandon Aaro for a little...vacation? Yes, that was what Pilot Krist had said.

Oyaz was one lucky son of a *kreso* to have found his *Dar Eth* so soon.

Aaro smothered a grimace. He'd been planetside when two of his battle-bonds met their life forces. Both Ulriq and Kanzo had kneeled that day. Danic's soulmate—as the humans termed it—had happened along with Oyaz's. Izzy's sister, Simone, had knocked Danic out with a...spade. Yes, that's what the gardening tool was called.

Aaro dodged a downward swing by rolling to the side and raised the blades in case Oyaz struck again. His limbs trembled. He lifted his chin to meet Oyaz's ice-blue gaze. The male was grinning, his shoulders rising and falling with his ragged breaths. Sweat slicked every muscle. Aaro glanced at his own drenched stomach where it met his military pants. Not even Danic had put him through this, and that male could fight. How Simone had managed to surprise him, Aaro had no idea.

Of the women Aaro knew, only one hadn't become a *Dar Eth*. Taylor had loved human Michel for so long. This intrigued Aaro. The *Ethera* that triggered pairings must take feelings into consideration. How did it choose who belonged to whom? How had the Durn engineered that but missed the gene that deteriorated the birth of females?

What Etterians knew about the *Ethera* wasn't well documented since it was considered too personal to share. A few of the medics had begun to remedy that. They'd learned so far that an Etterian male had to see the entire female or woman in her natural state. Thanks to Ulriq and Prince Enyl, training vids on how to mate with a woman had been issued to all males.

Most were itching to put that knowledge into practice.

Hence the sex-cybs. King Xeus had tasked a few elder males to test the progress of the void on these lifelike yet non-biological objects. Perhaps the encroaching darkness wouldn't shorten a male's life and sanity when he spilled his seed into such a...machine. Aaro's void had started to form later than usual. Gratitude warmed his chest. Many felt its presence when they were *damu* training on the planet, Gikaet.

Oyaz was spared such an emotionless death as only a *Dar Eth* could do. The males around them, with dark blue eyes matching Aaro's, confirmed their future—death on a battlefield to feel even an ounce of exhilaration. He sucked in a deep breath, cherishing the rush of enjoyment when he met Oyaz's swings with his raised blades. Yes, Aaro could understand the hunt to feel something, anything, and to sacrifice himself for such an experience.

He was young though, not as old as a few of the males in the common. Their time was running out. The number of women Etterians had rescued from Yithian and Maloidian clutches meant many males were finding their *Dar Eth*s. King Xeus was in the midst of negotiations with Earth to find more soulmates.

Aaro launched into the air, using his thighs for maximum height. From there, daggers flipped into icepick holds, he descended toward Oyaz. The male lifted his sword, the flat of the blade catching Aaro across the backs of his forearms.

Oyaz slid backward under the force. Battles had to be fought with Maloidian steel to be taken seriously, but also, a true opponent knew how to use weapons without inflicting harm. Still, Aaro would bear bruises until a medic could heal him.

Oyaz leaned in, his breath warm on Aaro's chin. "Izabelle has invited you to breakfast." He grinned as only a happy male could. "If you are interested in steak and salad?"

Images flicked across Aaro's mind, thanks to his O.D.I. instructing him. "My thanks. It looks good." He pushed off Oyaz's blade to nod at the males watching. Many would be enjoying such a meal this day.

With their preternatural hearing, all would have heard Oyaz's invitation.

Aaro spun the daggers and mounted them to the wall, pressing them in place. "Garix? Will he be joining us?"

"I have come to accept that she views him as a brother." Oyaz lowered his chin. "An *Eth* does not like to share his *Dar Eth*."

Aaro rested his hand on Oyaz's shoulder. "The women do that often. As such a brother to many, I assure you, Garix has no designs on your *Dar Eth*."

"I know this, and yet, it grates." Oyaz flipped the greatsword and clipped it in. He glanced at his O.D.I. "Tend to your bruises. I will see you within the hour."

Aaro stared at Oyaz's back until he disappeared through a doorway. He faced the medical nestled in the corner of the common, but a male impeded his path, his med-gun in hand. "Medic Flad."

"Sub-Commander." After running the device over Aaro, he stepped back and pocketed the med-gun.

"My thanks," Aaro said. "Trying steak and salad like the rest?"

"Yes." Flad rubbed his palms together. "I had pancakes with Garix yesterday."

Aaro's eyelashes fluttered, his O.D.I. detailing the strange meal. He chuckled at Flad's delight. "Indeed."

"It is the cinnamon, or so Garix assures me." Flad bowed his head and hurried to stand in line for the rehydrator.

With a towel he'd ordered from the replicator, Aaro strode to his officer quarters while wiping the sweat from his brow, neck, and chest. Energy pulsed through him, proving these morning sparring sessions were worth it. The mission loomed—to guard Earth, patrol space around it, and save any women stolen from the small blue planet. Circling an object would provide no mental stimuli.

He ran through his memories of the human women he called his friends. Their softness and sweet scents were always a memorable experience.

He tried not to think of them as he attended to his chore while cleansing. The explosion of pleasure was swift and fleeting. Would that change when he had a *Dar Eth*? He grimaced. Ava had mentioned that women could please a male multiple times in a day. Unlike Etterian females who could only do it once a day due to the painful swelling of their sex.

He donned the wrap and waited for the air-dryer to work on his unbound hair. His stomach rumbled in anticipation of the brown lump of meat and colorful vegetables. Human food was as diverse and delicious as their cultures.

"*Malia pa*," he commanded his hair, and once braided, he caught it and clipped the end.

Striding past his shelves, he paused to admire the artifacts and treasures he'd found or bought on the many planets and stations he'd visited. Finding each one had become cherished memories. The solid purple lumps along the top were Maloidian religious statues, most depicting a wrathful god bearing lightning. Some caught the exact color of their lilac lightning.

Few males had seen his collection.

He stroked the bulbous head of one statue, the stone lovingly smoothed. Below those were pieces of heated rock from Yithia, a planet with three suns. He palmed one then scoffed at imagining he could still feel residual heat. He ran his thumb over the curling fossil embedded in the stone. What he needed was more artifacts. No, what he craved was to explore worlds he'd never been to.

He ordered fresh armor from the replicator and donned the boots he'd dumped at the cleansing door. It took moments to place his sweat-drenched military pants in the aerator. Using the replicator shouldn't be taken for granted or abused.

From his quarters, it was a short walk to Oyaz's. He announced his arrival and waited. When the door slid open, the aroma that hit him was one he'd encountered before. He drew in a deep inhale. The barbecue on Earth at Michel's housing structure the day Ulriq and Kanzo had found their *Dar Eth*s. When the Yithians had attacked.

"Barbecue?" he asked as he entered.

Izzy laughed. "Close enough." She placed two plates on a raised table. "You're just in time, Aaro. *Giyua* or coffee?"

"*Giyua*, thank you." He settled into a chair known as a comfy. Colorful squares cushioned his back, so he leaned forward, resting his elbows on the edge of the elevated table. "I like this. It is practical." He dipped to study the elongated legs.

"Yup, was getting tired of eating off my lap." She danced to the rehydrator. "Garix is on his way. Oyaz?"

"I am here, *thamani*." In strange blue pants and a white tunic, he strode from the bedroom.

"What are you wearing?" Aaro asked before he could stop himself. Michel had worn similar garments. They did appear to be comfortable.

"Jeans and a T-shirt," Oyaz said and joined Aaro at the table as Izzy placed two more plates.

Garix, all seven-foot of solid Etterian muscle, strolled into the quarters through the open door. He gave Izzy a sideways hug before lowering his great bulk into a comfy. "Supreme commander, sub-commander." He thumped his chest in salute.

Izzy chose a comfy beside Oyaz, a plate of brown strips and white flat things with yellow centers in hand. "Bacon and eggs," she said, when she caught Aaro staring.

His O.D.I. hurried to educate him. "My thanks." He gripped the sharp knife and fork and started on his steak. On the first bite, a groan tore through him. He was amazed he'd forgotten how delicious their meat was? The salad, too, had an explosion of flavors, aided by the pale yellow sauce drizzled over the green leaves and red balls. He pointed his utensil at the sauce, still chewing and unable to ask.

"Honey mustard salad dressing," Izzy said, beaming between bites of her meal.

"Delicious." He shifted in the comfy. "Thank you for the invitation."

Oyaz kissed Izzy on her temple before facing Aaro and Garix. "In the event your commander is away—"

"We're going on vacay," Izzy squealed, bouncing in her chair.

Oyaz gave Aaro a pointed look. "That places you in charge in my absence, as per protocol, Aaro."

"As you command. For how long?" Aaro sipped his juice, trying to act as if this was a surprise. Anticipating Oyaz's absence, Pilot Krist had been directing issues to Aaro for two days now.

"About three weeks," Izzy said. "We're touring all the wonders."

Aaro frowned. *Touring? Wonders?* He sliced the meat before forking a sliver into his mouth.

"I do not know what to expect." Oyaz grinned. "It cannot be worse than what Maddox put us through."

"It's so much better. Cultural foods, music, beautiful statues, churches, amazing nature." Izzy clapped. "I've been packing for days."

"Packing?" Aaro popped a red ball into his mouth and hummed with delight when it exploded, filling his mouth with tart juice.

"Gotta have luggage." She shrugged. "Oyaz is so big that his clothes take up most of the space. Not to mention he doesn't have the appropriate attire."

Oyaz scowled. "Jeans will do."

"On the beach?" Izzy scoffed. "What if it rains? When we go skiing?"

Aaro's eyelids fluttered when his O.D.I. hurried to update him. He smothered a smile at Oyaz's disgruntled grumbling.

"Why can we not port home between destinations?" Oyaz's voice had taken on a plaintive tone.

"The traveling is half the fun." She rubbed her upper arms, barely hiding a shiver. "I hate zapping."

Zapping? Aaro coughed to cover a chuckle.

Garix nodded between massive bites of steak. "Illogical."

Izzy slapped him on his arm. "My reaction doesn't have to be logical." She raised her gaze to Oyaz's. "It's our first vacation, and I want to enjoy every moment of it."

Oyaz drew her into the curve of his body. Pink splashed onto her cheeks. Her eyes warmed, and something intense crossed between them. Aaro was torn, wanting to look away but mesmerized by the emotional display. This was love and was once considered a myth.

"Want an iced coffee?" Garix pushed off the table and crossed to the rehydrator.

"Please." With the plate empty before him, Aaro said, "Thank you for the wonderful meal, Izzy."

She beamed at him.

After shoving a tall glass of cold coffee at Aaro, condensation forming on the outside, Garix gave Izzy another sideways hug. He nodded at Oyaz and left.

Aaro leaned back in the comfy and rubbed his stomach. "May I request frequent updates? I would prefer not to find out too late that you've been kidnapped, stranded, buried alive..."

Oyaz chuckled. "I shall—"

"We'll send you digi-cards, Aaro." Izzy leaped out of her chair to clean up. Oyaz joined her, carrying far more at once than she could.

"Do enjoy your...vacay." Aaro left before he overstayed his welcome. When the door closed behind him, he hesitated in the passage. With a long pull from his iced coffee, he headed to his quarters. There was still a little time before he reported to the comm room to start his day.

As his battle-bonds found their *Dar Eth*s, one by one withdrawing from him, he'd turned to the archives, eager to research Earth and its inhabitants. In said journey, he'd stumbled upon a wealth of historical narratives. He was halfway through *Stolen Love*—a redemption story about a man who sailed the seas in search of bounty and found it in a lady.

At first, the man was without honor, or so the story claimed. Aaro had read on, hoping to discover the man's punishment for his faulty character. Instead, he'd learned the man had held the rank of lord and was treated most unfairly. Even though his profession of piracy was looked upon with disdain, the man did all he could to help those less fortunate.

Aaro nestled into the comfy, propped his booted feet on the table, and flicked the tablet's screen to 'turn' the page.

"Oh, Benedict, do not make such a vow," Elizabeth gasped.

He gathered her into his arms, crushing her plump breasts against his chest. "I swear it, milady, upon my honor and that of my father's. We shall be wed."

"No, I cannot expect you to—"

He silenced her with a kiss across her lush lips. "It is done, the decision made."

She trembled in his arms but met his gaze with courage he could admire. "My reputation is ruined. Marrying you will not restore my good name." Wrapping her fingers over his broad shoulders, she clung to him, a sob escaping her.

"Come, come, my sweet Elizabeth, you forget that love conquers all." He pulled her away to capture the tears from her cheeks.

"Sub-Commander?" Pilot Krist jerked Aaro to the present.

"What is it?" he snapped.

"Your shift began minutes ago. Do you require a medic?" Pilot Krist waited.

"I am on my way." Aaro glanced at the tablet before tucking it under an arm. Who knew he'd find such pleasure in reading Earth's history. He assumed this interlude in Benedict and Elizabeth's lives was just a snippet of what happened. Perhaps other stories told of their struggles after pairing? He would finish this one and continue his search. The archives had to mention them somewhere.

If the demands on his time weren't extensive this day, he might be able to sneak in another chapter.

AARO SMILED AT IZZY and Oyaz as they climbed into the *kuta* shuttle. Oyaz's attention lay fixed on Izzy, as expected of a pairing. Aaro rubbed his chest between his two hearts, hoping to assuage the warmth settling there. One day soon, he would find his lifeforce and *Dar Eth*.

He had to hope, that if he set his mind on Etteria and being honorable, his *Dar Eth* would come to him. With that, he strode along the passages to the comm room. The silence thickened, contrasting with the energy and excitement Izzy gave off. There was comfort to be found in the familiar drones and rumbles of the battleship. He squared his shoulders and studied the multi-vids above the console, trying not to glance at the tablet he'd left on the table.

"Any news from Operations?" he asked Pilot Krist. Etteria had to come first. Benedict about to mate with Elizabeth would have to wait.

"Nothing, Sub-Commander. Prince Enyl has asked that you comm him at your earliest convenience."

Aaro stiffened. "Why didn't you notify me immediately?" Anger was swift to rise. Keeping their prince or king waiting was never a good thing.

"He ended the comm, Sub-Commander."

Aaro grimaced.

Krist glanced at him over his shoulder. "He asked that it be in private."

As one, the comm room emptied, all except Pilot Krist. "I shall patch you through then head to the common."

Aaro nodded in thanks. He stared at the black vid until it flickered, forming Kanzo's face.

"Would you like a hot chocolate as well?" Krist offered, pausing for Aaro's agreement, before slipping out of the comm room.

"Aaro, it is wonderful to see you, my battle-bond." Kanzo beamed, his ice-blue eyes an external mark that he'd found his *Dar Eth*.

"I trust Lady Ava is in good health?" Aaro clasped his hands behind his back.

"Yes, better than well." Kanzo's gaze dipped, probably to his O.D.I. "Prince Enyl would like a moment." Kanzo's focus shifted off vid before he stepped aside.

Prince Enyl filled the display vid. As the first male to find his *Dar Eth*, his pairing had brought such hope to Etterians across the galaxies. "Sub-Commander Aaro, let me make this brief. John Wright of Cyborg Enterprises has asked for our assistance."

Aaro waited, not knowing who or what Enyl was talking about.

"As you may have heard, Etterians are testing these sex-cybs for our people. Since John Wright is human and the founder of Cyborg Enterprises, assisting such an influential man might bolster our negotiations." Enyl frowned. "E.S.A. is being difficult. They are wary of granting Etteria access to their females."

Ah, now I understand. "Do this as a favor to gain favor?"

"Precisely. Kanzo has commed the points." Enyl met Aaro's gaze. "Sixteen sex-cybs, Sub-Commander Aaro, and two engineers to be escorted to Maloid, Kulai, Sarvis, Etteria, and Yithia."

"I know, right? Like the might of Etterian is brought down to guarding sex-cyborgs. The horror." Princess Oriana grinned at Aaro, ignoring a grumbling prince beside her. "Just let me speak for a minute, please, Enyl. You're not telling the whole story."

Enyl scowled.

Aaro didn't lower his gaze though, content to admire Princess Oriana's pale skin and vibrant red hair. Such an amazing combination he'd never known existed.

"Aaro, the big issue is the engineers. Cyb Ent wants to make sure they're not harmed and are safely returned. If the Yithians manage to kidnap two unescorted women, Etteria would have to launch a rescue. If they're taken while under your protection, it will look as if Etteria gifted them to Yithia. This could become a political shit storm of note."

"Two women," Aaro repeated. It was a great honor to protect such treasures.

"The good news is that the sex-cybs may be used during your voyage. They are brand new and need to be broken in a little." Princess Oriana wiggled her eyebrows. "If you know what I mean."

"I hate it when you talk to my males about sex," Prince Enyl growled at his *Dar Eth*, his scowl ferocious to behold.

Aaro widened his eyes while pinching his lips to hide a smile. Their arguing never failed to entertain.

"They're walking sex dolls. You can be such a prude. Just send Aaro all the details, and we can get to the makeup sex."

The prince twitched. "What?"

Princess Oriana wiggled her eyebrows.

Aaro coughed to prevent a chuckle.

The prince typed on his O.D.I. before muttering, "All of Etteria is with you." The display vid blanked, ending the communication.

Aaro raised his gaze to the vid showing the blue planet and their salvation. Earth was so close, his *Dar Eth* somewhere on it. He took a calming breath. Etteria came first, and for Prince Enyl to comm him, meant this task mattered. He rolled his shoulders. Perhaps his *Dar Eth* was in outer space? His shoulders slumped an inch before he rallied and straightened his spine. Finding her on a single planet had been overwhelming enough, but now, to hunt her throughout the universe? How? Where did he start?

Krist strolled in and placed a steaming mug of sweet hot chocolate on the console. He sipped from his, keeping his focus on the display vids. "Adviser Kanzo has shared points. Do I set course?"

"Yes, we have a task of extreme importance to Etteria." Aaro smothered a grimace. He scooped up his mug and settled in the comfy beside the table at the rear of the comm room. His first urge was to notify Oyaz, but he was hesitant to do so. Had Prince Enyl wanted Oyaz to know, Aaro wouldn't have been commed.

"Open a ship-wide comm," Aaro commanded Krist. "*Valiant*, we have been sent on a diplomatic mission that will build bridges between Earth and Etteria. We do this for our future. I expect you to perform with utmost excellence as you have been doing. For this, you have my gratitude. I hope to bring you good news in a day or two." He glanced at Krist to end the comm.

"Good news?" Krist arched a brow.

"Sex-cybs," Aaro muttered.

Krist jerked back and typed on the console, summoning images and vids of these cyborgs. The males returning gathered around Krist, obscuring Aaro's line of vision.

"So lifelike…"

"Beautiful…"

"Are these machines?"

The males's questions and comments flitted through Aaro's thoughts. Indeed, they were attractive, these sex-cybs but couldn't compare to the vivaciousness of real human women.

"You have the comm," Aaro said to Krist in passing. What he needed was a chat with Taylor. As the only non-*Dar Eth* among his human friends, she was the safest to chat to.

In front of his display vid inside the privacy of his quarters, he commed her. "Taylor Montgomery."

Nothing happened. The screen didn't flicker.

He scowled. "Pilot Krist, my display vid has malfunctioned."

"One moment, Sub-Commander."

Aaro paced, casting glares at the black rectangle mounted to a bulkhead.

"It is fully operational, Sub-Commander."

"Thank you, Pilot Krist." Aaro paused and repeated Taylor's full name. The connection didn't go through. Had something happened to his friend? Gritting his teeth, he spat out, "Michel Dunois."

Relief flooded warmth to his toes when the screen flickered, and Michel's face came into view.

"Aaro, what a pleasant surprise." The blond man seemed happy, with no sadness in his crisp blue gaze. Taylor had to be well.

"Michel, where is Taylor? Why can I not reach her?"

The human man beamed. "Try Taylor Dunois."

Aaro froze. "What—"

"She married me last weekend." Michel raised his hand, wiggling the finger with a gold band around it.

"Ah, wonderful news." Aaro smiled.

Jacqueline, Michel's sister, and Ulriq, Aaro's battle-bond got married in a park. Aaro scratched his throat, remembering when he'd worn the constrictive Earthian garment called a tux.

"Yup. So, what's up? Should I be jealous?" Michel wiggled his eyebrows like Princess Oriana had done.

"No. I need..." What could Aaro say? Hope? Inspiration? He was an Etterian warrior, a commander, and a strong male. "To find out how you two are doing. Are things well?"

"Yup. We're heading planetside to visit with Vicky." Michel threw out an arm.

Petite Taylor pressed against him, her fingers splayed across his chest. "Aaro, it's so good to see you."

Without hesitation, Aaro grinned. Seeing her brought him such joy. "I am a sub-commander now and tasked to leave Earth for a while."

"You've been promoted? That's amazing." She patted Michel. "You can still call us, right? Traveling far away won't stop that, will it?" With a flick of a finger, she tossed her white-blue hair off her cherubic face.

"Of course." Aaro allowed the tension to ease from his taut body. "I must admit, I am excited. It has been a while since I visited the worlds on the itinerary."

"Oh," she cried out. "Do send us pics."

Aaro paused while his O.D.I. hurried to explain the meaning of 'pics.' Like Izzy's digi-cards? "I shall try."

Maybe if he held his forearm at an angle, the O.D.I. could capture a sunset on Kulai. Humans were odd, wanting to take vacations, pics to memorialize their experiences, and souvenirs as keepsakes. He glanced at his wall. Etterians weren't so different. Well, not him, at least. Perhaps this mission would help add to his collection.

"Thank you for accepting my comm," he said in farewell.

"Anytime," Taylor waved.

"End comm." Aaro rested his temple on the display vid.

That had been pointless for the most part, except for Taylor's request for 'pics.' She had given him something to look forward to. He pushed off the bulkhead and returned to the comm room. The slight nudge of the battleship confirmed their journey had begun. If all went well, it would be uneventful, but deep down, he hoped not.

Chapter Five

Leona scowled at her vid divided into six mini displays, all viewing various stages of sex. She snorted. Most engineers called it copulation, but not her, she didn't romanticize what she did or saw. A month in and she was an old hat. Worse, seven days in, and she was horny as hell. The constant sexual barrage was getting to her.

"Dammit," she muttered and tapped the data tab to soften how the cyb grabbed an algri's genitalia. Judging by the gurgling from 'Vid-4' that followed, the adjustment was much appreciated. She listened to the other sexual grunts and groans while she ordered a hot cocoa—her new drug of choice.

Never would she, as a naïve teenager, have thought this was where her degree would land her. The pay was good, the tokens almost double her former wages, and the sexual harassment halved. Humans were humans looking for physical connection, but Leona didn't do girls or cybs, for that matter. She would happily settle for the little harassment she got now to what she used to endure from her male colleagues on the *Riptide*.

She tapped 'Vid-1,' angled the cyb's hip by fifteen degrees and added ten percent more strength. The human man moaned. His thrusting into the cyb accelerated. Any future interactions with human men or algri would carry the changes she just made.

She consoled herself with the knowledge she was making the universe a better place, one fuck at a time. If only her mother knew. Leona frowned at the six screens with men in various acts of copulation. Two were Maloidians, in shades of yellow with their tentacled-hair stroking the cybs' faces. Three were human men with no care for the cybs beneath them. Any blatant disrespect would have the client's DNA added to the banned list. She tapped the vids to activate high alert on those men. The last vid showed the algri, green with multi-tentacles in the cyb's orifices which used to make Leona shudder with disgust. Now she made sure it was enjoyable for the clients regardless of the shape of their genitalia.

In the last month, she'd formed three rules:

    1. Do not fuck colleagues.

    2. Do not fuck the merchandise.

    3. Do not fuck the clients.

Sophia had helped with their mantra since the poor woman was in hot demand. When Tina staked her claim on the 'fresh meat,' the tension had ramped to such an extent Leona and Soph were forced to have lunch either in their rooms or the workshops.

Violating the rules meant Leona might as well quit her job.

Having any sort of a relationship with a colleague created tension in the workplace.

Fucking the merchandise didn't go down well with Cyb Ent, no raises, bonuses, promotions, or so her colleagues whined about.

Clients tended to treat real women like the merchandise, visiting at all hours, and using them as tools for gratification, with no respect, and no romance.

What Leona *had* enjoyed was when an Etterian scimitar visited the sex center. Shit. The station had come to a standstill. All the staff had watched a vid or ten. Most fascinating was the way the Etterians treated the cybs. With respect and gentleness, regardless that the cyb was just a connection of cybernetics in synthetic skin. They brought romance with them. It made every woman in the center sigh, even Tina. Leona didn't replay those vids anymore, couldn't since she was so sexually frustrated. Just the sight of their tight asses made her nipples hard.

She had always been a bit of a prude, worsened when she lost her virginity to Rex, the neighbor's son. Grimacing at that painful memory, she drank deeply from her cocoa. Not that she wanted to have sex now with so few, um, male prospects. It was just, that once she started to pleasure herself, where would it end? Using a cyb out of desperation? Various sexual toys? She shivered. It all seemed so pointless, like going down that path might cost her soul.

So, after day three and an explosive orgasm in bed, she'd scheduled her release like she did the cybs' maintenance. Every Wednesday after a warm shower. A quick flick and a roaring orgasm should bring her enough relief to last a few days. Well, that was the plan. After the Etterians' visit two days ago, she'd be lucky if she made Friday.

Last night, she'd awoken in a state of sensory overload, dripping between her legs and her clit throbbing. She'd been tempted to break her schedule, but the first weeks of any new routine were the hardest. If she succumbed, she might as well toss that plan out of the airlock. Instead, she'd gotten up and worked, doing stock take while watching an algri had certainly calmed her overactive libido. She kept a particularly enlightening vid on the data tab, just in case.

"'Vid-2' broke a toe," Soph said through the screen. A red circle appeared on Leona's 'Vid-2' screen. That girl had thrown herself into her new career, working hard and long hours, spending her spare time studying schematics, fluid dehydration, and rehydration formulae. Yet, she remained unfazed by all this sex. She was such a sweet girl, cheerful, stubborn, and persistent but learned quickly. Leona liked that about her since she didn't have the patience to explain stuff *ad infinitum.* Choosing Soph as her assistant had been the best decision ever.

"Accidental, Sugar," she called.

Soph popped her head into the cabin. "Thought so too but had to check."

She was dressed like Leona—a black jumpsuit covered in lubrication in various stages of drying, with multi-pockets stuffed with loads of gadgets and tools. She kept it zipped up, almost to her throat.

Leona's was defunct. The zipper had broken on the first day. She'd ordered a replacement and more sets, but in the meantime, the top half hung over her ass like a skirt, and it rode low on her hips, threatening to fall off despite the width of her hips. She wore a crisp white tank that barely reached her belly button, no matter how much she tugged on it. Her meager closet hadn't helped matters.

Her transmission pinged. With a glance at Soph, Leona shoved her hair out of her face. She undid her pony, re-gathered, then retied it. That was as presentable as she could muster.

"Allow." Her screen changed to the unexpected face of her employer. "Good afternoon, Big Daddy."

She had to admit to being curious. He hadn't contacted her since their initial meeting. His gaze touched on her bare midriff. Sure, her uniform wasn't crisp, nor in place, for that matter. But working on the cybs was sweaty work, and if flashing a little skin bother him... She shrugged. *I fix sex-cybs, for fuck's sake.* She almost pinched her brow. Her vocabulary had descended into the proverbial gutter. If only her finishing school heard her now.

"Sugar, glad I caught you. It seems Penny miscalculated your monthly compensation."

She blinked at him as distrust coiled in her belly.

"I have instructed her to increase your tokens accordingly."

Ah. Leona smothered a grin. Penny? As in the accounts ladies? "Thank you."

Soph bounced on the spot, her cheeks warming a pretty pink.

"Excellent." John cleared his throat. "I have a task for you."

So, here was the real reason for the comm. Leona forced herself not to twitch with impatience. "Happy to assist, Big Daddy."

His gaze shifted, and a shadow crossed his face. He waited until a soft click announced the person had left his office. His shoulders slumped.

"I have always admired you, Leona, despite who your mother is. The last month has proven you're Rigel's daughter." His facial expression changed into something fatherly, one she was familiar with.

He ran a frustrated hand through his hair, spiking it and making him look like the renowned scientist he was. "Since your arrival, ratings and personal purchases have skyrocketed. I assume it's the improvements you made to my cybs's behavioral mannerisms. Thank you for your dedication. Now we're in a bit of a pickle."

The unexpected praise and honest approach warmed her like nothing else could have. "What seems to be the problem, John?"

"You know how expensive each cyb is, and when I say we have a preliminary order for sixteen with guaranteed future orders in the thousands, it's an opportunity Cyb Ent can't pass up."

"Still don't see the problem, unless the client is the issue?"

Her question brought a tired but genuine smile. "Yithians."

"Shit," she whispered. Not that she'd seen one. Just what she'd heard on the news—sharklike aliens with tiger teeth and meaner than a pissed-off hyena. "I thought they didn't find humans attractive."

"We cannot deliver to the surrounding planets without 'gifting' a few to Yithia. They might use them as arena contenders, though." He frowned.

What a waste. All that engineering destroyed for blood sport? "I can't believe that's true."

"I agree, but tokens are tokens, and cybs are just robotics." He winced. "Well, I try to tell myself that."

"Even if they're arena fodder?" She had become fond of the cybs under her watch despite them being animated objects.

"Yes. My biggest concern is if they ask for an engineer."

"Which they have the right to, especially on large orders." She scowled, knowing Cyb Ent's protocol. An engineer traveled with a large order, although, she hadn't heard of one permanently transferring. Not to Yithia. She cast a worrying glance at a pale Soph.

"Leona, I can promise you, no woman in my employ will ever be stationed on Yithia."

"Thank you, John." She offered a smile. "It pleases me to hear that."

"Now comes the pickle."

She jerked back. *The Yithians aren't the problem?*

"I have managed to obtain military assistance with the delivery. Two cybs to Maloid, Kulai, Sarvis, Yithia, and eight to Etteria. You will be heavily guarded and hopefully never in danger, although I cannot guarantee that."

"Me?" she squeaked. "What about Chief Sugar? Shouldn't any of the chiefs do these deliveries?" Leona struggled to swallow past the lump in her throat.

"Tina broke her wrist last night." His deep scowl implied there was more to the story, and it wasn't one he was happy about. "I need a diplomat, Leona, able to wine-and-dine, to schmooze the clientele if needed."

No, she couldn't see Tina playing the hostess, and she didn't know the other Chief Sugars well enough to recommend them. Leona slumped. What the fuck? Leaving Callisto wasn't the plan. She'd planned to lay low, especially when Bradley had tabs on her. In the underground facility, he nor his spies could reach her. She hoped.

"Hence the promotion to Chief Sugar...for the duration of this mission only, if you prefer." John waited, expectant and yet still conveying an edge of desperation.

She sighed. "Fine, but I'm taking Sugar with me."

"Who?"

"Hello, Big Daddy." Soph stepped beside Leona and gave their employer a nod.

John nodded. "Oh, your assistant."

"Yes, on-the-job training." Leona folded her arms across her chest. If Soph wasn't going, then neither was she. What she couldn't tell him was that she would never leave Soph alone at the center.

"Very well, two would be better than one." He punched in a few buttons on his O.D.I. and offered another genuine smile. "The cybs have been prepped for transport and await your instructions in Bay '12.' I'm told the battleship *Valiant*, has been en route since I finalized this arrangement and should reach the center within an hour." The screen went black.

"Fuck," Leona spat.

Chapter Six

Approaching the moon the humans called Callisto went smoothly as expected. Clearance was given by a breathless woman. Pilot Krist had merely chuckled as he maneuvered the scimitar *Denessi* like a youngin's toy. He landed the ship with precision and opened the bay doors within the domed and pressurized landing bay.

Aaro read the list off the tablet. Thirteen cabins in a barracks were suitable as long as they were near to each other: nine for the sex-cybs, two for the engineers, one for storage, and one to be converted into a workshop. He had forwarded these requirements to Data Officer Ranh with a few amendments regarding the barracks. It was best to have the sex-cybs not too close to his males.

Having gone through his tasks and Oyaz's to ensure he could personally attend to the cargo, Aaro had just arrived in the bay, in time to watch the ramp lower. While he waited, he continued reading the Earthian historical archive, finding Benedict's removal of Elizabeth's gown a little...arousing. The man popped each button as if it was precious. Aaro might have torn the garment, sending the buttons flying.

He grinned. Perhaps seduction was meant to be slow, capturing every moment, touch, taste, and moan. With a glance at the bustling bay, he confirmed his males prepared for the sex-cybs' arrival. He flicked the tablet as he continued to read, eager to discover Benedict's skill in seduction. The man must have been a god on Earth.

With a caress, he slid his hand inside her bodice and beneath her chemise. Callused fingers probed the softest of flesh until a pebbled nipple pressed into his palm. She whimpered, arching into his hand. His name dripped from her parted and kiss-swollen lips.

Tension tightened in his core, and his manhood throbbed. A copper curl unwound and flowed over her collarbone, the color so bold and bright against her pale skin. His chest swelled, and he raised his gaze to meet hers. How he adored this woman. Everything she did was perfect.

With her bodice gaping, her cleavage called to him. He dipped and pressed a kiss there, the warmth and floral scent of her skin engulfing his senses. She plunged her fingers into his hair. Her nails scraped his scalp, summoning a frisson of heat to travel down his back.

He yanked her gown down exposing a breast and its taut nipple. Beautiful.

"Our guests are ready to board," Pilot Krist said through Aaro's O.D.I.

Guests? The announcement of the sex-cybs and their availability during the voyage had swept through the *Valiant*. He was more interested in the women. What would they be like? He was friends with four, and none of them were similar in character or physical attributes.

A little escort mission because of the Yithian threat seemed like a good enough diversion for his bored but battle-ready males. Sixteen sex-cybs would ease that boredom, as well.

First, he had to get them onto the ship.

He tucked the tablet under his arm and strode across the bay, pausing at the opening to scan the area planetside. His males had formed a protective circle around the platform, their backs toward the center, their stances vigilant. In the middle, humanoid cyborgs stood at attention in military style, a formation of three across and seven deep. Nineteen?

They shared the same height, long legs, large breasts, small waists, and plump backsides with wide hips, but their hair and eye color varied. They were adorned in expensive garments imported from Earth's Japan. His malehood twitched in admiration. Even from this distance, the synthetic skin looked soft and appealing.

Movement to the back of the cybs drew his gaze. A young woman skipped toward another woman he'd first thought to be a sex-cyb. His lapse could be forgiven since she was as tall and curvaceous as the cybs. Bags and various boxes at her feet awaited loading. He punched instructions into his O.D.I. Two cargo males ran past him to attend to his instructions. His chest swelled with a flash of pride at his males' promptness.

His gaze returned to the skipping woman, who was paler in hair and skin. She was animated, waving her arms up and down in her excitement. The other one, with her dark brown hair in a long tail, merely smiled at her before striding toward Aaro.

He focused on her features, absorbing the dark brows over blue eyes, a dainty nose into pert lips, and a small chin. His gaze traveled lower to the tight white tunic, her pebbled breasts straining the fabric, and her low-riding pants over long legs. She was beautiful. Something about her—

A white-hot pleasurable torment burst through him as if fire consumed the cells of his body. His breath rushed out at the unexpected heat, at the sweet agonizing bliss that hardened his nipples and made his malehood throb in ecstasy. His legs trembled. He thrust out a hand and caught the ridged edge of the bay opening, allowing him to fall to one knee with a little dignity.

A vision appeared, her black garment down to her knees, his hand at the base of her spine holding her in mid-air as he lapped her glistening feminine folds. In the image, she shuddered, crying out, her hands gripping the bulkhead with enough force to whiten her knuckles. As if he relived a memory, the taste of her blossomed on his tongue—tart, smoky, and addictive. His malehood dribbled.

Immense joy flooded him at discovering his *Dar Eth*.

With a deep groan, he pushed down his reaction with as much control as he could muster.

Standing, his hands still clenched into fists at his side, he kept his eyes closed and breathed in deeply.

Bliss burned through his stimulated body. A growl tore from him. *She is aroused.*

His eyes flew open to zero in on her.

He took an involuntary step toward her, only to realize she'd turned on a heel and was now walking backward up the ramp, her hips swaying with each step. The sex-cybs marched up the ramp at a slow enough pace she wouldn't have to dart out of the way. As she drew nearer to him, his gaze traveled the length of her. Her feet were encased in military black boots. The top half of the garment hung over her backside, revealing the smooth skin of her waist, with two dimples at the base of her spine. Her dark brown hair swung from side-to-side with each step. The closer she came to him, the more decadent her scent became.

Fighting for control, he jogged away from temptation, into the bay, then up the railing to watch her work. He needed the distance between them lest he did something impulsive like whisking her away to the officer's quarters. Etteria needed this mission to go well. Abducting then ravishing the engineer wouldn't be wise.

Once the sex-cybs were standing in what she determined was a good spot, she faced the bay. His males followed, crowding around their *guests.* When all were safely inside, the *kuta* door closed.

Aaro's gaze remained on her. The ringing in his ears persisted, and he gripped the metal railing hard enough to dent it. *My Dar Eth* circled his mind.

When the silence stretched on, and the other woman fidgeted, his *Dar Eth* spoke two words. "At ease."

Sixteen sex-cybs and one young engineer relaxed. The sex-cybs settled into poses designed to be seductive. His males shuffled, proving the poses effective.

"Welcome aboard the *Denessi*, miladies," Aaro greeted from the railing.

His *Dar Eth* tilted her head to make eye-contact. When their gazes locked, his world shifted. Air rushed out of his lungs, and a tightness took up residence in his chest. Every muscle in his body spasmed with the urge to claim her in an act as old as time.

Soon. He smiled, allowing his delight and eagerness to consume him.

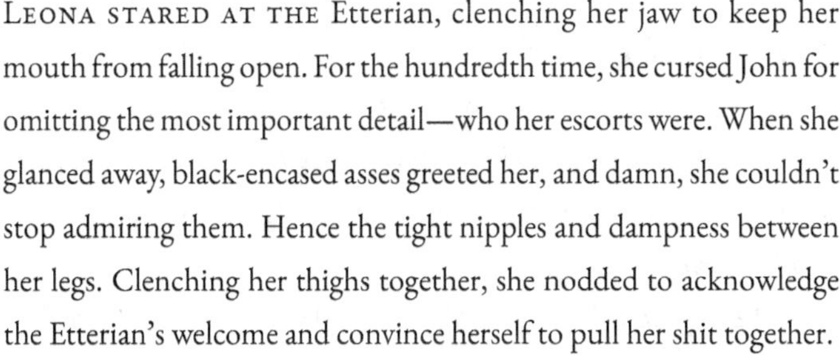

LEONA STARED AT THE Etterian, clenching her jaw to keep her mouth from falling open. For the hundredth time, she cursed John for omitting the most important detail—who her escorts were. When she glanced away, black-encased asses greeted her, and damn, she couldn't stop admiring them. Hence the tight nipples and dampness between her legs. Clenching her thighs together, she nodded to acknowledge the Etterian's welcome and convince herself to pull her shit together.

Despite her resolve, her gaze flew to meet his startling ice-blue eyes. She touched on his super wide shoulders, barrel chest tapering into a narrow waist, and hips into tree-trunk thighs that made her mouth water. This man was just as gorgeous as Nerx and Aldur. Then his smile had crept across his uneven mouth and blossomed.

Faced with his devastating handsomeness, she blinked, scrambling for something to say.

"Um. Thanks." She winced and mentally repeated: *He's just a man. Don't get excited. Calm down. Think of the algri and those tentacles...*

"It is a short journey to reach the *Valiant*. Care to observe from the comm room?" He indicated to meet him at the door near the back of the bay.

Leona faced her wide-eyed friend. "Soph? Wanna come or stay with the dolls?"

Soph chewed on her bottom lip, her gaze shifting from man to man. Leona surveyed the bay. A few men studied her and Soph, their dark blue eyes hooded. Others hurried about their tasks in the confined space able to fit the shuttle and the boxes mounted to the walls. "I'll stay."

Leona whipped her focus to Soph. "Are you sure?"

"Yup. Someone's got to babysit. Go, I'll be fine." She shooed Leona while reaching for the multi-tool in the left pocket of her overalls.

Leona faced the man who'd invited her to the bridge. He waited for her, infinite patience in his stance. His gaze was fixed on her face, not once dipping to her breasts straining her tight tank top.

Admirable.

As she approached, his eyes warmed, and a smile teased his top lip. Her heart fluttered, exploding butterflies through her adrenaline-saturated body. With each step bringing her closer to him, her senses heightened. Everything slowed as if she walked through mud, sluggish, but determined, her body bursting with warmth. He loomed, growing taller. His bronze skin caught the light and shimmered.

Stopping before him, she took a slow inhale, not wanting to be breathless when she spoke. Despite the effort, she still rasped, "Lead the way."

She tried not to stare at the Etterian's ass, hoping to offer him the same respect he'd shown her. Nor did she ogle his shoulders almost touching the sides of the passage. Which left the back of his head and the gentle sway of his long fishtail-braided black hair that was thicker than her forearm.

Come to think of it, all Etterians wore their hair the same. How odd. Earth's military men had buzz-cuts, especially those stationed in space—for many reasons, like hygiene and less shampoo needed. The Etterians went the opposite as if a thick braid wouldn't hinder their movements. How the hell did they even wear helmets?

The short passage flowed into a smallish room filled with screens. A battleship dominated the center vid. Its slick dark gray exterior and powerful guns stated its purpose.

Sure, she'd seen one a week ago on Lunar, but that was from a safe distance. Never would she have thought she'd be flying toward one and docking.

Excitement bubbled inside her, making her giddy. She bounced on her toes.

"Milady, welcome." The pilot thumped his chest, but when his gaze settled on her escort, he stiffened. Without another word, the pilot faced the vid. "Docking initiated."

"Pilot," her escort grumbled. "We do not endanger females."

The pilot nodded, then nudged a lever, slowing the ship's approach. "My apologies, Sub-Commander."

Leona tried not to show how impressed she was. *So, the gorgeous half-smiley man is a sub-commander?* His shoulder brushed hers when he inched closer to the console. His fingers twitched where they hung between her thigh and his.

She forced her gaze up and her eyes to focus on the tiny opening in the side of the battleship. How could docking in an alien ship distract her when the hairs on the back of her nape rose? When a shiver rippled down her spine and made her feet shuffle? When her breath lodged in her throat? The sub-commander was all she could think about.

Damn you, John. She squared her shoulders and folded her arms across her chest. Rallying her anger was her only defense against overwhelming lust. When she had a chance, she would give that man a piece of her mind. If it cost her the job, then so be it.

Blue shimmered over the vids when the ship penetrated the shield. Landing was with a nudge, almost imperceptible. Just like that, she was on board a freaking Etterian battleship. A plus to this adventure but not enough for her to forgive John for the too-short notice. Not to mention the little detail that she'd be surrounded by temptation for who knew how long.

"Milady?" The sub-commander gestured to the door.

Along the passage they went, except this time, she led the way. Had he been the slightest bit attracted to her and human, he'd be staring at her ass. She marched, clomping her boots on the grated flooring. Soph had the dolls facing the gaping door. Already their things and boxes had been unloaded.

With a nod from Leona, Soph commanded the dolls to disembark. All the controlled chaos in the warehouse-sized bay came to a standstill.

Aware of the attention their arrival generated, Leona faced the sub-commander, eager to be out of the spotlight. "Our accommodations, please. I need to settle my dolls."

She strode through the door, imagining his shoulder warming her chest when he brushed past her. With the punch of a few buttons on her O.D.I., a faint flutter of silk and bare feet meant the dolls formed a line. The chaos resumed when Leona, the sex-cybs, and Soph trailed the sub-commander.

After many twists and turns, he entered a wider passage lined with gray doors on both sides and stopped at the first one on the right.

"Storage. Your crates have been delivered." The door opened, but she blinked at it, too busy smothering the shiver running over her skin. His voice, so deep and husky, stroked along her senses as if he caressed her with those long-fingered hands.

Realizing he studied her face, she jerked forward to peer in. They had cleared the room of everything as she had specified. She stepped inside. Soph was close on her heels. Leona punched in commands, and two by two, they placed eight sex-cybs with their backs against the metal walls. With a mumbled, "Curtain call," she sent them into hibernation. Once done, she and Soph left the room, closing the door behind them.

"Is this security keyed to the three of us?" Leona asked.

"Yes, as requested," he rasped and pointed at the door opposite the storeroom. "Workshop." He swept out his hand at the table set in the center and the one wall mounted with screens. A flat surface to the back held a rehydrator and replicator. "The six cabins to the left and the five to the right have been prepared for habitation. All eleven are replicas. You may choose yours as you see fit."

Leona strode to the next room on the left, and when the door swished open, she gasped. This was an officer's cabin, with its own living room, bathroom, and bedroom. Her gaze shot to his. "I didn't expect this."

Soph poked her head around Leona's shoulder and peeked in. "Damn," she whispered. "I wish I was a doll."

Leona laughed. "For this, you would let an algri—"

"Ew. Point made." Soph squirmed.

"You do four and I'll take five, Sugar." Leona flicked her fingers, dividing the dolls.

They made light work of the remaining sex-cyb placement under the Etterian's watch. She tried to ignore that he was there, but he loomed, his presence sucking the air from the rooms. Holy shit, his eyes were stunning. When she couldn't resist anymore, she glanced at him, her gaze stalling on the magnificence of his ice-blue against his bronze skin. Thankfully, Soph wasn't as distracted and handled most of the preparations.

Once Leona had tested the security access panels, she entered the cabin that was to be hers.

The man followed her. "Does the accommodation meet your requirements, milady?"

"Yes, thank you." She forced herself to face him and held out a hand.

"Sub-Commander Aaro et Zaro." His hand engulfed hers, and heat unlike anything she'd experienced before zinged up her arm. She was torn between closing the gap between them and pulling out of his grip.

"Sugar, you should see the bathroom," Soph squealed.

Leona didn't break eye contact with Aaro, allowing herself the moment to drown in his eyes. "Why don't you check out your cabin?"

"In a minute. The sub-commander said they were identical. Gotta confirm it first." Soph disappeared into the bedroom.

"Are both your names Sugar?" Aaro frowned.

"No, it's our rank." Leona inched closer, drawn to his illusive spicy cologne. "Although mine is Chief Sugar. I just got promoted."

"Congratulations," he offered. "Then what *is* your name?"

"Oh. Um..." Her eyes widened. Her cheeks burned while he waited. "I *do* know my name."

He grinned and scattered her fragmented thoughts. *Wow.* "You do?" he teased.

She loved the charm oozing off him. "Yes, it's..." She grimaced. "I'm..."

"Leona Williams," Soph called from the bedroom before popping into the seating area.

"I'd almost forgotten." Leona prayed no one noticed her flushed face. "Soph, how about you head to your cabin so I can talk to the sub-commander?"

"Oh, all right. The dos and don'ts of sex-cyb usage. Rather skip that, thank you very much." Soph backed out of the cabin.

Aaro graced Leona with his profile while he addressed Soph. "Your things are in the storeroom. My males did not know which quarters you would choose."

"Got it, thanks." Soph bounded out of the cabin.

"She is enthusiastic," he observed, returning his gaze to Leona's upturned face.

She hadn't looked away from him. Even his profile thrilled her. The door of the cabin opened again to Soph clasping Leona's bag. He took it with one hand. The door whooshed shut on her disappearing form.

"I often wish I had an ounce of her energy." Leona tried to take her bag, but he set it against the wall. Shaking her head to clear her mind, she ventured farther into the cabin and took a seat in a white chair. It adjusted to cup her backside. The sensation made her shiver. "What times would suit you?"

"For?" Aaro didn't sit but leaned one shoulder against the bulkhead and stared at her, his ice-blue eyes assessing, admiring, and intense.

Her chest constricted under his vigilance. "For your men—

"Males."

She frowned at his correction. "…To have at my dolls. Eight cybs, two shifts." Not comfortable with the way his gaze caressed her, she fidgeted, then leaped to her feet and approached the rehydrator. With a cup of rich, hot cocoa in hand, she sat in the same seat she'd vacated and sipped the sweet liquid. "I don't wish to disrupt what must be a well-oiled machine." She hummed as the beverage calmed her. "The average Etterian takes approximately fourteen minutes so the disruption may be minimal. However, I don't want to deliver over-used dolls to the clients."

He scrutinized her, crossed his arms over his chest, and angled his hips away from her. "Only fourteen minutes? That is indeed sad."

She hid a smile by taking another sip from the cup. "I need at least ten minutes between sessions. Each doll has built-in self-cleaning. For the first few sessions, Sugar and I inject lubricant. Once the doll has stored sufficient ejaculation, it will be able to create its own lubrication. During the process, any sexually transmitted diseases are neutralized. It's quite ingenious."

He straightened, pushed himself off the wall, took a step toward her, then hesitated. "Alodon's balls, milady," he rasped then cleared his throat. "First two hours at shift-start?"

"Yes, that is acceptable." She jumped up, placed the cup on the table, and strode to the door. If she didn't kick him out, she'd beg him to fulfill all her Etterian fantasies. The poor man. Worse, what if he rejected her advances? She scowled. Right, like that was her biggest concern.

He punched in a few commands on his O.D.I. and waved the door open. "The next shift starts in three hours."

She caught his cologne and drew in a deep breath. When she spoke, her voice was hoarse. "We'll be ready."

The second she was alone, she squeezed her thighs together and rested her temple against the cool wall. Avoiding an interspecies incident wasn't going to be easy. Unless she could steer clear of Etterians and especially Aaro for the entirety of this trip. Not hard at all.

She scoffed and pushed off the wall. A cold shower might be a good start.

Chapter Seven

Leona tapped her O.D.I. trying to speak with John. Babe's holographic face appeared, pixelating badly. *What the hell?* As far as she knew, they were still planetside.

"Big Daddy, please," Leona said.

"He is on another call, can I—"

"Cary, he's sent me into this without warning. I'm so angry, I could kill him." Leona pinched her brow. *Damnit, not what I meant to say but true, nonetheless.*

The poor woman focused on Leona and sighed. "This is a bad connection. Find something stronger while I clear his schedule."

Leona grimaced and hurried over to the screen mounted to the wall. She flicked the call to it, but nothing happened. Tapping it only summoned archival menus. *Well, shit.*

"How the hell do you work, you stupid alien tech," she screamed.

"Milady, may I be of assistance?" a voice asked, reverberating through her cabin.

She squealed. "You're eavesdropping?" Hell, not once had she considered she'd be without privacy. There went her schedule. No way would she relieve her...tension if they listened in.

"No, milady. A disturbance was logged for your quarters." The man hesitated. "It is a security precaution in case someone is injured."

Note to self, no loud moaning when I orgasm. "How do I make a *private* call?"

"Address the display vid with the individual's full name and any available device close to them will connect."

So simple and yet not common knowledge. "Um, thanks."

"I am Pilot Krist et Garist if you need me, milady."

"Thank you." She winced. What else could she say? When he spoke no more, she faced the screen and gritted out John's full name.

His face flickered into crisp resolution.

Anger surged through her in waves. "You could have told me," she snapped. "Seventy-two minutes? I swear, when I see you face to face—"

"You're dressed like that?" His gaze swept over her in horror.

"My point exactly." She crossed her arms over her chest, trying to hide her state of arousal.

"My apologies, Leona. You do look a little...flustered."

She snorted. *He damn well means stimulated. Hell's bells, my nipples can cut glass.* "What would you expect when you're surrounded by asses so tight they could ricochet bullets?"

He started to laugh with a rumble at first then a full-out guffaw.

She continued, ignoring his mirth. "Everything has been settled, the cybs are in place, and a preliminary schedule has been worked out with the sub-commander."

"Good. While you're there, take the chance to sample a few Etterians. You don't watch their vids like the other women. Just one algri on repeat? Never thought you swung that way, girl."

She gaped, willing herself not to blush. "You monitor our vid choices?"

"Of course, how else am I to know what women want?"

All the women in his factories were his lab rats? The why was obvious, but surely he knew what women's needs were after all this time? She stared at him for a minute before narrowing her eyes. "You're making male sex-cybs."

He barked out another laugh. "Damn, you *are* good."

"Well, if you build them like Etterians, then you'll have the perfect product." Any remaining anger vanished. She paced, her mind accepting the challenge and running with it. "You won't be able to have male or female staff working those factories. They'd sample the goods, for sure."

"I thought of manufacturing my cybs to do the grunt work, but they're not sentient, can't think on their feet, so to speak. Also, cybs are expensive. Surveys have shown that the clientele will always think of Cyb Ent's products as sex toys."

"Then we'll hire older people." She punched her hand. "You could start a sister company to market security cybs as bodyguards, male or female or gender neutral." She paced again. "Couriers that can alter the color of their skin to blend in. They can fly single-body crafts, no life support needed."

"Another company... " John hummed. "That could work." His smile widened with every one of her ideas, inspiring her onward.

She bounced as she crossed her room. "Repair cybs that are stored in the outer structure of a ship or space station. Or law enforcement cybs—"

"You'll be visiting me when you've completed these deliveries, Leona."

Her gaze shot up to meet his. "Happy to assist, Big Daddy."

Her screen blanked. End of transmission.

She danced around the cabin, put away her meager belongings, then took a cold shower before heading to the workshop. There, she spent the majority of the three hours setting up the work surfaces, calibrating the screens, and organizing the lubricants. She entered each cabin and placed cameras as per the Cyb Ent protocol regarding the care and maintenance of each sex-cyb. Returning to the workshop, she synchronized the cameras to her main screen and tested their maneuverability. After all, the cabins were larger than the rooms at the cyb center. Once she was happy with the viewing access, she called Soph, and they lubricated the dolls before waking them from hibernation.

A few minutes before the shift-start, the Etterian men began to arrive. It was sweet of them to have showered, and their eager expressions broke her heart.

"If you encounter any issues, please find us. Soph or I will be in the workshop. Each cyb needs to be prepped for the next man so give us a little time before rushing in, and remember, enjoy it. There's no hurry." Taking pity on them, she opened the doors before the scheduled time. She punched in the command, 'Show Time' and headed to the workshop, to do what she always did—monitor the feeds.

Hours ticked by. She'd gone from never watching Etterians to being forced to gawk at their gorgeous asses. Hell, they had the perfect bodies, the kind honed in combat and not the gym. Faced with their physiques, the subtle differences came to the fore. All had black hair and bronzed skin, but the variances lay in the angle of their eyebrows, the shape of their eyes, noses, or mouths. Dimples and angular-to-square jawlines varied to some degree.

Their heights were between six feet to seven, though that didn't matter when they were horizontal for the most part. And penis-wise, they looked similar to humans. She supposed that might be why she liked them. Algris and Maloidians weren't the norm and felt...wrong. There was no other way to explain it. Perhaps due to her sheltered childhood and brief walk on the promiscuous side in college, she wasn't wild enough to try something different, especially a new way of fucking.

As if tutored in the art of love making, Etterians were gentle, almost reverent.

Soph sighed and clasped her hands to her chest. "Wow," she mumbled.

"Yup," Leona said, dragging out the 'u.' She typed on a tablet, capturing the ideas she'd listed to John earlier. Something had to keep her mind off the vids. The only thing that would drag her focus to the sexual acts was a doll malfunction. She downed another hot cocoa and smacked her lips, considering a slab of chocolate, instead. Or maybe a shot of brandy in the next cup.

Damnit, as soon as this session was over, she'd return to her cabin and take care of herself. Fuck her schedule. Who was she fooling anyway? John had doomed her to this torture.

"Milady?"

Leona smothered a squeak and faced the Etterian dominating the workshop's doorway.

"May I have a copy of the recording?" He gestured to a screen.

She stiffened, cast a wide-eyed glance at Soph, then rolled her lips, not sure how to respond.

"Why?" Soph asked.

"I need to perfect my technique. I cannot do so without studying my performance."

Leona blinked at him. He wanted to study his what? "Um, sure." She flicked a thumb at the split vids. "Select yours."

He ventured deeper into the workshop, tapped 'Vid-4,' and raised his forearm. The holographics of his O.D.I. flickered. With a bow, he exited.

"Watch himself perform?" Soph whispered, two red splotches on her cheeks.

"Yes, for our *Dar Eth*s," another man said. A long line of men queued behind him, no doubt wanting the same thing.

"*Dar Eth*s?" Leona mouthed while they streamed in, grabbed their recording, and left. She hurried to her cabin and faced the black screen. "Pilot Krist et Garist?"

"Yes, milady."

"May I have a screen mounted to the inside of each cyb's cabin, please?" She stilled and studied her screen. Aaro had said the cabins were replicas. "Wait, does every cabin have a screen?"

"Only the officer quarters."

She frowned. *Is that a yes or no?* "Not the cybs' cabins?"

"They are officer quarters, milady."

So, a yes. "Cancel that request, Krist." She darted in and out of the emptied doll cabins, setting the screens to show the recording of each session.

"Milady?" A man frowned, standing in the doorway while he waited for her.

She hurried past him and addressed those in line. "I've synced the screens to the cameras. Help yourself to your recording as you leave." Well, at least they wouldn't bother her and Soph every damn time they were done.

"Wise," Soph muttered after the last man left. "I can't get shit done with all this in-and-out nonsense."

"Yup." Leona flicked a thumb at the door. "I'm tempted to shut it."

"Same." Soph huffed the hair off her face. "Still, I bet we're the envy of every damn woman on Callisto."

"Sure." Leona ran her thumb along her jaw. "I wonder what happened to Tina."

"You go ahead and think about that," Soph gritted out. "I'm not wasting a moment of my time on her."

"Whoa, where did that come from?" Leona faced her. When the younger woman didn't say anything more, Leona rested a hand on her hip and tapped a foot. "Sugar, what did you do?"

"She...wouldn't take no for an answer," Soph stammered. "So, I...I took her down."

Ice drenched Leona from her ears to her toes, but before she could shiver, a fiery fury swept over her. "She did— You did—" She clamped her lips to end her stuttering.

"It's all right, Sugar. Thankfully, security witnessed it all." Soph dipped her chin to her chest. "I don't think Big Daddy knows I was involved." She offered a stiff shrug. "He probably thinks any Sugar was the cause."

Leona threw an arm across Soph's shoulders. "I doubt he deals with every incident that happens. Just..." What could she say? 'Don't be alone with Tina' sounded redundant. "You took her down?" *Oh, I so want the details.*

Soph smile was wicked. "I should be sorry, but when the snapping of her wrist echoed in the showers, I relished it." She twitched her nose. "Does that make me bad?"

"Not in my book. That makes you kickass." Leona hugged her, squeezing the air out of her. "Well done, Soph. Now I don't have to worry about you too much."

"Thanks, Leona." Soph chuckled. "Wanna discuss Etterians studying their own porn?"

"Nope." Leona giggled as she pulled away. "I do want to know what a *Dar Eth* is."

"Same." Soph hopped over to the rehydrator to order a soda. "Maybe it means 'wife' in their language."

"Makes sense." Leona tapped the digital clock in the bottom right corner of the screen. "Almost end of the first session. For some strange reason, this morning has dragged."

"Yup, and in seven hours we repeat. Got any plans for the interim?"

"The usual. Swap out the dolls, lubricate, then shower and nap." Leona studied the split screens and the last batch of men grunting and huffing, anything to hide what she planned—some sexual relief.

"Oh, a nap sounds amazing." Soph bounced on the spot. "One's done." She grabbed the lubrication gun and bolted. The poor Etterian had yet to close his pants.

Leona laughed and ordered another hot cocoa.

Chapter Eight

"Opacity: mirror." Aaro blinked at the reflection of his ice-blue eyes in the passage's bulkhead the moment it switched from gray to mirror. Warmth flooded him. He threw back his head to laugh. Indescribable joy pulsed in his chest. Never had he felt this good nor this intensely. The past hour with Leona, from meeting her to now, had blurred. He could almost believe the *Ethera* hadn't struck him down. His eye color didn't lie, though.

It is true.

He was paired and his life spared *if* Leona accepted him.

With a mental finger, he prodded the dark void buried in his core. It lay dormant as if it waited.

"Sub-Commander," Data Officer Ranh greeted when he passed Aaro to the comm room.

"Opacity: default," Aaro commanded the bulkhead. It shimmered to metallic gray—like Maloidian steel. He strode behind Ranh and assumed the comfy against the back wall of the comm room. Beside him was a high table with a tablet lying on it.

"Um, Sub-Commander, how do these sex-cybs look?" Pilot Krist asked, his gaze fixed on Aaro.

"Did you not watch the sec-vids?" Aaro scanned the room and took pity on the males in the comm. "Human-like with skin appearing as soft as an Eiltar's fur."

His males gawked at him but remained silent. He frowned. What more did they expect him to say?

"Congratulations, Sub-Commander." Pilot Krist grinned. "On your pairing."

Ah. "Yes," Aaro said, at a loss on how to respond. "At ease." He pulled the tablet closer and summoned *Stolen Love*. Sifting through the endless comms was an option, but to ignore the staring, he needed something distracting.

Benedict gripped the railing and raised his face to the morning sunlight. A breeze tossed his hair across his eyes, but it didn't matter, not when Elizabeth's scent engulfed him. He snuck a glance over his shoulder, somehow knowing she'd be there.

In nothing but her shift.

He gritted his teeth, torn between covering her beautiful body and savoring the way the transparent cloth draped over her curves.

"Woman, what—?"

"I want you," she said, her shoulders square despite her clasping and releasing the fabric of her shift.

A shiver raced through Benedict, the kind that burned like fire and made him ache for more. "What do you know about the flesh, milady?"

Aaro scowled, not liking the way Benedict spoke to her as if she was a simpleton.

"That one taste isn't enough?" She harrumphed. "Now that London is in our sights, you do not share my craving? I suppose any of your crew will do."

Red tainted Benedict's vision. Another man touch what was... His? He could not have her and keep her, that he knew. His life was not for the faint-hearted, nor for one as delicate as his Elizabeth.

Tomorrow, they would dock. He had this one day, one last chance to taste those sweet lips, to relish her softness against his body.

"I will always want you," he rasped, closing the distance between them.

"Pilot Krist et Garist?" Leona's voice slicing through the comm room snagged everyone's attention.

Aaro stiffened, caught his breath, then lowered the tablet to the table.

Krist swiveled his chair to face the console. "Yes, milady."

"How does she know your name, pilot?" Aaro growled, pushing off the comfy to approach the console.

"Milady had an issue with the display vid in her quarters," Krist whispered.

Aaro frowned. "Where—"

"May I have a screen mounted to the inside of each cyb's cabin, please," Leona continued. "Wait, does every cabin come with a screen?"

"Only the officer quarters," Krist said, his gaze fixed on Aaro.

"Not the cybs' cabins?" Leona asked.

Krist faced forward. "They are officer quarters, milady."

Humor filled Leona's voice. "Cancel that request, Krist."

"More screens?" Aaro repeated when she said no more. It didn't help that he was in the middle of Benedict drawing a fulfillment from Elizabeth. Alodon's balls, he should've waited until the privacy of his quarters to read that scene. Now, all he could imagine was pinning Leona beneath him.

"For the recordings," Krist said, punched the console, then pushed off when his O.D.I. pinged. "My turn." His step held an extra bounce.

Aaro scowled. "Turn for?"

Krist rubbed his palms together, nothing daunting his good humor. "A sex-cyb, Sub-Commander. Medic Flad has the schedules if you want to book a time."

The least amount of disruption Leona had said? There went Aaro's primary pilot.

Aaro swept out his arm, gesturing to the wall of display vids. "Who—"

"Pilot Saan will cover for me." Krist thumped his chest. With a laugh, he left the comm room.

"How many of you have tested these objects?" Aaro faced the males gathered around the table in the war room leading off the comm room.

"Most educational," Ranh said. "Though, not all of us have had our turn, hence Krist's question. Skin like Eiltur's fur is a perfect description."

A few males nodded, their smiles blooming like the magnus sunrise over the crimson oceans on Etteria.

"Krists's inability to sit still might be tied to the number of hot cocoas he has consumed." Ranh gestured to the display vids. "Lady Leona agreed to let us keep our recordings for research purposes."

Medic Flad strode in, a grin splitting his cheeks. "I came to find out if you would like a session, Sub-Commander?"

Aaro shook his head. The only woman he wanted wasn't his to claim, yet.

"Aaro..." Flad gripped Aaro's upper arms and held him still to stare into his eyes. "When? Who? I never thought another of *my* males would find his *Dar Eth*."

Flad hadn't been on the *Gladio* when Oyaz had met Izzy. Since this was the first pairing on the *Valiant*, Aaro allowed Flad's familiarity. As the elder, he deserved respect and a little leniency. A pairing happening had to be a shock. They'd been myths, after all.

"Leona, the dark-haired woman." Aaro squeezed and released the male's shoulder.

Flad tapped his O.D.I., his fingers dancing merrily over the holographic lettering "Please, walk with me to medical. I would like to do a full scan to document all you are enduring."

Aaro smothered a groan. The last thing he wanted was to be prodded and probed. "You could command me, Flad." He spoke the truth. A medic could remove a superior from their post if their ill health demanded it.

"True. Instead, I ask, as your battle-bond, as a sub-commander who understands how vague our archives are on this subject."

Put like that, it would be unfair of him to not do this. "Very well, Flad." Aaro led the way, gathering his thoughts while he strode to the nearest common. Once in medical and sprawled on the medical emergency device or med-E.D., he lay there, staring at the white ceiling.

"Start from the beginning," Flad said while punching instructions into the med-E.D. reserved for severe injuries.

"I saw her, nothing more. The pain was...exquisite." Aaro winced, unable to convey the sweet agony that had taken him to his knee. He cleared his throat and tried again. "It was as if a thousand explosions burned along my veins. I had visions of her in an intimate position."

Flad nodded like discussing lovemaking was normal. "That should bring hope, that mating her is inevitable."

"I cannot command her to my bed, Flad. My interactions with women have taught me that as a human, Leona knows nothing of the pairing, of what the *Ethera* means. I must find a way to tell her without risking a rejection." Aaro gritted his teeth. "I am avoiding her for now and praying to the Maker that a little distance will grant me some control."

Flad tutted. "The scans do not lie, Aaro. Your hormones, blood pressure, and adrenaline fluctuate at alarming rates. Can you regulate your heart rates?"

Aaro drew in slow calming breaths and called on decades of training, but still, his heartbeats pounded in his ears. "No."

Flad typed on the med-E.D.'s panel. "From what information we have gathered so far, you do not have long until the *Ethera* will take over and force the situation."

Aaro scowled. Like he didn't know that? He'd witnessed it first-hand with Ulriq, then Kanzo. Jack had been eager to pair with Ulriq, but Ava had fought the *Ethera*. Same with Tory when Teric had knelt for her. She'd resisted the very idea of a soulmate. To humans, choice mattered even when the *Ethera* never failed to make the perfect match.

"Perhaps using a cyb to perform your morning chore would buy you time." Flad met his gaze.

Everything within Aaro rebelled against the idea. He understood the validity of the suggestion, but Leona watched the vids. His male-hood throbbed at the thought of her gaze upon his naked form. No, he couldn't bring himself to do it. He had chosen to stay away from her for his sanity. Now, it seemed the only solution to eventually claiming her was to spend time with her, as much as possible.

Maker. He lifted his hand to stare at his trembling fingers. All he could promise was to try.

"Thank you, Aaro." Flad deactivated the med-E.D. "When your control deteriorates, please, let me scan you again."

Aaro sat up and swung his legs off the side of the bed. "For you, old battle-bond."

As Aaro strode from medical, he used his O.D.I. to locate Leona. When it pinged, indicating she was in the workshop, he veered in that direction. Had she been in her quarters, he would have returned to the safety of the comm room. With the threat of Lady Soph interrupting, he couldn't succumb and seduce Leona, regardless of how much he wanted to.

He stepped into the passage and paused, taking a moment to sniff the air. Residual scents of matings, lubricant, and the not-unpleasant perfume that was Lady Soph couldn't smother the lure of Leona's natural essence. He strode past the sex-cybs and storeroom to the workshop, its door wide open.

There she stood, a hand splayed on the table, the other cradling a cup to her chest. Behind her on the display vids were various scenes, the muted moans of mating reaching his sensitive hearing.

"Malfunction in the metatarsals of the left foot. Check with the supplier," she said into her tablet.

A grimace twisted her features, so fast that, had he blinked, he would have missed it. He leaned against the edge of the door, folding his arms and crossing his ankles, content to admire her. A slow smile formed. If he had his way, he would close the distance between them and save her bottom lip from her teeth. His heartbeats leaped at the thought of kissing her. Would she gasp? Would his boldness anger her? He was eager to find out but wary of driving her away. Every step he took might bring their mating closer or push it further out of reach.

She rubbed her neck and, with a sigh, raised her face to the ceiling. Under her closed eyes were shadows as if sleep was elusive. Her braid fell over a shoulder, darker when her hair was damp. He sniffed, inhaling her freshly washed skin and—

Fire lanced through him. His knees weakened. His malehood hardened. A lingering scent of her fulfillment clung to her. He opened his mouth to ask... No, to demand, but no words formed. His voice lodged in his throat.

She opened her eyes and settled her gaze on him. Her cheeks pinkened like the hahyt blossoms of home. "Sub-Commander, I'm sorry, I didn't see you there." She ran a palm over her hip, distracting him for a second.

"Why do you scent of fulfillment?" He charged into the room, pausing to grip the table.

"What?" She jerked back. "What's that?" She swept a curl off her temple.

"Finding pleasure," he gritted out.

"Oh." Her cheeks bloomed again. "You can smell—" She cupped her mouth, her eyes wide. "I... After a shower..." She huffed, slammed the cup down, and gripped her hips, challenging him. "It's none of your business."

His shoulders slumped, and he let out a breath. She hadn't mated with anyone, had simply taken care of her chore. Good. He didn't need to kill a male today. "How did the shift go?"

"Just like that? Like you haven't just insulted me." She threw her hands in the air. "Why not ask me about the weather?"

He frowned. "All battleships are climate controlled."

"Oh," she cried out, stamping a foot.

Liking this passionate side to her, he tried to hide a chuckle. "You found release by *your* hand. This is acceptable."

She blinked at him, her mouth opening and closing. "It is?" she squeaked. "No, don't answer that." Offering her back, she faced the bulkhead, her fingers buried in her hair. Her shoulders rose and fell with her ragged breathing. "So, your men...behaved well." She snatched the tablet and tapped on it.

"Leona, come here." He pointed to the spot at his boots.

She stiffened, her gaze flicking between his face and the floor. "Why?"

"Please." He held his breath, waited, hoped, and prayed she'd choose to trust him.

She stared at him, placed the tablet on the table, then crossed the room, stopping a foot from him. A smile threatened to spill free, which he managed to rein in. This close, he could trail the dots on her cheeks, faded but there. He looped an arm around her and held her against his chest.

She cried out and threw her hands up to his biceps while glaring at him. "What are you doing? Let me go." She slapped his arms.

"It is called a hug," he said, not releasing her despite her futile attempts to make him.

She wiggled for a minute, then with a huff, rested her temple over his left heart. As time passed, the tension in her body eased. At last, she slumped against him with her breathing deepening.

"I *did* need this," she mumbled.

Her scent engulfed him, drowned his senses, and soaked into his skin. He gathered her closer, inch by inch, unable to resist doing so. The softness of her in his arms was breathtaking as if he had found joy, peace, understanding, and enlightenment all at once.

"What you need is rest." He splayed his fingers between her shoulder blades. "Do you have time now?"

"I was going to, but the...uh, fulfillment energized me."

"I shall escort you to your quarters." He stepped back, dragging his palms down the back of her arms to her elbows and fingertips.

"What?" She jerked out of reach.

He clasped her hand and pinned it to his chest. "Escort, no farther than your door, *ensa*." He grinned. "Trust me."

She harumphed but let him lead her out of the workshop, watched him lock the door, then she trailed him along the passage to her quarters. At her door, he faced her, cupping her exquisite face to stare into her blue eyes.

"Rest well, Leona," he whispered. "Comm if you need me."

She tugged her hand free, trailing her fingers down his torso. "Thanks, Sub-Commander."

"Aaro," he rasped, strangely desperate to hear his name on her tongue.

She stepped into her quarters, then glanced at him. "Aaro."

The moment he was alone, he pressed his palms and temple to the door. Drawing in slow breaths calmed his heart rates enough for the roaring in his ears to subside. With a tremble, he pushed off the door and returned to the comm room. This time, he ignored Benedict and Elizabeth. Instead, he focused on the endless requests and information that formed part of his position.

He needed something monotonous to keep his mind off Leona and her enticing scent.

THE MOMENT THE DOOR swished shut, Leona leaned against it while holding her inflamed cheeks.

"Wow," she whispered. Her heart thudded a tribal beat she hadn't heard in a long while. Well, not since her first crush with Rex. *And look how that turned out.*

Catching Aaro staring at her had done something to her internal wiring. Her thoughts had zigzagged, zooming through her mind until all she could do was gape...like a virgin.

"That amount of sex appeal has to be illegal. Damn you, John." She pushed off and veered to her bedroom.

When Aaro had commanded her to stand in front of him, she'd sensed it meant more than submission to his authority. Etteria's military might infinitely outweighed Earth's. For the sake of diplomacy, she could acknowledge he had power over her.

A hug wasn't something she'd expected.

She'd fought him, assuming he wanted intimacy and, with his strength, could take it.

The longer he held her, asked nothing of her, the more she succumbed to the solid muscle engulfing her in a sense of security. His addictive cologne helped. Holy cow, he smelled of citrus and cinnamon. She giggled at something Mel would've said. *Damn lickable.*

Undoing her boots and tossing them aside, Leona crawled across the bed. No blanket adorned it, but like he'd said, the battleship was climate-controlled. She snorted. Closing her eyes would hopefully convince her body to sleep. Except for the stunning images of Aaro rising to the forefront of her mind. She tamped them down and wiggled, trying to find a comfortable spot. Snuggle, huff, slide hand under pillow, roll over, and repeat. No matter what she did, she couldn't let it go. What were his motives? Why her? Could she trust him? He'd claimed to want nothing more than for her to find rest, but could that be a ruse?

She thumped the pillow and sat up. Why was she overthinking this? As a considerate host, he was probably ensuring she was happy. Nothing more. Flopping back, she settled, and on a hum, let her eyes close.

She smirked, torn between obedience and defiance. What would he do if she got up? Would he throw her over his shoulder and toss her onto the bed?

A thrill shot through her. The temptation to test his resolve was almost irresistible. She yawned and let herself imagine propositioning the man for a little sexy time. Would he be interested?

Come to think of it, not a single Etterian had hit on her. What about Soph? On a battleship this size with who knew how many soldiers on board, they had to be a little desperate for female companionship, right?

Leona clenched her teeth, silently cursing Soph, who, no doubt, *was* napping already. What would end this sexual torment? A good fuck? A week ago, she'd been at peace, sipping coffee while admiring the Etterian battleship looming over Lunar Base. At that exact moment, all had been right in her world with a good job, minimal sexual harassment, no Bradley on the horizon, and no lustful urges she needed to fight.

Her present situation could be worse. Bradley could be forcing her to wed him, her mother gleefully splaying a hand to her chest while dabbing her non-existent tears with a delicate touch.

No, facing danger in any form was preferable to that. Being a little horny was bearable.

What she needed was a shot of vitamins. Something to bolster her body. Meeting Medic Aldur implied medics had to be on a battleship. Leaping to her feet, she hurried across to the black vid. She winced. Whatever the cost, she had to try.

"Pilot Krist?" Speaking to herself, with her voice dominating the space, made her feel stupid. She shifted from side to side and glanced around as if she wasn't alone or could be overheard.

"Milady?" Krist's voice made her yelp then giggle at her silliness.

"Do you have a medic?"

"You are unwell, Lady Leona?"

She paused, loving the reverent title. It took a shake of her head to clear her mind.

"I am en route," Aaro said.

She shivered, recognizing his raspy voice in an instant. "Shit," she growled. Not once had she considered her conversations with the pilot wouldn't be private. Having been on the bridge, she should have realized this. *Idiot.* "I'm well. Not injured or any-thing."

"Medic Flad is on his way," Krist said, ignoring her assurances.

"Dammit." She stamped a foot. Squaring her shoulders, she opened the door to her cabin and waited.

Aaro striding toward her, his braid whipping behind him, was the stuff of erotic fantasies. His brow furrowed with concern. It would ease soon enough. Still, she could admire the sheer mas-culinity of him.

"What happened?" he demanded, cupping her arms while run-ning his gaze over her.

"Just need a vitamin shot." She raised her hands to rest against his pecs and stopped herself in time. Her fingers twitched at the lost opportunity.

"I told you to sleep." His tone was resigned, and when he rubbed her arms from elbow to shoulders, she leaned toward him, seeking his warmth.

"Can't," she muttered, caved, and touched him. It could be her imagination messing with her that he trembled beneath her hands. It might be insanity when his fingers clenched around her arms, drawing her closer.

"Milady?" an older male called as he hurried along the passage. There were no designations on his uniform to mark him as anything other than an Etterian soldier.

"Medic Flad, Lady Leona requests a...vitamin shot?" Aaro frowned, hesitated, then stepped aside.

Pacing her room would have been easier than dealing with whatever this was. "I'm tired but can't sleep." She pursed her lips, wondering if it was adrenaline still flooding her body. "I need a boost of some sort."

"A sedative, perhaps?" Flad flicked a glance at Aaro then ran his O.D.I. over her. "Serotonin low, vitamins and nutrients fine, hormones fluctuating."

She tensed and smothered a groan. Heat exploded across her cheeks. Aaro and now Flad would know about her aroused state. *Dammit.*

Flad offered a polite smile. "It is to be expected."

"It is?" she squeaked.

He squared his shoulders like he prepared to face off an army. "Your hormones are unstable due to your arousal. I anticipate it will worsen."

She opened and closed her mouth. Nothing in her schooling or surviving her mother had prepared her for this scenario. "Worsen?" She gasped. "How— Do you— Can you help me?"

Flad shook his head. "I have added vitamins and a serotonin boost to your cleanser." With a pointed look at Aaro, he strode off.

Pinching her brow, she prayed a black hole opened beneath her feet and dragged her in. Part of her whispered that Aaro had known about her...condition. Still, she swallowed past the lump in her throat. How mortifying.

"I need to shower again?" She flicked her gaze at Aaro and froze.

Agony twisted his handsome features.

"Aaro?"

He shuddered, raised his gaze to the ceiling, and drew in a ragged breath. "If you are well, milady?" He didn't glance her way, even when he lifted his hand to touch her, paused an inch from her chin, then withdrew.

"Leona," she said.

He lowered his gaze to meet hers, seizing the air in her lungs. Intense emotion swirled in the bright blue depths of his eyes. A frisson of need trickled down her spine and settled in her core. She opened her mouth to ask if he'd be interested in something casual with her.

His gentle touch along her jaw trapped the words in her throat. Then he was gone, leaving her standing there, shaking, yearning, and stunned. Her last glimpse of him was of his incredibly broad shoulders disappearing around the corner.

She swept her hair off her face and blinked at her trembling fingers. A shower, a coffee, and work. That's what she needed. Perhaps, when she'd tamed her arousal and gathered her wits, she would be grateful she hadn't said a word to her sub-commander.

Chapter Nine

Aaro went over the same sentence. He couldn't bear to read onward.

Every time Benedict spread Elizabeth's thighs, Aaro imagined doing so to Leona. Her imaginary cries, pleas, and whimpers were all too real as if he recalled memories.

It had taken all his strength not to beg her to let him taste her. The *Ethera* had started their connection, building it, and until they consummated their pairing, the void would be in limbo. He wasn't foolish, having witnessed stubborn Kanzo's struggle. Besides, it had only been a day, and had Leona not been in such a state of constant arousal, things might have progressed at a slower pace.

Consummation was the only way to help her, but doing so would seal her fate. Yet, she'd save him from a dark and lonely life. *If* she stayed with him. Could he tell her? Would she choose him after such a short acquaintance? Aaro's human studies had taught him women didn't believe in instant love. They had to decide their future.

He gritted his teeth and shifted on the comfy, hoping to ease his aching arousal. As a sub-commander, he could invite her to his quarters for dinner. Perhaps honesty would be the best approach. And if she was amenable to it, she would be his *Dar Eth* in the truest sense.

Empowered, he leaped to his feet. "Krist, you have the comm."

En route, he ran through scenarios: what to say, or how she might react.

"It's the rotating ball joint." The workshop door opened, and Soph stepped out. "He's almost done. Will lubricate at the same time." She nodded at Aaro in greeting as she waited outside one of the cybs' cabins.

He peeked into the workshop's door that had remained open. Alone, Leona stared at the six-paneled display vid. Her focus mesmerized him. She touched 'Vid-1' and typed on her data tab. An answering moan from a male brought forth a nod from her. She picked up a cup and froze, blinking at Aaro standing in the doorway.

"Sub-Commander." Her gaze snagged on the display. She put the cup down and tapped the data tab. "Shit." She touched 'Vid-3.' "Soph?"

Soph raised her gaze while wiping down the cyb. "What?"

"You're right. It *is* a defective ball joint. Got another in room '1.' I'll notify the factory."

"I'll search storage. We packed a variety." Soph waved a cloth. "Might be able to replace them."

Leona returned her attention to the displays. "Twelve percent more arch and twenty percent more volume," she mumbled. A feminine moan emanated from 'Vid-4.'

"What are you doing?" Fascinated, he crossed the room to face the six panels. "Do you monitor each one for the duration of the sessions?"

"Yes. We must always be ready. The dolls do malfunction, and we've encountered disrespectful clients, as well." She flashed him a smile, hitching his breath. "Not Etterians, though."

"What do you change on your data tab?"

She shrugged. "I like to improve their performances, make them more responsive and human. Just this morning I added sounds like moans and groans. Soph and I were in hysterics, recording examples the cybs could evolve on their own." She touched 'Vid-5' then her data tab. "Watch. Let's increase the angle of her hips by five degrees on the second thrust and decrease the movement speed by thirty percent."

The male the cyb was riding arched off the bed and roared his release. The cyb cried out, sounding like Leona.

"Each amendment is recorded in their cybernetics. All existing and new dolls will respond accordingly."

Aaro blinked, trying to appear casual when he curved his hips away from her. His malehood throbbed at the words dripping from her pink lips. *Alodon's balls.* Didn't she realize how her subject matter affected those around her? Judging by her relaxed expression, she did not.

He met her gaze then shifted his focus to how pale she was with a fine sheen coating her skin. Her hands shook, and her decadent arousal drenched the small space.

"Did you not shower?" He faced her, but she stepped away from him.

She closed her eyes and took a deep breath. "You smell so damn good," she whispered.

A wave of ice then heat flooded his body. He activated his O.D.I. to regulate his armor beyond the usual. When she met his gaze, her expression was one of innocence as if she hadn't revealed her attraction.

"I did shower, had a coffee, and am now working."

"Your arousal has deepened, *ensa*." He sniffed and groaned, his fingers twitching with an eagerness to touch her.

"Damn." She gaped. "I didn't know Etterians had such an amazing olfactory..." Her eyes widened, and she grabbed the data tab. "What do I smell like?" When he hesitated, she raised her gaze to his. "Tell me, please." She waited, her finger poised.

He inhaled through his nose, swelling his chest to the maximum. "Sweet, fruity, like an exotic flower. Smoky and delicious."

"Thank you," she rasped, typing on the data tab despite the flush on her cheeks. "With the chemicals in each cyb, the closest scent they can generate is...vanilla." She punched the tab.

Across all screens, his males groaned.

Leona flashed Aaro an arched brow. "All we need to find out now is what our other clients like to smell. Y'know, an algri versus a Maloidian." She did a little dance on her toes, the action bouncing her breasts.

"I've never thought about scents before. The dolls reek of lubricants and synthetics." She scrunched up her nose. "Must be awful for you."

"Me?"

"Etterians," she said and swept out an arm.

"Leona." His patience was dwindling.

"Aaro," she said, her good humor tugging at her sensual lips.

"I would like to invite you to dinner."

She studied his face, tilting her head as she did so. "Ah, the captain wining and dining the guests?"

He grinned after the O.D.I. flashed images to explain her words. "In a way. There is something I need to discuss with you."

She stilled. "So, no Soph?"

"Just you," he said, desperate to have her alone and focused on him.

"Sounds serious."

"It can be." He cupped her shoulder and stroked her silky skin.

"Oh?" She shifted closer to him, her breasts almost touching his chest. "Dinner with the sub-commander? I can't say no to that," she whispered, peering at him through the veil of her eyelashes. "What time?"

He stepped back to thwart sinking into a kiss. "After shift end."

"Sure."

He suppressed a shiver. "I will collect you." He inched away, despite everything within him urging him to close the distance between them.

She smiled. The sweetness in her expression was his undoing. He lunged, looped an arm around her waist, and pinned her against a bulkhead. Her gasp merged with her arms tightening on his shoulders, all registering her submission.

She had no idea how irresistible her scent was to him. How addictive the weight of her in his arms was. The way her softness pressed against his body. The warmth of her breath on his chin.

He met her gaze and dipped, slanting his mouth across hers.

Maker. He groaned and swept his tongue in, tasting her as he'd longed to do. Not that he knew what to do. Except for how Elizabeth had described Benedict kissing her. Aaro slicked his tongue along Leona's. Her moan, her nails digging into his back, her leg wrapping around his hip, and rubbing her sex along his arousal, all culminated in blinding desire. He broke the kiss to run his lips along her jaw then nibble on her earlobe.

"Fuck," she cried out as a shiver rolled through her.

With his body layered over hers, he relished every one of her reactions. Pinning her in place, he rested his temple on hers while dragging in gulps of air. "Dinner, talk, then fuck."

She laughed. "Aye, aye, Sub-Commander."

He chuckled. She knew her history. Elizabeth had said something similar to Benedict. *Alodon's balls, the Ethera has chosen the perfect woman for me.* "Will you be all right until dinner?"

She scoffed and pushed at him, silently asking him to release her. He did so, creating a little space between them.

"Yes," she said. "I'm aroused, not ill." Her honesty floored him and ramped his heartbeat. "It's been building for a week, and today tested me. For now, I won't focus on the actual act, just the mechanics of it." She flashed him a self-mocking smile.

He blinked at her, struggling to hold onto his control like fingers cupping water.

She shrugged and sucked in a sharp breath, pulling the front of her shirt away from her taut nipples. "I'll watch an algri and a doll. That should restore a little peace."

"Did you not ease your suffering earlier?" He frowned. She couldn't have lied about that, not when he'd scented her fulfillment on her.

She arched a brow. "Once is enough, you say?" she teased. "It's been a week of torture. I have yet to grow accustomed to the amount of sex I watch."

"Perhaps twice a day might help." He ignored his erratic heartbeat and trembling hands. The way her pants clung to her backside...visions of tasting her shredded what little control remained. "Until this evening," he said and bolted for his sanity alone.

Chapter Ten

"Well, well." Soph smirked when she stepped into the workshop.

"It's everything you think it is." With a start, Leona realized she was still leaning against the wall. She relaxed her posture and suppressed a moan when her core twanged. Damn. Aaro hadn't just kissed her, right? He'd done so with such mastery. She fanned herself with no effect. Expecting to self-combust at any moment, she used both hands, relishing the slightest breeze. Her face burned. From a dinner invite to sex, that had escalated quickly. She was ashamed of her behavior but so delighted with the outcome. "My one to your countless."

"My zero." Soph chuckled when Leona gaped at her.

"No, I don't believe it. Not one man on this ship?"

"Yup. From hot-off-the-press to doesn't exist, it's enough to give me a complex." Soph giggled. "Admittedly, it's only been a day, but I'm loving it." She closed the door behind her and ventured deeper into the workshop. "They're literal, these Etterians. They've bombarded me with downright dirty questions on the ins-and-outs of sex, right to the nitty-gritty, and no sexual innuendoes intended." She dipped her chin. "I almost caused an interspecies incident when I mentioned the possibility of tit-fucks." Her cheeks bloomed. "I don't mind what we do and what we train the dolls to do, Leona. I'm just not sure I have the necessary experience or patience to explain sex ad infinitum to aliens."

Leona pressed four fingers to her mouth, trying to smother a laugh. When she'd mentioned lubrication to Aaro just that morning, he'd looked like he'd been in pain.

"They're like children, wanting to know the dolls' inner workings while waxing how awesome it was to ride them. I'm split between a sex therapist and a Dear Diary podcast." Soph climbed onto a stool and rested her elbows on the table. "If we hadn't discussed this so much in the last week, I doubt I would've survived today."

Leona grimaced. "Sorry, Soph. I'll be happy to take some of the slack."

"Thanks. Was going to suggest how-to talks. Do you know they view porn as instructional vids? I damn near swallowed my tongue. Talk about giving them too-high expectations."

"Shit. Let me chat to Aaro—"

"Oh, so that's how it is? After a day?" Soph wiggled her eyebrows.

Leona ignored her. "Perhaps we can vet what they watch. I'll emphasize the importance of real women versus fiction. Ninety percent of what these porn stars can do are beyond my skills."

Tingles spread outward at the thought of discussing this with Aaro. Would he listen? Would he expect her to watch vids alongside him to point out the unrealistic acts?

"I asked a random male what those ridges on their cocks were. He told me it's called a 'denit.' And he said it as if were discussing the weather." Soph tapped her chin. "I bet it would feel like a ribbed dildo. Anyway, I'm almost jealous," she said. "I haven't had anything between my legs for weeks."

"It's just dinner for now with a promise of more." Leona studied the last occupied vid, the way the man cuddled the doll against his chest. "I need this."

"I know you do." Soph offered a smile. "They're sexy as all hell, so go for it." She rolled her lip under the other. "Just one thing you need to ask yourself, what are you going to wear?"

Leona stilled, mentally sorting through her meager wardrobe. "Shit."

Soph glanced at Leona's tank top. "Use the replicator."

"Going to have to." Leona shrugged even though she was far from nonchalant. Paying for the cognac and fresh fruit juice at the Sky Lounge had taken her below her self-imposed threshold. Still, the urge to dress for the occasion was too tempting to resist. Dinner with a sub-commander was a formal affair, and she had to dress accordingly. "Let me take care of the last doll. Then you can help me choose."

Soph squealed. "I'll prep the dolls for tomorrow."

She jumped up and rushed out of the workshop leaving Leona to monitor the vids. A man orgasmed in the background. Soph had the right to suggest she dress well. Too stunned by Aaro's interest, the thought of what to wear hadn't concerned her. She was an attractive woman and had no illusions about it. But for a man like Aaro: strong, competent, authoritative showed interest in her... It boosted her confidence. Then again, it was her or Soph. Maybe Aaro saw Leona as on his level? An oily sensation coated her excitement. He'd been clear on his expectations for tonight. She squared her shoulders, determined to get to the bottom of this attraction tonight.

Did it matter, though? Sex with him would build on the Etterian-human relations *and* get her laid. A win-win, but she would be using him. She pushed off the table and headed to the last doll.

The cabin was empty. In the center stood the cyb, staring at the door. The man had dressed her with such care. Leona's heart fluttered. She had no doubt an Etterian could crush bone in his grip. And it wasn't just Aaro's men who were this gentle. Those Etterians who'd visited the sex center had shown similar reverence.

She removed the kimono and tossed it on the bed. Out of the closet, she took a sterilizer spray and cloth. It took minutes to wipe the cyb down, redress, and comb her glorious red hair.

"Hey, Red, how was that for you?" she asked.

With a chuckle at her silly expectation the doll would respond, Leona stripped the bed, swapped the soiled sheets for fresh ones, then remade the bed. Vanilla saturated the cabin with an appealing muskiness that reminded her of Aaro. Tapping her wrist, she escorted Red to the storeroom, and thus ended her shift for the day. With one last glance, she locked the storeroom and workshop.

Soph bounced outside Leona's cabin. "Something tight and slinky." Soph ran her hands down her own body. "How about in red?"

Leona laughed and let her in. "Too much, maybe."

Soph made a beeline for the replicator while Leona dropped into a chair to unbuckle her boots. She'd showered enough today, and she didn't have time to apply cosmetics or perfume. Her natural fragrance would have to do.

Soph pointed at the replicator. "Put in your sizes, Leona. This is the one."

"How much?" Leona pushed out of the chair and settled beside Soph.

There, on the glass's display, was a gown in deep purple. A cowl draped in the front and another hung low at the back. The silk dress would reach to Leona's toes. Slits split the fabric to mid-thigh on both sides.

"Yes," she gasped, shoving aside the thought of no-bra being a blatant enticement. "Hair up or down?" she asked and ordered the gown. Nowhere did she see the cost. She'd mention this to Aaro, not wanting a nasty bill after the job was done.

"Damn." Soph grasped the purple fabric off the black glass and held it to Leona.

Like the appearance of something out of nowhere wasn't miraculous. The algris or the Maloidians had introduced this and O.D.I.s to humans. While Leona stripped off her overalls, she had to admit she couldn't be more grateful for the use of such technology. The gown shimmered over her when it fell into place, caressing her skin like a lover.

"Panties." Soph ordered black lace underwear and tossed them.

Leona caught them out of the air. She winced, preferring something more...comfortable. "Fine." She whipped off her shorts to wiggle into the G-string.

"Shoes?" Soph arched a brow at Leona's bare feet.

Shit. It had been a year since she'd abandoned socializing. But it wasn't that long ago that she'd forgotten how to walk in heels. "Please."

Thankfully, she didn't need to shave, having opted for permanent hair removal when she was a teen. Underarms, legs, and pubes had been clean-shaven since her rebellious phase. She snorted. Like running away from Mom at this age didn't count?

"Soph, something that won't hook on the grated flooring. Purple wedged pumps? Peep toe?" She flicked through the choices and settled on transparent pumps. The door chime had her sliding her feet into the new shoes. "Well?" She twirled on the spot.

"Knock his boots off...literally" Soph giggled, skipped to the door, then opened it. She squeezed past Aaro who stepped aside.

He stared after her, his lips curling with repressed humor.

It allowed Leona to ogle the man dressed in jeans and a tight white T-shirt. *Holy shit.* His hair draped down his back in its usual thick braid, and his military boots still adorned his feet...for now. Those jeans molded to his narrow hips and thighs, emphasizing the extraordinary length of his legs. The T-shirt looked as if it was painted onto his angles and dips. *Fuck.*

"Ready?" she rasped, then swallowed, hoping to return her voice to normal.

His gaze whipped to her. While he admired her, his chest muscles bunched and released. His blue eyes swirled with intense heat that sparked an answering warmth deep within her. She pinched her thighs together when he swept a tongue across his bottom lip as if he remembered their kiss.

"Maker, Leona, you are exquisite."

"I assumed the dinner was formal." Despite the zing of joy his admiration brought her, she gestured to his jeans. "I can change."

"Do not dare to do so," he growled, stepping into the cabin and crowding her.

She lifted her chin in the hopes of a kiss, only for him to place his hand at the base of her spine. With quick movements, he ushered her along the passage and away from relative safety. Her skin prickled. Her nipples pebbled under the silk, and for the life of her, she couldn't stop focusing on the friction emanating from his hand. In the narrow passages, men stepped aside when they passed. A frisson of heat pooled in her chest at their blatant admiration, but not once did their attention make her skin crawl. Like they studied a work of art. Odd that.

Aaro paused beside a door. "My quarters." He palmed the lock and led her inside. The space was a replica of hers, cold and impersonal, except for a wall of strange objects. She strode there, browsing but not touching what looked like tribal fertility statues in amethyst or agate. Chunks of obsidian rock and fossilized orange algae were added to the display.

"These are extraordinary, Aaro."

"I collect when I can." He palmed a statue. "From Maloid, along with genkoo—their food source for millennia."

She ran her finger along the face of the statue he held. "I hope they have other foods. Variety is the spice of life, or so they say."

"They?"

She grinned and settled in a chair, crossing a leg over the other at the knee. Doing so exposed a swath of bare skin. Any attempts to cover up would be met with futility so she resisted the urge. "It's an idiom. No one knows who 'they' are."

He replaced the statue and chose a chair opposite her, though he balanced on the edge. Restrained power tensed his body. She half-expected him to bounce a knee.

"We have survived on *kreso* for generations. Even though we export *omeika*, it is not a preferred meal." Before she could quiz him on *kreso* or *omeika*, he pushed out of his seat and approached the rehydrator. "Something to drink?"

"A glass of chilled dry white wine, please."

He held out a glass to her a minute later, a cherry soda in his other hand.

"Thank you." She accepted the drink and took a long sip, needing the wine's fortitude. "Tell me about yourself, Aaro."

He stiffened before sitting. "Nothing different than all males. Separated from my blood-bonds at four, trained to control my emotions as expected of our *damu*. When I reached eighteen, I traveled to Gikaet, like all our males do, for further training. After four years of service, we are assigned to our posts. Only recently was I promoted to sub-commander. My supreme commander found his *Dar Eth*. They now tour Earth in what Izzy calls a honeymoon."

Leona blinked. Questions circled and collided. "Four years old? Why?" She'd heard of medieval times when the parents sent their sons at age six to become pages, squires, and finally knights. Etteria as a nation did this to their sons?

"Centuries ago we were a volatile people, triggering wars that decimated our numbers. King Pius approached the Durn for guidance. They were incredibly intelligent and had technology and knowledge beyond ours. Their solution was to genetically modify our DNA and, along with an extensive training regime, taught us to control our emotions. The *Ethera* came into being." He grimaced. "It worked, but the Durn hadn't anticipated the decline in the number of females born. The fewer pairings, the higher the death toll. I believe the existence of the void within each Etterian hadn't been a factor in the Durn's calculations."

Her mind reeled. "The *Ethera*? Voids? Pairings?"

"When a male meets his female, the *Ethera* sparks to life. It strips their control, allowing them to feel without repercussions."

She sat up and clasped the glass to her chest. "What?" *Is this the soulmate thing they believe in?*

"If no pairing happens, no *Ethera* is triggered. Therefore, any emotions, such as love and lust, bring the void closer. From a certain age, all Etterians stop searching for intimacy." He gripped and released the can, making it crackle in his hand. "I am sorry if this is confusing." He took a long pull from his soda, his Adam's Apple bobbing as he swallowed.

"Intimacy? Like sex?" Sliding her glass on the table, she gripped the sides of the chair, her gaze fixed on him. *Whoa, he's serious.* She couldn't scoff and dismiss his beliefs, not when it sounded like they had science backing this *Ethera*.

"Yes. Fulfillments with anyone other than my soulmate strengthens the void until I feel nothing, driving me to find exhilaration and finally death on a battlefield."

"You can't be serious? Soulmate?" She snapped her mouth shut, not wanting to appear disrespectful.

"Your human term for it."

For there to be a human word meant it had to have happened. Although, humans could be romanticizing the experience.

"It's real?" *No sex ever until he finds this perfect person?* "Wait, then why are your men fucking my dolls."

His breath whooshed out, and he ran his palms up and down his thighs. "Your cybs are inanimate objects. They do not trigger the void's expansion. Neither does my hand."

"Oh." Her shoulders slumped. To fuck Aaro could kill him. At that moment, she ached to be his soulmate, to save him. "The Durn can't help a second time?"

His stillness solidified the importance of his response. "Few remain."

"Shit. So, Soph was right? *Dar Eth* means wife?"

"Yes, in a way. There is no divorce in our culture. To do so is to doom each other to the void. We are also learning that an *Eth* and *Dar Eth* cannot be parted from each other for extended periods."

"Ah, hence soulmate." She scooped up her wine and cradled it, needing the chill of the glass to ground her. "And fewer girls born mean fewer *Etheras* and more deaths?" She stared into her glass, no longer enjoying the wine. "Izzy's a soulmate?"

"She and other humans have triggered the *Ethera*."

"Oh," Leona gasped. "So, Soph and I could..." She rolled her hand. "Y'know, um, find ourselves paired against our will? Worse, if we don't honor this, we doom our...*Eths* to slow and painful deaths?"

When he nodded, she placed the glass down and layered her hand over his resting on his thigh. "That sucks, Aaro, that you don't get a choice. I don't know how I'd deal with that if it happened to me."

He didn't say anything just kept his gaze on her.

"I mean, it's my life. I don't want some fate choosing who I can or cannot love." She squeezed his hand. "I'm not disparaging your *Ethera*, though. It's part of your culture and should be valued. So where do we find your *Dar Eth*? How do you know how long you have? Is there a way to tell she's the one?"

"I have time, *ensa*." He flipped his hand to capture hers and brought her fingers to his lips. Her breath hitched when he kissed her knuckles, trailing fire in the wake of his lips along her skin.

"Good," she rasped. *Sex's back on the table.* "You're not my first Etterian."

His eyebrows shot up.

"I met four of you on Lunar Base." The thought of Medic Aldur dying dampened the memory. They were headed planetside. She hoped he found his *Dar Eth* soon. "Nerx, Aldur, and others saved me from a...tricky situation."

Aaro stilled. Power poured off him when he inched closer to her. "You were in danger?"

"In a way. All I've ever wanted was to be able to steer my life. I left Earth so my mother wouldn't marry me to this asshole. He found me on Lunar Base and tried to force me to leave with him." She slipped her hand free and patted Aaro's in parting. "It's why I chose the position with Cyb Ent, far away from Bradley." She took a sip of wine. "I won't always have an Etterian to save me. Might be wise to learn a few self-defense moves." The idea of being in pain made her grimace. The last time she'd had any muscular soreness was when she'd drunkenly bet she could outclimb anyone in her class. Conquering a climbing wall was a far cry from escaping Bradley's clutches.

"We shall begin tomorrow."

"What?" she squeaked.

"I shall train you in Hatimaye. If Princess Oriana can master the fighting style, so can you."

"Right." Leona brought the wine to her lips, trying not to imagine Aaro pinning her to the floor. "Where?"

He frowned. "Afraid of failure?"

"Being sweaty in front of an audience isn't appealing."

He rose, forcing her to tilt her head to maintain eye contact. "Fair enough, *ensa*. I shall prepare a separate area." He offered her a hand which she accepted by sliding her fingers across his palm. With the gentlest of grips, he hoisted her to her feet. "Dinner?"

"Please." This close, his spicy cinnamon scent scattered her wits. "Kreso?"

He grinned—the kind that crawled across his face like the first dawn on a dark planet. *Shit, now I'm waxing poetic.*

"I have tried your Earthian food. It is as good. I will not be offended if you prefer something familiar."

"As long as my body doesn't have a violent reaction, I'm willing to try anything."

"Our physiology is surprisingly similar." He clasped her hip to squeeze past her.

She cradled her wine to her chest and watched him order. Two plates appeared with lumps of gray meat covered in green sauce. Not a vegetable accompanied the meal. He carried the plates to the low table, then veered off to tap the vid. The table extended upward, and the chairs slid in when he dragged his finger across the screen.

Handy. She settled in her chair and aligned the utensils he pulled from a hidden drawer below the rehydrator.

"The knife is dulled Maloidian steel. Be careful, though. It is sharp enough to cut through bone."

She sliced the meat, marveling at its succulent texture and ostrich-like flavor, beautifully balanced by the sweet berry sauce. Humming after every bite, she closed her eyes to better savor each mouthful. "I can see why you like this, Aaro, but for generations?"

"We have other foods but prefer this and plan our stores accordingly."

"It's real meat?" she asked around another mouthful.

"No, not in space. The sludge reserves are designed to carry higher concentrations of protein."

"Ah." It was all genius and sparked Leona's curiosity. The food on Callisto, was it real or sludge? Had the algri introduced the rehydrators and Maloidians the replicators? The buzz wasn't clear on this. Yet, how had the sludge knowledge been transferred? How else could humans maintain the levels in the tanks?

"Dessert?"

She stared at their empty plates with the powerful urge to climb over the table and kiss Aaro. There he sat, all rippling muscle, that chiseled jaw, those high cheekbones, and his eyes blazing a neon blue. She was proud of herself for surviving this evening with decorum.

"Let's talk if you don't mind," she said. "It sounded as if you wanted to discuss something specific?"

"Yes. We reach the planet of Sarvis in six days. This pleases me. The algri are an emotionless species and should not hinder our delivery. A little longer to Yithia—"

She stiffened. "That's second?" Fear rippled along her skin, raising goosebumps.

"My concerns are how best to proceed without endangering you and Lady Soph."

"I'll leave Soph on board the *Valiant*. That's one less human to worry about."

He bowed his head to acknowledge her offer. "Good. For diplomatic reasons, it is best not to bring many warriors." He inched to the edge of the chair, resting those powerful arms on the table. "I am hoping we can deliver and leave."

"Same." She shivered, recalling the one image she'd seen of a Yithian. Sharklike, long teeth dimpling their wide lips, and venomous spit? Nope, she'd happily skip the entire planet.

Aaro's gaze roamed her face, dipped to her collarbone, then lingered on her cleavage. "Perhaps dress less revealing." He glanced up.

Ah. He's trying to protect me. Or is he playing the diplomatic game to avoid trouble?

"I thought you were a sex-cyb when I first saw you." He chuckled.

Ice skidded down her spine. *He did what now?*

"It is a compliment, Leona."

She gritted her teeth. Why was being described as an overly priced sex toy supposed to be flattering? Did he view her as one? Something to fuck and discard?

"I have many women as friends, and none are like the other. I pray to the Maker that my males do not believe the sex-cybs are indicative of all humans. Etterians are black-haired and blue-eyed. Your differences in shape and color intrigue us."

She released a slow breath. Okay, he wasn't insulting her on purpose. She was as tall as a doll, but that was where the similarities ended. "What would you like your *Dar Eth* to look like?" She studied him, watching his every expression.

"Like you," he rasped. "Before meeting you, I had no preference."

Her heartbeat fluttered, sparking pulses to her stomach and lower.

"No matter what she looks like, I will love her regardless."

Her heart melted like fudge in the summer sun. "Love? What if you can't?"

He frowned. "The *Ethera* chooses well. It took into account Taylor's love for human Michel. Every pairing I know of has been perfect."

Leona sighed, allowing her cynical heart to imagine what a soulmate would be like. Someone who understood her and loved her no matter her mood swings, stalker, and mommy issues? "I can see the appeal."

Aaro smiled. "It is what all Etterians long for."

He stood and offered his hand again.

Just like that? Come with me to my lair? She accepted, rising to stand beside him. He tucked her arm through his and ushered her to the vid. With a few taps, maps appeared, zooming in from one planet to another.

"From Yithia, we will reach Maloid in two days. Kulai is next and the farthest." His fingers tightened when he glanced at her. "After that, Etteria. I would love to show you my homeworld, *ensa*." He cupped her cheek and ran his thumb over her bottom lip.

"How long in total?" She grimaced. Not once had she thought to ask.

"Fifty-eight days to Callisto."

She gaped. *Two months?* "The quicker we deliver, the better."

"Expecting trouble is wise. I suggest you familiarize yourself with their cultures."

She gulped. "No need to offend if it's avoidable." *Damn*. John had said he needed a diplomat. She swept a hand down her body. "Should I wear their clothes?"

His gaze followed her gesture. "Dress as an Etterian. If any question it, I will claim you are mine."

Everything within her stilled, like something in her heart clicked. Claiming her as his? She liked the sound of that too much when she didn't have the right to. "What if you meet your *Dar Eth*?"

He laughed. "We have not found them among these species." He caught a lock of her hair and toyed with it. "Your dark coloring and blue eyes might convince them. Most have not seen an Etterian female."

"They're that rare?"

"And well-guarded." He tucked the curl behind her ear, running his fingers along the shell.

She shivered and wished she could close the distance between them. Every cell in her body craved his. "What is this between us?" She splayed her fingers over his right pec, relishing the texture of his muscles beneath her touch. "I've experienced attraction, but this is too...intense." She met his gaze.

He layered his hand over hers, pinning it in place. "You in that garment, Leona, are testing my control. Everything about you ignites my desire." A pulse ticked along his jaw.

On impulse, she rose onto her toes and pressed a kiss there.

A groan lodged in his throat. He gripped her hip and yanked her against him, releasing her hand to do so. "Leona," he whispered.

The way her name dripped off his tongue sent chills through her.

"Aaro," she said, kissing his chin, then the other side of his jaw.

Guilt twinged across her heart. Could she sleep with him even though it brought the void closer? What she knew about this *Ethera* was too little to make a decision. Not that she thought he was lying about having time, but what if after one fuck the void took him? She doubted he had a clock ticking his life away, but what if he misjudged how long he had?

He spun and held her to the wall, and without hesitation, she hooked her leg around his hip. Lust demanded she ignore her doubts and concerns, and go for it. With desire pounding at her senses, she could do nothing but succumb. When he skimmed his mouth down her neck to plant a kiss on her collarbone, she trembled.

He cupped her breast, and she whimpered, driven to arch into his touch.

"Please," she whispered. Though what she pleaded for, she couldn't pinpoint.

He paused, leaned back, and studied her face. "What is it you want, *ensa*?" he asked as if he had no idea how much he tormented her. A smirk tugged at his lips while he thumbed her nipple with the gentlest of strokes.

Fire zinged outward, catapulting her thoughts into a dead zone. "That. More of that."

He chuckled and continued to touch her, cupping and squeezing her breast through the fabric.

She huffed, shoved him back, then wiggled out of the offending thing. When he stilled, his focus intense, his eyes swirling that riveting blue, she considered that standing naked in front of a man was perhaps the craziest thing she'd done.

She glanced at the gown pooled at her heels. No, she couldn't go back. Hiding her body would accomplish what? He wanted her. He'd said talk then a fuck, and dammit, he was either a man of his word or not worth her time.

"Maker, *ensa*, you are..." He brushed her hair off her shoulder. "More beautiful than anything I have ever seen."

His rasping voice was a caress across her skin, tightening her nipples, and sending a flare of heat deep into her core.

What could she say to that? For he was sincere, of that she had no doubts.

"Are you planning on just looking at me, Aaro?" Resting a hand on her hip, she tilted her head, challenging him.

His smile was so breathtaking she struggled to hold onto her courage. "Oh, I hope to do many things with and to you, *ensa ra ensa*."

"Show me," she said, splaying her fingers across his chest.

Chapter Eleven

Aaro's mind reeled. He *should* tell Leona. She had a right to know. But with her standing there, bare and magnificent, he couldn't risk it. Perhaps he could appease the *Ethera* without losing her?

She was far from timid, as evidenced by her undressing. If he told her now, she'd walk away, naked or not. Might not even give the *Ethera* a chance.

He trailed his gaze over every curve, then followed with his fingers, needing to learn the exact texture of her exquisite skin. Those pert breasts so free and ripe, and that tiny piece of cloth hiding her sex from him? He drew in a deep breath. So succulent, and delicious, her smoky arousal filled his lungs to capacity.

He shuddered and leaned forward, pinning her to the bulkhead. Resting on his elbows, he layered his body over hers. No, it wasn't enough. He gripped the collar of his T-shirt and ripped it off, dropping the fragments to the floor. The softness of her skin, the scent of her, and the muted thump of her heartbeat culminated in his mind, heart, and body, and hardened his malehood.

"Are you certain, Leona?" He wanted to make damn sure she was ready for this. "There is no going back." He dipped to capture her lips in a delicate kiss, one where he tested the plumpness of her bottom lip with his tongue. "I want to claim you as mine."

"You can do that?" Her eyes widened. "As in sexually?"

"Yes." It wasn't a complete lie. He could, as allowed by the *Ethera*. Perhaps she would grow fond of him then the existence of the *Ethera* wouldn't matter. Even his omittance wouldn't bother her if she loved him.

His hearts stilled. Loved him? Yes, he wanted that with every beat of his two hearts.

But not telling her was dishonorable. He opened his mouth to lay it bare, to take a chance and trust the *Ethera*. "Leona, I am—"

She feathered her mouth across his.

The sensation so fleeting formed a lump in his throat. "Your *Eth*," came out in a whisper.

She hummed as if she'd heard him, her arms tightening around his neck.

Just one moment, a memory, then he'd tell her again.

He swooped in and kissed her, flicking his tongue into the warm cavern of her mouth. Make her his in every sense of the word: that was his mission. He gripped her hips and lifted her, breaking the kiss to latch onto a nipple. So sweet, he sucked harder, needing the taste of her skin to soak into his tongue. Dragging his mouth to the other, he lavished attention there too, while relishing her groans and gasps. She squirmed, kneading his shoulders with her fingers.

"Aaro," she cried out and wrapped her legs around his torso. The damp heat of her sex against his stomach registered along with the intense fragrance of her arousal.

He growled and slipped a hand between her thighs. One stroke across her silky sex drew a whimper from her. Another summoned a cry. She panted, her cheeks flushed while he flicked his thumb back and forth across what Elizabeth called a 'nub.' Stroking downward, he found Leona's channel and slid a finger in.

He focused on her face, on those kiss-swollen lips. When he kissed her, she curled her tongue around his and sucked. His malehood throbbed in unison, painful and tight in the confines of these human blue pants—a poor choice on his part. Her breathing labored. Her heart stuttered, then on a mewl, she stilled. Her head fell back, her eyelids closed, and her mouth parted on a husky moan.

Her channel squeezed his finger as a wave of heat coated it. Her heartbeat tapped out a beat against his knuckles.

"That..." She met his gaze, and the smokiness of her blue eyes ensnared him. "...was incredible, Aaro."

She'd found her fulfillment, drenching the room in her decadent scent.

He rested his temple on hers, his breathing harsh. "Leona, I must tell you something."

"Tell me in the morning," she said, pressing a kiss to his neck while she stroked his chest to cup his malehood.

The spark of need was his undoing. He yanked off her small garment and dropped it. Then dipping, he scooped her into his arms. He took two steps and swiveled, needing that sliver of cloth lying discarded on the floor. To mark this evening, he wanted to keep the torn garment.

He tossed her over his shoulder and grabbed the cloth, shoving it into his pocket. With a hand on her bare backside, he hurried to his room. He lowered her onto the bed and stepped back to undress.

She licked her bottom lip when he removed his boots and jeans. "You're the sexiest man I have ever met," she said.

"Oh?" He arched a brow, not realizing that being considered the sexiest was a thing.

"Gorgeous," she whispered, rising to her knees to drag her nails down his stomach. "May I?" she asked, raising her gaze to his.

When he frowned, unsure what she meant, she wrapped her fingers around his malehood. He shivered, his breath gone. Her touch was so soft, like he'd anticipated *and* remembered from his vision. She ran her hand up and down his length, pausing to rub his denit. His eyesight blurred. Pleasure struck and rattled the thread of control he clung to.

"*Ensa*, I cannot endure..."

She hummed as if acknowledging he'd spoken. What he had not expected was her feathering her lips over the head of his malehood. So exquisite. He curled his fingers into fists and willed himself to stand still, to not make any sudden movements. Not that he thought she would harm him, but he wanted to savor every second of her mouth on him. The sweep of her tongue was his undoing. He grunted and lunged, pushing her back onto the bed. Then, with determination, he climbed over her, trapping her beneath him. She was his. She had to realize this.

She met his gaze and smiled.

He paused again and cupped her cheek, losing himself in her eyes. "May I?" he asked.

"Sure," she smirked.

With a nod, he lifted her leg and angled his malehood at her entrance.

"Oh," she gasped, her humor replaced with a need that had to match his in potency. "Please do."

He thrust in, plunging to the hilt, and lost his hearts. In an instant, the *Ethera* pummeled him, circling his soul, thoughts, goals, and loyalty, then dragged them to one focal point—his *Dar Eth*. She had no idea what she'd just become to him. Neither had he known what consummating their pairing would mean. He kissed her temple, her cheekbones, then captured her mouth for a slow kiss.

"*Ensa*," he rasped.

"Aaro," she said and hooked the other leg around his hip. This sank him deeper. Never had anything felt this incredible.

"Forgive me, Leona, for I cannot hold back." He withdrew and rammed in, driven by a desperate ache to share this with her, this moment, their union that she didn't know the importance of. Soon, he would tell her.

"Can you feel that?" she asked, her eyes wide, her awe clear.

He stilled because he knew what she meant. The *Ethera* tugged at his core like a ribbon of light banded his hearts and soul to hers. "What is it, *ensa*?" He had to ask, hoping she was experiencing the same thing.

"A strange warmth," she said, fluttering her fingers over his face and jaw. "As if I've known you forever." She flicked a dismissive hand. "I'm being silly."

He kissed her again, needing her taste and the softness of her lips. She was his world now. Resuming his thrust and withdrawal, he chased the dancing sparks of pure joy. She didn't hold back but matched his rhythm, chanting his name while stroking his neck and ears.

She cried out, then along with rippling spasms, heat flooded his malehood, drenching him.

It was the catalyst. Pleasure washed over his body, ripping a roar from him. He forced his eyes to remain open and his gaze fixed on her. Tremors replaced the initial jerks and twinges. He lowered her leg to gather her close.

"I don't know if I'm a cuddler," she said as she snuggled into his arms.

"Same," he said after his O.D.I. informed him of the word's meaning. With her, he wanted to hold her and spend hours in bed.

"Do you show all your dinner guests such a good time?" she teased.

He chuckled. "Only the most beautiful."

"Charmer," she said.

"Cold?" He tightened his arms around her, making sure his body warmth covered her.

She kissed his chin. "I'm cozy, you?"

"I am where I most want to be," he said.

Her eyes widened the tiniest bit as if his words surprised her. She dipped her chin to hide her face, but he caught the shimmer in her eyes. What had he said? Despite the guilt hounding him for not revealing the *Ethera*'s existence and its purpose, now he'd insulted her without meaning to.

"I am sorry, Leona. I did not wish to offend—"

"You didn't, Aaro." She cupped his jaw and met his gaze. "Your words were perfect. They gave me hope."

He frowned. "What is it, *ensa*?"

"We've just met, and I can't go around wishing for something impossible." She wiggled out of his arms to sit up. Not that he minded with the light playing across her magnificent body. "Let's enjoy these two months and see what happens afterward."

"I agree to time together. Nothing would bring me more pleasure." He feathered his fingers along her cheek. "But I do not like this sadness in your voice."

"I'm sorry," she said, splaying her fingers across his chest. "I'm ruining the moment. I just meant I'm looking forward to getting to know you, Aaro." She slipped her arms around his neck and pressed her body to his.

"As am I, *ensa*." He wouldn't push it, not wanting to force her to reveal her thoughts. Only when she truly trusted him would she share. And she was right. They had plenty of time for him to convince her to stay with him. Still, if the opportunity arose, he'd tell her.

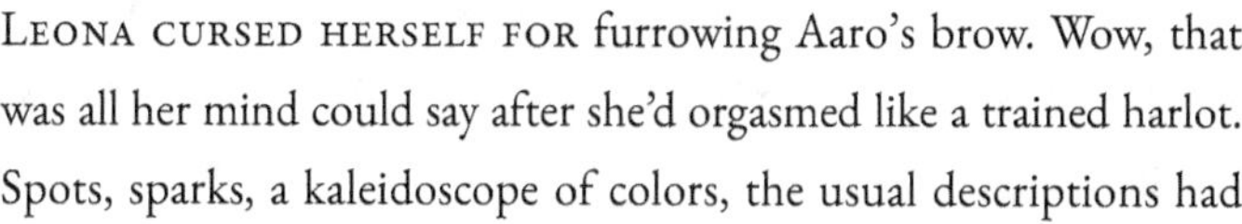

LEONA CURSED HERSELF FOR furrowing Aaro's brow. Wow, that was all her mind could say after she'd orgasmed like a trained harlot. Spots, sparks, a kaleidoscope of colors, the usual descriptions had bombarded her when he'd first thrummed an orgasm from her. Then he'd pounded into her with that impressive erection of his. And those ridges on the length of his cock rubbed all the right spots.

Rex had been a waste of her time. Aaro would ruin her for all men. Hence the despair that she couldn't keep him. This journey would be time spent with him then a devastating goodbye. And it wasn't his fault, this sweet man who said the perfect things at the right time. It was as if the universe and God had designed the ideal man for her. Sure, like she'd said before, they'd just met, but damn, they were off to a spectacular start.

She shivered when he swirled his fingers over her skin, kneaded tense muscles, and smoothed across the callouses on her palms and heels. His lips followed. Urged by his tug on her foot, the stretching out of her arm, she sprawled onto her stomach for him.

He worshipped every inch of her. She relished the attention, letting him do as he pleased, even as a slumbering heat rekindled in her core. Pinching her thighs did nothing to appease the fresh throb striking a tribal beat across her clit. That strange warmth curled in her heart again. Whenever she could she watched Aaro, admiring the flex of his muscles across his chest and the focus he showed in his self-appointed task. Something was happening here that she couldn't put her finger on, but he was at the center of it. She wanted to be his. Or did she just want someone? Maybe she was tired of being alone? If that was true, she could've settled for Bradley.

She rolled onto her side to better appreciate Aaro stretched out before her. This man had a body even Adonis would envy. With those broad shoulders and massive biceps, he'd carried her as if she weighed nothing.

"My turn," she whispered, her lips itching to taste his skin as he had hers.

Without a word, he lay on his bed and tucked his hands behind his head. He gazed at her like she did her morning coffee—with reverence. What did that mean? Damnit, she couldn't ask him. It had been a day. What would tomorrow bring? Would she still feel this intense for him or more so? And this odd warmth inside her? Maybe a trip to Flad might not be a bad idea. After she explained what patient-doctor confidentiality meant, she'd ask him about this sensation deep inside her.

It could be love.

Her heart leaped. Hope rose like an avenging angel, but she swatted it down. It could also be indigestion, lust, or something alien, maybe a parasite? Casting these pointless thoughts aside, she started with Aaro's toes. He had six on each foot. She stared at them and laughed, loving this oddity. Well, odd for her, but not for him. No hair covered his defined and rock-hard calves. Even his knees had muscles. Strong lines cut into his thighs, no doubt for muscle groups she didn't know the names of. His cock bobbed when she stroked his hips, rippling her fingers over his many abs and the spot where he should've had a belly button. Up she traveled and across his nipples, as sensitive to her touch as she was to his. She flicked her tongue around a taut nipple and moaned at the heat radiating off his velvety skin. He flexed his chest but said nothing. Only his flaring nostrils revealed he liked her touching him.

"Tell me if you don't like something I do," she said and waited for his nod.

Then down his torso she went, spending time kissing, licking, tweaking, and tasting. What she wanted to do was investigate those ridges on his cock and that he only had one scrotum. He had no hair anywhere except on his head.

"*Ensa*," he muttered.

"Yes?" She arched a brow but didn't glance at him, her attention on those ridges. With her forefinger, she rubbed them, wondering if they were bone or flesh.

He hissed, his body tightening.

When he said nothing, she brought her face closer, to an inch from his cock, and stroked him again. Already droplets had formed on the head. She captured one and smoothed it between her fingers. It had the same silky feel as hers. Popping a fingertip into her mouth, she sucked. She barely registered the sweetness before he lunged, flipping her onto her knees.

Doggy style wasn't one of her favorites. She tried to tell him this, but he entered her, and all her thoughts scattered. The second plunge stole her breath: so intense and addictive. She half wanted to demand he stop. But she couldn't, not when it felt so good. He rubbed along her inner walls with every thrust. Never had she experienced anything like this. Unable to resist, she let instincts take over and arched, shoving her ass higher.

His grip on her hips became forceful, holding her in place as he pistoned in and out of her. Her breasts swayed, but she didn't care. Her cheek chafed across the linen and grew hot, but to hell with that. As long as he didn't stop. Orgasm after orgasm shot tremors through her. She descended from one only to be hit by another. No words formed in her mind; only mewls, cries, and whimpers escaped her lips.

He wrapped himself around her, bathing her in warmth, and stilled for a few moments.

"*Ensa*, you are perfect," he whispered, his breath on her ear summoning a shiver.

She was raw, not physically, but deep inside as if her soul was exposed to whatever sorcery he wielded. Principles all fell away.

"Now, *that* was a fuck," she said, twisting to glance at him.

He chuckled and kissed her shoulder. Sweat slicked their skin. It didn't matter. Lying there naked and ravaged was all her addled mind could cling to. This was sex, pure, unadulterated, something her dolls couldn't ever provide. They offered a service. She, as a human woman, was the full sweaty, gooey, sticky package.

"Care for a shower?" She wiggled her brows.

He grinned, looking like an all-glistening-and-bronzed sex god. "Yes, then it is to bed for you. I want you refreshed for tomorrow's first training session."

She groaned and dropped her temple on the bed. "Don't remind me."

"I will be gentle."

She met his gaze at the seriousness in his voice. "I never expected you to be anything else, Aaro. It's just that it's been a while since I've done anything like exercise."

"Ah, then I will handle your post-training care."

"Oh?" she managed when he hoisted her into his arms and carried her to the bathroom. "And what would that entail?"

He twitched to the side to meet her gaze. "Food."

"And?"

He frowned. "What else?"

"A full-body massage, chilled drinks, mind-blowing sex, cuddles, kisses, and dessert."

He laughed, the sound so heartfelt and warm that she smiled. "Indeed, *ensa*, I shall endeavor to ensure your post-training care is of the highest standard."

As he lowered her, he trailed his hands over her body before stepping into the cubicle. His gaze remained on her, like she was the center of his world. Odd that. Maybe she was the only woman he knew? No, he'd said he had other friends.

Was she his friend?

A yawn snatched her from her thoughts. Now that she was satiated, exhaustion dragged on her. Her limbs became leaden, so she leaned against his chest and let him hold her. Dipping between sleep and wakefulness, he'd repositioned her at the air dryer, then on his bed. He drew her into his arms again, and within moments, she knew no more.

Chapter Twelve

Leona awoke to the gentle nudging apart of her thighs. She mumbled something about sleeping a little longer, but the hot tongue running along her clit snapped her eyes open. A moan followed when Aaro did it again. She splayed her legs like a spatchcock chicken, uncaring that it made for an unladylike pose. The man was busy, and he should have the best access.

A flush of heat rippled up her spine and hardened her nipples, sending tingles outward.

She sank her fingers into his thick braid. When she scraped her nails over his scalp, she received a twitch across his shoulders as a reward. *Mm, so he likes that?*

With flicks of his tongue, he drew her focus to the building heat and need. She released his hair to prop herself up on her elbows. Watching him feast on her, this gorgeous man, was an aphrodisiac on its own.

He met her gaze and groaned, sending a vibration along her sensitive skin. She shivered.

"I like it when you watch me devour you, *ensa*," he said, his words almost muffled.

She couldn't respond, not when he found a spot that tensed her body, sent a spiraling joy along her senses, and tilted her hips to grant him better access.

When he hitched his thumb in her entrance, she cried out and arched off the bed. Exploding lights of pleasure slammed into her.

Before she resurfaced, he raised her legs and rested her thighs against his chest. With her knees almost touching her breasts, he plunged into her. So close to her last orgasm, fresh pleasure barreled along her insides. He locked his gaze onto hers and didn't glance away.

Her eyelids wanted to flutter shut with each orgasm, but she dared not. As if some unspoken request from him lay between them. It should've been awkward, vulnerable even. Instead, his intensity matched what he invoked within her. Last night had been sex. Now was making love. His thrusts slowed. He stroked her cheek, played with her hair, or stole kisses, all while wringing orgasms out of her.

When it was his turn, he roared her name. Right then, she knew she'd never be the same.

"Morning," she whispered when he collapsed on top of her. Although, he didn't crush her like she expected from a man of his bulk.

"Morning, *ensa*." He held himself in a push-up, supporting his weight with ease. "I like having you in my bed."

"Well," she ducked her chin to her chest, "if you wake me up like this every morning, I like your bed too."

"Since you are here, I suggest we start on your training."

She groaned, throwing an arm across her eyes. From an orgasm to torture? "I don't have any clothes," she muttered.

"Choose from the replicator." He play-swatted her ass as he pulled out of her.

She pouted at the loss of his warmth. He stepped off the bed, his cock still erect. "About that. I didn't see any costs."

"Whatever an Etterian needs, Etteria will provide." He strode naked to the wall, touched a ridge on the top corner of a panel, and a door opened. Inside hung suits of armor and a stack of towels sat on a shelf.

Before she could rise, he dipped a knee on the bed and dabbed her thighs. She shivered, torn between relishing his gentle strokes or closing her legs. His nostrils flared, his focus on the most private part of her body, then when he licked his lips, she bit hers to smother a gasp. Damn, the man was sexy as hell.

He stepped back and, with flicks of his hand, cleaned himself off, as well.

As he dressed, his gaze on her, she tried to gather her thoughts. His magnificent body disappearing beneath black pants and vest was as enticing to watch as him stripping.

"Anything? What if I want a diamond necklace?" She arched a brow then pushed herself off the bed to stretch.

His breath hitched. "Tempting me will not defer your training."

She jerked to the side and tossed him a glance. With a sweep of her hand, she gestured to her nudity. "This?" she scoffed. "What about...?" She twirled and thrust her ass out, giving him an eyeful of her sex where he'd buried his face minutes ago.

"There is time for all that you ask," he said, looping an arm around her waist to yank her against his armor-clad body. "You are mine, Leona, and I need you safe. Unless you wish that I guard your exquisite body every second of the day?" He licked his lips, and his ice-blue eyes glowed with desire.

"No." She slumped. "You're right to insist. Let's be prepared for anything." After stealing a kiss, she pulled out of his embrace to head to the replicator. Choosing suitable gym clothes didn't take long, and she wiggled into them under his vigilance.

While braiding her hair, she followed him out the door and along various passages. Despite her best efforts, she dipped her gaze to his ass too many times to count. The front of him had been her sole focus, but later, as he promised, she planned to give his exquisite butt cheeks some much-needed attention.

The air grew staler the longer they walked. The temperature chilled her, and she shivered, wishing she'd 'summoned' a sweatshirt too. And a bottle of water wouldn't go amiss. When he stepped into a dark common room, he tapped his O.D.I. Lights flooded the space, almost blinding her. He took position at the center of a massive blue padded mat.

Within five minutes of stretching, her hair stuck to her face and neck. Her tongue stuck to the roof of her mouth, and the only thing she could think of was water.

Then he started with passive, semi-passive, and fighting stances. His patience was phenomenal as he explained the purpose of each, with subtle changes to the placement of her feet, to where she rested her weight, to how she formed fists. Punching a wall-mounted pad rippled power along her arm. The flush of control was addictive, so she did it again, and again. He adjusted her stance, showing her how to swivel on the ball of her foot thus bringing the full weight of her body behind the punch. With every move, she had to keep her left fist in front of her face. By the time he called an end to the session, her limbs were rubberlike.

He tapped the rehydrator on the nearby counter and ordered a bottle of water. Condensation glistened on the side. When he offered it to her, she hooked her fingers around his neck and dragged him down for a sweaty kiss. With his solid muscle against her body, she was tempted to sprawl him on the mat and have her way with him. But her sex twanged, no doubt needing a break.

She pulled away, taking the water with her. "I'm ravenous," she said before tilting the bottle to her lips.

"Me too," he rasped, his heated gaze conveying what he meant.

She smirked and nudged her head at the door. "A shower, then breakfast?"

He glanced at his O.D.I. and scowled. "It is later than expected, but I can cleanse then eat. Perhaps this night a little post-training care?" With a chuckle, he ushered her through the door and along the first passage

She liked that he'd remembered her silly request, not that any woman in her right mind would turn down a full-body massage or dessert.

He glanced over his shoulder at her. "Cleanse with me or in your quarters?"

She studied his biceps and any visible skin that didn't have a drop of sweat anywhere. "Well, if there's no time for a quickie, then separate showers might be wise."

"True. I cannot resist you, female, even when there is something I must discuss with you."

"I'll take that as a compliment," she said.

He snatched a kiss outside her cabin door, then abandoned her. Tension stiffened his shoulders when he marched off, that amazing braid of his swaying behind him. She'd forgotten to ask him about it getting in the way of day-to-day tasks. But give a girl a break. He'd blown her mind and dominated her body with his skill as a lover. Yeah, which meant she hadn't remembered to mention his species using porn vids as tutorials.

Had he been disappointed with her? After all, she was no porn star.

He was so sweet. If she asked him how well she performed, he'd be complimentary.

Striding into the bathroom, she stripped and tossed the clothes on the floor. The shower spray hit her hard, and she hummed in pleasure. She was lucky to be able to walk without limping or wincing. Damn, the man had game.

Skipping another horizontal session meant she had a little extra time this morning to document more of her ideas. She'd been bombarding poor John with almost daily texts. Not that he'd complained yet.

"So, how was it?" Soph asked from the bathroom doorway, her arms folded across her chest. A wicked smirk added a devilish eagerness to her face.

"Amazing," Leona groaned while ringing water out of her hair.

"Figured it all went well when I heard nothing from you."

Guilt lanced through Leona at having left poor Soph to her own devices. "Sorry—"

"None of that. Us girls gotta get what we can get when we can get it."

"True." Leona chuckled. "What did you do last night?"

"Since I'm eager for the sordid details, I'll rush through my salacious activities." Soph sat on the closed toilet seat. "I watched movies, stuffed my face with buttered popcorn, and threatened my body with diabetes with the amount of chocolate I devoured. Halfway through the first movie, I fell asleep in a chair."

"Movies? And don't get me wrong, popcorn sounds awesome." Leona patted her grumbling stomach as if to appease it.

"Listen, being ravished is far more preferable to gorging myself on romcoms." Soph flicked a hand. "Now, spill."

Leona stepped out of the shower and punched the blue button. A blast of warm air hit her from all sides, muffling anything said. She giggled at Soph's glare. "Go order us breakfast," she yelled at her assistant.

Soph huffed and darted out of the bathroom, granting Leona a little privacy. She didn't want to share last night with her curious friend. Aaro was hers, and she wanted to savor that. She could share some of what she learned, though.

After hitting the gray button, she let the toweling robe snap shut around her body. Striding through the door into her living room, she inhaled the aroma of coffee and bacon like a starving woman.

"You were right. *Dar Eth* does mean wife," she said by way of greeting. She snatched a strip of bacon from the closest plate and slumped into a chair.

"So they're learning how to sleep with their future wives?" Soph sipped her coffee, pausing to lick her lips. "That's adorable."

"Yup," Leona said. "Last night was quite an eye-opener. In a nutshell, each Etterian has a darkness inside they call the void. Without a mate, that void will kill them."

"What?" Soph squeaked, almost spilling her coffee. "Mate?"

"*Soul*mate." Leona picked another bacon strip. "And they're rare. Although, he did say they're finding them among us humans."

"Okay, thanks for the heads-up." Soph swirled a finger, gesturing around the cabin. "I'll hide here, then. I'm enjoying not being 'wooed.'"

"I can believe that." Leona grinned. "Worse than that is the sixty days this journey is going to take."

Soph gaped, her fork halfway to her mouth with scrambled eggs balanced on it. "Shit." She stared at the eggs, her face pale.

"We would have been as long on Callisto before we could take a vacation."

Soph lowered her fork and scooped more eggs on and off then on again. "I know, but Callisto's a lot closer to Earth than wherever the hell we're going."

"Thea is fine, Soph. If your sister would let us, we could move her closer, but that still wouldn't be enough. Some of these planets are weeks away."

"Shit," Soph said again. "Did you know about this?"

"Nope. Found out last night. Yeah, I'll take Big Daddy to task. Aaro thinks—"

"Aaro, is it?" Soph giggled, cupping her hand over her mouth when she sprayed bits of egg across the table.

Leona sipped her coffee. "That you should stay on board when we deliver the dolls. One less 'female' to protect."

"Fine by me, besides, it's not as if these men will stop using the dolls while you two are planetside." Soph buttered a toast point and leaned back in her chair. "Anything else?"

Leona slumped. Soph's acquiescence was a load off her shoulders. Had her friend wanted to visit other planets or species, Leona would have spoken to Aaro about somehow sharing this experience with her. But, as usual, she'd made Leona's life easier.

"The replicator is free of charge," she offered by way of thanks.

Soph frowned. "Weird."

"I know, right? He said something about Etteria taking care of its people."

"What about big items like couches? There's nothing like that on the menu, but still, larger furniture would be better for movie nights and falling asleep." She rolled her shoulders then rubbed the nape of her neck.

"You know what, ask him, or make a list and ask Krist." Leona met her friend's bright blue gaze. "I can't be remembering all of this."

"No doubt he blows your mind. Want me to take over some of your responsibilities, especially those that require brain power?"

"Oh, the sass." Leona laughed. "But I'm good. We can take care of the dolls in our sleep."

"True. The factory hasn't come back about that defective joint. I'll follow up with them later today. You know them, gotta have their morning brew a few times before they answer."

"How about movie night tonight?" Leona offered, though she wasn't sure if Aaro had something planned. She dipped her chin to her chest to hide a smile. Damn, it was good and strange to have someone in her life.

"So, no details? You're gonna let me waste away not knowing anything?"

"Biological contact with anything other than their hand brings the void closer." Leona scooped up the dirty plates and carried them to the replicator.

"What?" Soph squeaked. "But you slept with him."

Leona winced. "Yeah, he said he was safe."

Soph gaped, then closed her mouth with a snap. "That explains why none of these gorgeous men have hit on me." Jumping to her feet, she danced around the chair to face Leona. "It also explains why a doll has such an impact. They're so much better than their hands. And," she paused to suck in a calming breath, "it explains their curiosity and twenty-million questions."

Leona gasped. "Forgot to mention those porn vids to Aaro. I'll do that at the first opportunity."

"Yup, can't expect you to ask him when he's *busy*." Soph wiggled her pale eyebrows.

Heat bloomed on Leona's cheeks despite her best efforts. They serviced sex dolls, for shit's sake. But talking about a lover was...personal. "I'll get dressed and meet you in the workshop."

"Sure thing, Sugar." Soph winked. "I'll prep the dolls for the day. Don't want to disappoint their fans."

Leona stared at the door after Soph left. Her mind reeled at all that had happened in the last few days. But at least her constant arousal was no longer plaguing her, not when Aaro was such an attentive lover. With a bounce in her step, she hurried through her clothing choices, then headed to the workshop.

Could he be falling for her? She'd caught him saying, "Leona, I am—," but he hadn't finished.

With a scoff, she worked through her morning routine. It was too soon for him to feel anything. And yes, he'd said they needed to talk, but she suspected it was all business. She grinned. Which meant she better keep his mouth busy if she wanted to avoid any unstimulating subjects.

Chapter Thirteen

WHEN LEONA HAD JOKINGLY demanded a post-training pamper session, she had no idea Aaro would deliver. He'd done his research too. What man did that? Taking up space in his cabin was a massage table, covered in white sheets with a towel at the foot. Beside it was the dining table, adjusted for height, and on top of it sat a bottle of oil. Across the rehydrator counter was an array of platters with tall glasses of sparkling champagne beside them. Candles burned, and actual music played in the background. Violin strands thrummed and tingled her ears. Floral fragrances tickled her nose, and her mouth watered at the promise of strawberries and cream.

Aaro waited for her to kick off her shoes. He said nothing while he removed her shirt and jeans. But when she didn't touch her underwear, he hooked a finger between her cleavage and snapped her bra open. She gasped. Her breasts bounced free. Her nipples tightened as if they could recall the number of times he'd teased them. Another yank tore her panties. She stood naked before him. He took his time, admiring her with his glowing blue eyes.

Damn. She'd never grow tired of that expression.

"Come," he rasped, then gripped her waist to hoist her onto the massage table that reached him mid-thigh.

She splayed her legs to accommodate him, but he didn't take the opportunity for something a little more sensual. Instead, he urged her to lie on her stomach. He draped a towel over her backside, then with a little oil from the bottle, he kneaded and rubbed her back.

As the tension eased from her body, she moaned. Trying not to drool used all her concentration. He didn't neglect an inch of her, from the nape of her neck to her toes. Off went the towel when he massaged oil into her thighs. His fingers came close to touching her sex. She spread her legs a little wider, hoping for a touch. Every brush stiffened her muscles in anticipation, and every time, he missed her by what felt like an inch.

When he stepped back and asked her to roll over, she whined. Banishing her disappointment came with a flood of hope. Maybe now, with her exposed breasts that he adored, he might thrum an orgasm from her. She ached in her core, between her legs; her need pressing against her senses until every touch slammed against her control. She was so close to demanding he fuck her. If it wasn't for her finishing school training, she would have succumbed by now.

Again, he started at her shoulders and worked down her arms to her fingers. Then up to her collarbone, down between her cleavage and around her breasts, circling her nipples until at last, he brushed his fingers across them. She whimpered, arching into his touch. But he didn't linger, and she didn't mind, not when he skirted her waist to her sex.

She gritted her teeth when he traveled down her legs instead of aiming for the part of her that ached the most. Time passed, worlds formed and died, and still, he massaged her toes and feet. At last, he massaged up to her inner thighs, nudging her knees apart with his knuckles.

With a finger, he caressed her seam. He touched where she most wanted it, and her breath caught spreading her thighs wider. He brushed over her clit. She swirled her hips, in effect, rubbing herself along his finger. She pinched her lips, closed her eyes, and concentrated on hitting the right spot.

At his chuckle, she flicked her eyelids open and glared at him.

He removed his hand and circled the table, stopping at the foot. Then he clasped her ass and dipped his head to slide his tongue where his finger had just been.

She cried out, quivering in his arms. Cold tingles traveled from her ears to the base of her spine. Flattening his tongue, he lapped at her clit until stars and spots formed in her vision. She couldn't breathe. Everything tightened, from her core to her thigh muscles as she climbed the mountain. The cliff was close. She buried her fingers in his hair and clung to him.

He rumbled, and the sound vibrated through her. When he plunged two fingers into her, she screamed, splintering in his arms and under his expert mouth. He didn't stop but continued to lick and nibble her, his fingers buried deep and stroking her G-spot.

The man was a sex god. She'd thought it before, but now she believed it. He flipped her over and, with an arm looped under her hips, hoisting her against him. Her knees slipped off the sides. While he stroked her exposed sex, he nibbled and kissed her butt cheeks like she longed to do to him.

With her ass against his lower abdomen, he angled himself at her entrance. One thrust drew a gasp from her, and she pushed back, meeting every one of his penetrations. She couldn't breathe, couldn't speak, could only ride the swells of pleasure he drew from her.

He layered his chest to her back, reached beneath her, and cupped her breasts. Not once did he falter. When he stiffened, he buried his face in her back and roared.

She was truly a woman well-fucked.

Time ticked past, and neither of them moved. He placed kisses between her shoulder blades, and occasionally muttered, "Maker."

She loved that he was as shaken as she was. He shuddered when he withdrew. She slumped, flopping face-first onto the table, her limbs spent. Over her, he draped a toweling robe, then scooped her into his arms. Onto the closest comfy, he sat with her on his lap, his face tucked into the curve of her neck. His breathing had yet to calm, and his heartbeat thudded against her shoulder.

"Just...let me hold you, *ensa.*"

She wasn't complaining. Without hesitation, she snuggled against him. He was following the list and doing it so naturally. Did he even have dessert planned?

At some point, they'd have to do other stuff than sex. Although, she was torn between being ravished and getting to know the quiet man holding her. His wall of memorabilia said there was more to him than an alien sub-commander who knew his way around her body.

"Do you want children, Aaro?" She hadn't meant to ask that, hadn't given it much thought, to be honest. The idea of kids, when her father would never bounce them on his knee, hadn't appealed to her. If the man she fell in love with did want children, would she give in to please him?

"I do, though, for Etterians, males are statistically more likely to be born than females."

Ah, yes, that mutated birth rate. Still, little Aaros running around would be cute.

He pinched her chin and raised her gaze to his. "And you?"

She shrugged. "I haven't thought about it. Although, the way my mother's been chasing this Bradley-thing, it's on her mind." She shuddered. "If I do have kids, I don't want them near her."

"They will be well-guarded."

She twitched. Had he just assumed she'd be having his off-spring? That was kind of arrogant of him. But she could see him being a pillar of strength to their children, a constant, unbreaking force.

"Do you have any siblings?"

He grinned. "A sister, though she is far younger than me and not a female I know as well as I would like."

"I'm an only child." She tried not to reveal how often she'd hoped for a sibling to share her life with. Or how many times she'd been glad that she was the only one to suffer through her parents' messy divorce. "Are your parents still together?"

"Yes, though it is unusual for a female to stay in a relationship when she first births a son. They are fond of each other. Even though they are not blessed by the *Ethera*, because of my sister being born to their union, they will remain together in the hopes of birthing another female."

"Well, that's...sad." *Like an arranged marriage backed by the government?* "What if your father finds his soulmate, will he leave your mother?"

"Yes, or vice versa, though the chances of this happening are slim."

"I don't like the way your planet's handling this, Aaro. I understand why but still, to be valued for your womb and nothing else..." She drew in a shuddering breath. "It sucks."

"Indeed, but do not feel too sorry for our females, *ensa*." He tightened his arms around her and pressed a kiss to her temple. "They receive anything they ask for and are deeply valued in our culture."

Did he mean only if they had daughters? "What happens to the women who birth sons?"

He hesitated then said, "They move onto the next male."

Leona squeaked and clambered off him, whipping the robe around her to cover her nudity. "You have got to be kidding me. What if she doesn't want to 'move' on?"

"Her wishes are taken into consideration. Most believe they are duty-bound to birth females. As we males serve Etteria in all capacities, they serve how they can."

She growled, pacing the room to vent her frustration. "And they know they have a choice?"

"Of course. Our king is not heartless, Leona. And now that he has found his *Dar Eth*, he is going to great lengths to ensure more and more pairings happen."

"Oh," she said, her shoulders slumping.

He chuckled, caught the edges of her robe, and tugged her closer. "I adore this passion you have for the rights of our females. This pleases me, *ensa*."

"What's your sister's name?" she asked and draped her arms over his broad shoulders.

"Taro," he said. He buried his face in her hair. "She is a handful and diligent at her studies, or so my mother says."

"Do you see your family often?"

"No, it has been decades since I went home. I hope to change that soon." He peered at her, an intensity swirling in his eyes.

Leona stilled. There was a message in his gaze she couldn't read but somehow knew it was tied to her. She opened her mouth to ask. Her stomach rumbled. Within seconds, Aaro had her seated in a chair and a fruit platter placed before her. She dipped strawberries into whipped cream. The tartness of the fruit with the smoothness of the cream coated her tongue. She closed her eyes and moaned, savoring the flavors. It had been years since she'd last had fruit.

With her forefinger on her lips while she chewed, she ogled him when he licked a dollop of cream off his thumb. Fuck, he was gorgeous and so easy to be with. He didn't bombard her with pointless stories as if trying to prove how masculine, wealthy, or influential he was. It struck her that all he did was enjoy her company and body without making any demands.

"The day we arrive at Sarvis, we will skip your training session. Boarding the *kuta* to the visitors' station is scheduled for 0700. Is that too early?"

"No," she managed round a sliver of mango.

"Good. I would prefer to arrive before the scheduled time to ensure nothing unexpected occurs. I am glad you have an O.D.I, Leona, for should we be separated for whatever reason, I will be able to track you." He tapped her wrist, activated the holographic letters, and a rainbow of colors flickered as he flew through menus and choices. "I have enabled the algri, Yithian, Maloidian, and Kulaian language protocols."

"What?" she gasped, wiping her fingers on a paper napkin to touch her wrist. "Does that mean...?"

"That you can speak and understand them, yes." He smirked no doubt finding her awe amusing.

She slapped him on his upper arm. "I didn't know this thing does that. I've just been using it for banking and communication." She sipped from the flute of champagne he pushed across to her, her gaze fixed on him sprawled in a chair. He was naked, gloriously bronzed, with an erection that made her core clench in anticipation. Not that he showed any awareness. If she wasn't hungry, she'd be feasting on him.

Exhaustion pressed on her too, tugging at her limbs and her focus. She could sleep for sure. It could be the training, the long days staring at rutting males, or spreading her thighs repeatedly, but today, she was drained. Adding the alcohol only loosened her further.

"Let me take that, *ensa*," Aaro said, jerking her from her daze. He slid the glass from her fingers and placed it on the nearby table. Up she went, scooped into his arms. She rested her temple on his right pec and let him carry her. Warmth poured off him, adding to the cozy haze fogging her mind.

He draped her onto his bed and climbed beside her. Without hesitation, she snuggled into his embrace, laid her head on his arm tucked under her, and dozed off.

Days passed, blurring from waking with Aaro in her bed or vice versa, to training, to work. She delayed spending the evenings with him until after dinner, wanting to make sure Soph didn't feel neglected. Sarvis was tomorrow, and nerves had Leona hopping from foot to foot.

She browsed the archives on Sarvis, needing to know she wasn't visiting a carnivorous planet where she'd be the meal of choice. Although, the algri weren't an unknown species. The images of their homeworld seemed surreal. Organic-shaped buildings occupied every square inch of their continents. Floating cities traveled their oceans of deep green waters. One weak sun warmed their world with days longer than their nights. They wore no clothing, and their names were impossible to pronounce. Shit, she hoped she did Earth proud.

"What are you doing?" Soph asked, striding into the workshop. For once, Leona wasn't watching sex play out on all the mini-vids.

"Research. I don't want to offend, so Aaro said I should dress like an Etterian woman." She tapped her chin. Later, she'd asked him to choose an outfit for her. Hopefully, it was something she could move in. Images of Victorian gowns came to mind. No way could she run in one of those.

"I don't see why you're so nervous," Soph said while ordering hot cocoa for them both. "We've met algri before, seen their...um...mating techniques." She gestured to the display vids.

"Those are outliers. It says here," Leona tapped the screen, "that only the most adventurous leave their planet. It's not the norm and is frowned upon." She shrugged. "I guess you could say the algris traveling space are exiles."

"That's sad," Soph said

"Yeah. So let me not piss off any I meet."

"I'm glad I'm not going down there. I prefer my feet on solid metal." Soph gave a decisive nod.

"And surrounded by a battleship of soldiers?" Leona arched a brow.

"That too." Soph winked.

"How are the sex education sessions going?"

"They still like to hold my hand at every opportunity, but now the questions have gone from sexual to what makes a woman happy." Soph chortled. "Hell, some days, *I* don't even know. We're a mystery to ourselves sometimes. There'll be days where I cry for no reason. How do I explain that to these men? Or how to convert our unhappiness to joy?"

"If there was a handbook, every human man would have it memorized by now."

"Fact," Soph cried out, then giggled. "Me too. On page 3985, it states that to cheer a woman up, large boxes of chocolate or bouquets are needed."

Leona chuckled. "And if she glares at you through the veil of her eyelashes, run."

"A woman shouldn't have to state she wants attention when a flash of a breast is enough to convey her needs."

Leona swallowed her laughter, remembering Aaro's expression when he undid her shirt last night and discovered the white corset she'd worn to surprise him. The poor man had reacted a little aggressively. She shifted on the chair, trying to ease the deep ache in her core along with the craving for him that never went away no matter how much he adored her.

"Anyway, I'm starving. What's for lunch?" Soph cleared her throat. "Battleship to Leona."

Leona jerked back to reality. "What do you feel like?"

"Pizza."

"Again?" Leona groaned. "What I could do with is a nap."

"Then do it. I've got you covered."

Leona hesitated then slid off the chair. "You're right."

With a squeeze to Soph's forearm, Leona headed to her cabin. The late nights were catching up to her. She smothered a yawn and climbed onto her bed, sliding her hands under the pillow. Her mind reeled with algri facts, excitement at visiting a new planet, and what Aaro had planned for tonight. Her chest swelled, and she smiled. Was she in love? If this was it, she'd revel in it. Everything good came to an end, and when it did, she didn't want to regret missing one moment of it.

Chapter Fourteen

"You are asking me to clothe you?" Aaro froze, his ears ringing despite his supernatural hearing having caught every word. He crossed the room and swept Leona into his arms. "It would be my pleasure, *ensa*," he said, his voice hoarse. To clothe her stated to all that she was his, and for her to ask him, meant she'd accepted this as fact.

She laughed—her unfettered joy sparked an answering fire within him. "You said I should dress Etterian. I'm assuming you know how."

"I do," he said, pressing his temple to hers.

He stole a quick kiss, for to linger would need hours, and now wasn't the time. Lowering her feet to the floor, he held her in a hug as he'd done that first time. Without hesitation, she slid her arms around his waist and clung to him. Her long sigh of contentment said it all. Trailing his touch down her arm to her fingertips, he escorted her to the replicator. There, he punched in his requirements. On the glass, her gown formed in the colors of his family—the deepest pink of an Etterian sunset. She would look exquisite in it. Thin black rimmed the cuffs of the sleeves and along the seams. He offered it to her, his hands trembling. Maker, he prayed she adored the garment.

"Shoes?" she asked as she accepted the bundle.

"I will order those. First... Try it on, please." He wanted to beg her to hurry. This was foolish, but every day spent with her had been bliss so far. And seeing his *Dar Eth* in his house colors was a dream come true. Even if she chose to leave him. He blinked against the overwhelming darkness that thought summoned.

She smiled and placed the garment on the counter. Then with slow movements, she flicked the buttons open on her blouse. It parted, and he held his breath. After that white undergarment she called a corset, he never knew what awaited him when she undressed.

Excitement flooded his veins, and the urge to kiss her hit him. He pinched his lips and forced himself to remain still. She toed off her shoes and shimmied out of her skintight pants. Standing in nothing but her tiny strips of cloth, he admired her as he always did when she bared herself to him.

I am a blessed male.

The moment she slipped into the wrap, his thoughts quieted. Something squeezed his chest, slowing his heartbeats. *Alodon's balls, she is exquisite.*

"This is...so luxurious," she said, stroking and crushing the fabric between her fingers. "What is this?"

"A ceremonial gown only *Dar Eth*s wear."

She froze and raised a wide-eyed gaze to him. "But—"

"It is why they will believe you are Etterian and mine."

"Ah," she said and glanced away.

Sadness flittered across her face. She was so easy to read, his female. The words lodged in his throat. He should tell her, should cross that line, and reveal she was his for an eternity. Though, with what roiled inside him and with every second spent with her, forever wasn't long enough. He'd love an eternity with her.

Tapping the replicator, he summoned a matching pair of slippers. He knelt and slipped each on her delicate feet, but he did not rise. Instead, he trailed his fingers up her bare calve, to clasp behind her knee.

He met her gaze. "You in this gown brings me so much joy, *ensa ra ensa*."

"Oh?" She cupped his face and brushed a kiss across his lips.

"Yes," he said, his voice too guttural, but he didn't care.

Touching the magnets, he opened the gown, exposing her to his hungry gaze. He glided the fabric back until he could cup her backside. Then leaning forward, he pressed a kiss to her stomach, relishing the softness there. She sank her fingers into his hair, and he groaned, hugging her tighter.

What Benedict felt for Elizabeth couldn't compare to what Leona invoked in Aaro. For theirs was more than an archival documentation of a couple he would never meet.

"Aaro?" Leona kissed his temple. "What's wrong?"

"Nothing. I find you breathtakingly beautiful in every sense."

She squirmed. "I'm not always this... I have bad days too."

"Ah," he said. "You believe we are in this honeymoon phase Izzy mentioned."

Leona slumped and lowered herself to kneel before him. "Yes." She stroked his cheek, her touch infinitely tender. "I don't think you care, though."

"I do not," he growled. "You at your worst is better than never having known you."

Tears shimmered in her eyes.

He frowned. "Did I hurt you?"

"No," she croaked, then chuckled. "I'm just a little emotional. I'm nervous about today."

He didn't say a word, just tucked her into his embrace and rested his chin on the crown of her head. Nothing, and he swore this to the universe, would harm her.

She pulled out of his arms and stood. "I'll prep the dolls. Fetch me when it's time."

He nodded, watching her leave in his house colors. Every male she passed would know to whom she belonged. His chest swelled. *Maker.*

All was ready. The *kuta* would hold a few warriors, no more than four as per protocol. They would each carry a blaster, but Aaro would have preferred to sheath his greatsword down his back had it not been overkill.

Thankfully, the algri were far more accommodating when it came to Etterians, allowing them their weapons and procedures. Adviser Kanzo had done wonders negotiating with the Sarvis representative. Still, Aaro didn't want to offend, so a blaster would do.

He paused before his wall and scooped up the latest addition. Encased in glass was Leona's black sliver of cloth she'd worn to cover her sex. He couldn't scent it, but that he had it was all that mattered. It took center stage in his collection.

Grabbing the tablet off the table, he left for the comm room. They approached the visitors' station within the hour. He'd collect Leona and Soph closer to the time if they were interested in observing their descent.

"All is well," Pilot Krist said when Aaro entered. "Ambassador Ghesthsoooa awaits our arrival."

"You will pilot the *kuta*, Krist. I want you at your best. Nothing must harm my *Dar Eth*." Aaro tucked the tablet under his arm and settled with his hands clasped behind his back and his legs spread wide.

"I assumed as much, Sub-Commander." Krist's fingers flew across the console. "I have sent a warrior to escort Lady Leona and her cybs to the holding bay. From there, the warrior will bring her here, if that pleases you, Sub-Commander?"

"My thanks," Aaro grunted. "Make the offer to Lady Soph as well."

"Will do," Krist responded, typing more commands into the console. "Done."

The display vids filled with stars against a black-blue background. A large orb circling a weak sun sat center stage, the battleship *Valiant* baring down on it. A white spec circled the green-white planet. Disappointment coated this trip, for Aaro would not be venturing to the surface. No artifacts awaited him.

When Leona entered, looking breathtaking in the ceremonial gown, Krist rose out of his chair to nod at her and Soph. "Welcome, miladies."

"Is that it?" Soph asked, pointing at Sarvis. When Krist nodded, she said, "It's pretty."

Leona settled beside Aaro, bringing her scent with her. His fingers twitched to touch her. He relaxed, placed the tablet on the table, then returned to her side. Without anyone noticing, not that he had to hide it, he captured her hand, lacing their fingers. His heartbeats stuttered. Logic dictated he shouldn't feel this much this fast. He shouldn't long to see her, to wrap his arms around her, or inhale her scent.

He'd need to let Flad do a full assessment again. Whatever the *Ethera* did could be construed as magic. Aaro snuck a glance at Leona, catching the awe opening her eyes and mouth. If only Flad could scan her too. They knew nothing about the *Ethera*'s ability to influence humans. But how to ask her without revealing why?

"Ready for this, *ensa*?" he whispered, dipping to bring his lips close to her ear.

A tremor shot along her arm to her fingers clutched in his hand. "Yes," she rasped, flicking her gaze to his. The ceremonial wrap draped her every curve, accentuating the heaving of her bosom. No wonder Benedict had been ensnared by Elizabeth, for the in and out movements of her chest would be as mesmerizing as Leona's.

Her cheeks flushed a coral at his scrutiny. "I *am* ready, Aaro."

"I believe you." He smiled, hoping to put her at ease. "I merely like looking at you."

"Oh," she mouthed. "You saw me just this morning." She gestured with her hand to the rest of her.

"I did. I plan to again. Still, you are a beautiful woman." He feathered his lips over the tip of her ear. "And mine."

"Battleship *Valiant* requesting docking." Pilot Krist cut into the desire narrowing Aaro's vision. "We will be sending our *kuta*."

Aaro straightened. With the importance of this mission before him, he couldn't afford to be distracted. Needing to ensure Leona's safety, he had to remain attentive to any threat or situation.

"Maker, female, I want done with this and you in my arms," he gritted out, then stepped away from her, dropping her hand.

"Battleship *Valiant*, your arrival is anticipated," an algri warbled. "Please proceed to Bay 423."

"This is so exciting." Soph danced on the spot.

Leona wiggled her eyebrows. "So many algri with all those tentacles, Soph."

Soph shuddered and tossed a glare Leona's way. "No. Thank. You."

"Think of the questions they'll ask you," Leona teased.

Soph grabbed Leona's hand. "Oh, while you're there, find out if they have a scent preference."

"Good idea," Leona said. "Anything else?"

The younger woman released Leona and peered at the display vids. "Taste too, might as well see if we can influence the flavor of the doll's skin and lubrication."

Leona tapped on her O.D.I. "That's brilliant. If successful, I'm letting Big Daddy know it was your idea."

Soph groaned. "Please don't."

"He doesn't bite, babe." Leona's tone softened.

"I know, it's just..." Soph gazed at Leona. "I haven't told Thea where I work. I don't want her to find out before I get the chance. So, if I keep to the shadows, it'll buy me time."

"Fair enough," Leona said, dragging Soph into a hug.

"It is time to depart," Krist said as Pilot Saan settled into his chair.

"I'm not going." Soph stepped to the side of the comm room. "If someone can take me back to the workshop, I've dolls to monitor."

"Come with me, milady," Data Officer Ranh said, gesturing to the doorway.

"Good luck, *Chief* Sugar," Soph said with a wink before trailing Ranh.

"No pressure," Leona muttered.

Aaro held out his hand which she accepted, then with a shortened stride, he led her along the passages to the nearest bay—the same one where he'd first seen her. Up the ramp he ushered her. Two cybs were strapped to the back wall of the *kuta*, a crate at their feet. He wasted no time in securing Leona to a fold-down seat. No accidental jarring from asteroid debris, nothing would place her in harm's way. He stroked her jaw to her chin, then gave her a playful pinch. When she smiled at him, he sank into the seat beside her.

"Strap in," she said, reaching across him.

His chest swelled that she cared. For this reason alone, he obeyed.

"Good," she said, settling back against the bulkhead. She ran her palms along her thighs, threatening to part the gown. Thankfully, the magnetic clasps held firm.

"The ambassador awaits our arrival," Aaro said to put her at ease.

She drew in a deep breath then glanced at him. "Thanks."

He captured her hand to rest it on his thigh. "Watch the forevids." He gestured to the front of the *kuta*. Krist occupied the pilot seat as he navigated out of the bay and toward the visitors' station.

Her breath caught when they sped closer. "I sense nothing. No engine vibrations, no sound." She glanced to the rear of the *kuta*. "Sol is your power source, right?"

"Yes, though how its energy is so well harnessed, I cannot say."

"I mean, it powers the *Valiant* too. You'd have to store the sol in great quantities." She thrummed with restrained excitement, confirmed by the beaming smile she leveled on him. His gaze traveled over her face, noting the luminosity of her eyes and the sheer joy in her expression.

The *kuta* jerked. She squeaked and squeezed his thigh.

He layered her hand with his. "We have docked."

The *kuta* door opened to the bright interior of a docking tunnel. White lined the floors, walls, and ceiling. He blinked, adjusting his visual sensitivity. Unbuckling the straps, he pushed out of the seat to free Leona. She rose before he did, shoving her breasts into his face.

He clenched his jaw, willing himself not to react. Had they been alone, he would have buried his face against her soft belly. He stood and didn't reach for her hand. Here, now, she had to stand on her own as Cyb Ent's representative. She gazed out the door, squared her shoulders, then released the cybs.

Leona typed on her O.D.I. as she marched down the ramp. The cybs trailed her, their curves on display in those flimsy garments.

Aaro fell in behind them. Two of his males and Krist would remain with the *kuta*. Another two would join him. "Remain vigilant," he commanded them.

"We will defend your *Dar Eth* with our lives," Elite Warrior Siio said, clutching his blaster to his chest.

Aaro nodded, gratitude unfurling in his chest. He had good males.

Leona stepped into the welcome center lined with tall strips of display vids and weak sunlight. Views of Sarvis filled the walls. A closer inspection revealed the vids to be glass and not imagery.

It made sense since this wasn't a military station requiring defensive protocol and architecture.

"It's picturesque, Aaro," Leona whispered without glancing over her shoulder at him.

The crowds parted to watch them pass. A mix of Maloidian, algri, and Yithian filled the room. He studied as many as he could, searching for a hint of ill intent. Resting his hand on his blaster still strapped to his thigh offered a pathetic sense of control. But he grasped it, needing something to calm the desperation pounding at his instincts.

"Ah," an algri warbled, coming to stand in front of Leona. "Leona Williams, Chief Engineer of Cyb Ent, welcome. I am Ambassador Ghesthsoooa."

Leona bowed her head. "Ambassador." She swept out her hand. "I hereby deliver the sex-cybs as promised."

"Are all Earthians as built?" The ambassador stroked a tentacle down a cyb's arm. He turned two of his six eyes on Leona. "Like you?"

"I suppose," Leona said, although she'd stiffened her posture. "We have a variety of skin tones, and hair and eye colors. If these are not to your preference—"

"My apologies, Leona Williams. I meant no offense. I am merely curious. I have not met an Earthian before. Will you escort your...sex-cybs to their destination?"

Aaro frowned. "That was not part of the plan," he growled.

"Again, my apologies, Sub-Commander Aaro et Zaro. Their new home will be on this station. I believe the location should bring peace of mind to Leona Williams and Cyb Ent. We aim to care for these...automations in good faith."

"Please, lead the way, Ambassador." Leona tapped her O.D.I. and activated the cybs.

As one, they all trailed the algri as he scurried along causeways, through crowds, musical performers, and a flamboyant algri in a strange robe addressed a growing crowd.

Leona held her head high and glided at a steady pace after the ambassador. She had the grace of a queen, his female.

"Tell me, Ambassador, who will be maintaining your sex-cybs?" She didn't extend her voice, nor did she hurry to catch up to the algri.

"We have chosen someone with suitable skills. You may convey any instructions to her." The ambassador drifted through gaping glass doors to a padded common room with hard indented seats. A young algri in mottled greens awaited them. Her six-eyed gaze shifted from Leona to Aaro to the cybs. Ridges along her neck confirmed her as female. Aaro couldn't remember the details, but once an algri reached a certain age, as in centuries, they chose their permanent gender. All were female until then.

"Jeeonaaausi," the ambassador waved a tentacle, "please make yourself useful."

"Hi," Leona smiled. She withdrew a tablet she'd tucked into the pocket of her ceremonial wrap. "All you need to know is in here, from minor maintenance to cleaning. They're prepped and tested. Any defects need to be reported to me or the factory. And if you have any concerns or queries, contact me directly." She tapped her O.D.I. "I control them from here. May I?" She waved her arm, mimicking the transfer of data across implants.

"Please," Jeeonaaausi gurgled in a higher pitch.

Leona swiped her wrist over the tentacle Jeeonaaausi offered. "Monitor the feeds, specifically for abuse or malfunction." Leona hitched a thumb at the crate a warrior carried. "These are spare parts should you need them."

"Thank you." Jeeonaaausi tapped her O.D.I. and the cybs straightened. With the tablet clasped in one tentacle and the crate in two others, she hurried through the closest door, the cybs sashaying after her.

"Your signature here," the ambassador revealed a tablet upon which Leona placed her hand.

After a beep, she lowered her hand and bowed to Ghesthsoooa. "Thank you for your time, Ambassador. I hope you will enjoy your gifts."

"Good day to you, Leona Williams."

Leona marched out of the common room and through the crowds. "That was painless," she whispered when they'd reached the docking tunnel.

"Want to linger?" Aaro asked despite the urge to have her safe on board the *Valiant*.

"Searching for something specific?" She gestured behind her.

He glanced at a relics shop they'd just passed. "Perhaps one stop?" He grinned.

"Why not?" she said, looping her arm around his.

Elizabeth had done the same to Benedict. Where that male had drawn her closer, Aaro captured Leona's hand and cradled it to his chest. In the windowed shelves were transparent rocks as big as his hand. Pinks, purples, hints of greens, and a sliver of blue shot out from its center.

His males surrounded them, their gazes outward.

"They are magnificent, Aaro." She leaned closer, her nose almost touching the glass. "Which one?"

"You choose," he said, although he preferred the pinkest rock that had first caught his eye.

When she tapped the glass over the correct one, he beamed. "It's almost the color of this gown." She raised her arm, splaying the sleeve to compare colors.

"Yes," he rasped.

"Get the little one too, for Taro." She stroked the glass above the rock's smaller twin.

A deafening hum bombarded his hearing, and his vision spun. That she would think of his sister... *Maker*. "I shall," he managed past the lump in his throat. "Is there anything you like?" He scanned the display, desperate to find her something.

An algri waddled through the shop's entrance. "Perhaps this?" He held up a piece of jewelry. The pink stones were the size of Aaro's fingernails and were joined in a loop.

"What is it?" he asked even as his males closed the circle around them, no doubt distrusting the algri's sudden appearance.

"A bracelet?" Leona took it from the algri and draped it over her wrist.

The stones were so pretty against her skin that Aaro swiped his wrist over the paypoint.

She gaped, her gaze flicking between the beads and him. "Aaro, you didn't need to—"

"I did, and it brings me so much joy to bless you with a gift, *ensa ra ensa*."

"Let me pay for it." She nibbled her bottom lip, reminding him of his plans for later.

"Then it is not a gift. The giving is something Etterian males never have an opportunity to do."

She gasped when the algri looped the jewelry around her wrist. "It's lovely." She rose on her toes and pressed a kiss to Aaro's cheek. "Thank you."

With his purchases tucked under his arm, Aaro ushered her to the *kuta*. Warmth bubbled inside him like the champagne that had tickled his throat last night. He'd never known this much happiness. After locking the boxes in storage, he crouched to strap Leona into her seat. She watched him, her focus intense. What was she thinking behind those big blue eyes?

No words were spoken on the return trip, but the air thickened between them.

As soon as the ramp lowered, she unbuckled herself and left. He hurried after her but not before thanking his males for performing their duties well. It cost him precious seconds, even though their surprise was worth it. Before the *Ethera*, only his duty to Etteria mattered. And until his males had found their *Dar Eth*s, he would ensure they knew their value.

"Leona," he called, striding after her. He caught her and pinned her to the bulkhead. Males streamed past them, but he didn't care.

"That went well," she said but didn't meet his gaze.

"What is the matter, *ensa*?"

She sniffed and raised her gaze to the ceiling. "It's been a while since someone gave me a gift, Aaro. And you asked for nothing in return. I..." She cleared her throat even as a tear slipped free. "I don't know how to handle such a gesture without distrust." She cupped his cheek and offered him a tremulous smile. "Thank you. I will always cherish it."

"Alodon's balls, female," he growled. "I aim to bless you often."

She chuckled through her tears. "And I shall accept your gifts with more grace."

What kind of life had she lived where receiving anything came with a cost? "I do ask for something in return," he said. When she stiffened, he hurried to add, "that you share your time with me."

"I do that anyway, Aaro."

He grinned. "I know."

She huffed but at least she no longer cried. "You're being silly."

He stole a kiss. "As a male infatuated, I can be any way I please."

"Infatuated, huh?" She pinched her lips to hide a smile but failed.

"Indeed." He stepped back and threw his arm across her shoulders. "Later, I shall demonstrate how much I adore you."

"I'll hold you to your word," she said, splaying her fingers across his stomach.

Chapter Fifteen

Aaro abandoned Leona at her cabin for which she was grateful. She needed a few minutes alone. When she stripped out of the gown, she ran her hand over the soft fabric, then draped it across her bed. The bracelet slid back and forth with her movements. Pausing, she held it to the light and admired the various splashes of pinks in the depths of the stones. He hadn't hesitated, paying before she could register his intention. And with his shit-eating grin, she hadn't wanted to castigate him for his impulse. It *had* been thoughtful, and she'd meant it when she said she'd cherish it forever.

Nor had she lied. The last gift she'd gotten was from her father the week before he'd died. Most gifts ran on a tit-for-tat system, a you-scratch-my-back sort of thing. This bracelet had come with nothing but a request to continue as they were. Her heart thumped, skipping a beat. She couldn't put her finger on when, or how, or why, but she was fast succumbing to Aaro's sweet nature. How had such a man become a sub-commander? Surely that position demanded a mean, military-focused individual?

He took his tasks seriously, always lost in that tablet. She imagined the amount of paperwork he had to work through was extensive. Tonight, she'd show him the same attention he'd lavished on her. A massage would be first. No doubt, his responsibilities had to weigh on him.

She giggled, bouncing as she dressed in her uniform.

What she tried not to think about was the next delivery: Yithia. But after this morning, her confidence in Aaro had grown. He'd been vigilant and had taken many precautions, until that curio shop. She chuckled, delighted that he'd found something. His wall of oddities mattered to him, something he might seek comfort from on long interplanetary journeys. That, she could understand. If he didn't fill her nights, she might have been forced to take up a hobby. Soph had mentioned acrylic painting, just for splashes of color.

Leona grabbed a chicken-mayo sandwich and an iced chai then left her cabin for the workshop.

"So, how was it?" Soph asked, a slice of pizza in hand. By the looks of the solidified cheese, she nibbled on leftovers.

"Good, interesting, and Sarvis is even more stunning up close." Leona sank into a chair. "It's a pity we didn't head planetside."

"Nope, no thanks." Soph popped the last bite into her mouth and grabbed a paper napkin.

"To each his own." Leona shrugged. "Left the cybs in a female algri's...um...tentacles. I expect her to contact me with questions soon enough. I'll ask her about scents and tastes once we have some sort of relationship going."

"Wise, build trust, then milk her for details to exploit her species." Soph laughed. "The human way, for sure."

Leona smiled. "I hadn't thought of it like that, but then again, I couldn't just ask the ambassador what he wished cum tasted like. Do they even have cum?"

Soph grimaced. "I thought it was that slime-jelly. The cybs need full sterilization after an algri's had their way with them."

"True, though it would be awesome to know for sure. Anything odd happen?"

"All good. Wanna come over later for a painting party? Gonna start on decorating my dismal cabin." Soph pushed her plate aside. "I asked Ranh about big replicator orders. He said they have a massive one in storage and that it has a separate menu. He's taking me later to order canvases."

"Oh, that does sound like fun. I'll watch the dolls if you want to go sooner." Leona gestured to the workshop. "Why don't we paint here? We're bored anyway, might as well dabble during our shifts."

"Good idea. We can listen to the vids while mixing colors." Soph bounced on her toes. "I'll ask Ranh, see when he's free."

Leona forced herself not to roll her eyes. A week ago she wouldn't have considered suggesting this, but with the reverence Etterian men showed the dolls, there wasn't much she and Soph needed to do.

In truth, every time she watched a vid, it reminded her of Aaro. Within seconds, she'd be fanning herself and pinching her thighs together like some sex-starved spinster. At some point, she had to reach enough-is-enough, but that hadn't arrived yet and didn't seem to be on the horizon either.

And days spent painting with Soph might free up Leona's nights for Aaro.

Hours later, Soph returned with the works: canvasses, brushes, paints, and even easels. Ranh smiled at Leona in greeting before stacking the items in the corner of the workshop.

Soph waved him off then skipped to the pile. "We'll start tomorrow. I think we'll need the entire day to get the hang of it." She beamed. "I plan to spend tonight sketching some ideas. Mind if we skip movies?"

"No problem," Leona said, hiding her amusement.

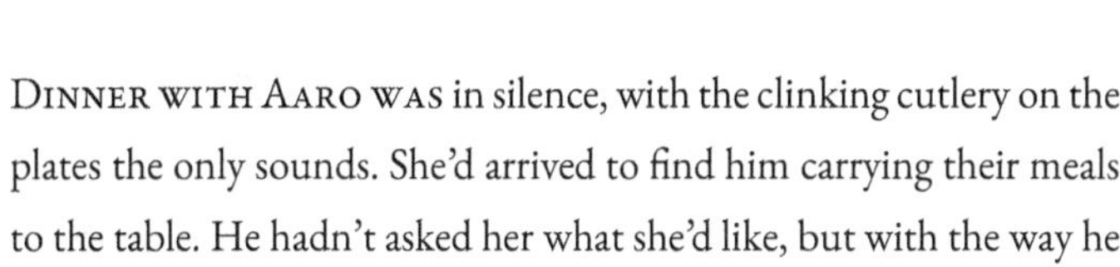

Dinner with Aaro was in silence, with the clinking cutlery on the plates the only sounds. She'd arrived to find him carrying their meals to the table. He hadn't asked her what she'd like, but with the way he ogled her, food wasn't important.

And here she'd hoped to lick him all over. It seemed like he had other plans.

"You all right?" she asked when he dumped the plates on the replicator.

"Just craving you," he said, his back to her.

Craving? Yes, that made sense. Not an hour went by that she didn't think about him, and often, her body would twinge in longing or she'd catch a whiff of his cinnamon-scented cologne when he wasn't even near. Lasting hours between seeing him was becoming harder. What madness was this? It had to be alien in nature, for sure.

She stood, needing to work out the restless energy bouncing her right leg. Her gaze caught on the pink rock placed on the end of the top shelf. Odd, she thought he would've placed it dead center. Instead, a clear block holding a black something took up the most prominent position. She leaned in to better see what thing he'd encased in glass or plastic.

A gasp slipped from her lips. That was her…G-string? She glanced at him then at the block again. A giggle threatened to escape, but she swallowed hard. Was this supposed to be a joke?

"Aaro," she croaked then hurried to clear her throat. "Why do you collect these?" She gestured to the wall in general.

"They're my most treasured memories," he said, striding toward her.

But her panties? Surely an image of her would be better? She opened her mouth to suggest it when he grabbed the clear block and held it to his chest like a cherished childhood toy. Shit, he *was* serious. That slip of black lace was tied to their first lovemaking. Since he was Etterian and not human, she didn't think he kept her panties as a memento for finally fucking her.

She pinched her lips, imagining the corset finding its way there. Maybe he didn't know of digi-frames slide-showing pics of her? Maybe she didn't understand his need to capture precious moments. The latter was more probable.

"Does anyone…um, see your collection?" Heat exploded across her cheeks at the off chance of someone recognizing her underwear.

"No. These are for me." Grinning at her as he returned the 'ornament' to its place, he nudged his chin at the empty wall to the right of the main door. "I would love to fill that space with more memories of you."

"I'd like that," she said. Desperate to change the subject, she asked, "I've been meaning to ask you, does your braid get in the way of daily tasks?"

He whipped his head and caught the thick rope to run his hand over the ends. "No. We learn from a young age how to care for our honor."

She'd raised her hand to touch the tips then froze. "Your what now?"

He chuckled. "Our honor is visible in the length of our braids. Dishonor means losing a foot of hair."

She gaped. If humans had outward signs of their honor, dating would've been so much easier. She ran her palm over the tail of his braid and groaned. It was softer than silk. "How do you care for your hair? Wouldn't washing, drying, and combing take time?"

"The water has all your body needs, from shampoo to soap to brushing your teeth."

"Your teeth? How?" She feathered the tail along her neck, shivering in reaction when it tickled.

"We gargle," he rasped and stepped forward, crowding her until her backside hit the bulkhead. "If you keep doing that with my hair, *ensa*, it will land you flat on your back."

She drowned in his eyes even as she flicked his hair over her taut nipple tenting the summer dress she wore. He snatched a hard kiss, then, before she could gather her wits, he tossed her over his shoulder. As he carried her to his bedroom, her gaze fixed on her entombed panties. Perhaps she should start her own wall, especially if it was for her eyes only. Making Aaro wear a speedo then encasing the item in glass did have some appeal. Although, the types of questions Soph would ask... Leona swallowed a giggle. Okay, maybe putting the wall in her bedroom might be wise.

"WHEN YOU SAID TRAINING, this isn't what I had in mind," Leona muttered, doing her fifteenth push-up. Her arms trembled, and on every descent, she collapsed on the mat, making it harder to lift herself off the floor. Punching and kicking was exhilarating, venting any frustration, anger, hell, even pent-up sexual energy.

"Complaining will earn you no leniency," Aaro said, his arms folded across his bare chest. In nothing but military pants and boots, he cut a fine figure. Even in the meager lighting, his bronze skin glistened, especially along his Adonis belt. *Yummy.*

"If my whining isn't working, what about a little skin?" She flipped onto her back and gazed at him.

He frowned. "I do not understand."

She sat up and peeled off her sneakers and socks.

"We are not done with the session," he said, though his focus snagged on her feet.

"I wouldn't suggest we are." She smirked and stood, then hooked her fingers into the waistband of her sweatpants and panties to shimmy them off.

"Leona," he warned but strode closer.

"I haven't done my sit-ups yet, Coach Aaro." She pouted and sat on the mat, spreading her knees wide. Giving him a clear view of her sex, she leaned back, then sat up. "One."

"Maker, female, this is..." He knelt between her thighs and cupped her jaw before she could descend. The kiss he gave her scattered her thoughts. Any more plans to torment him abandoned her. With his masterful tongue, she whimpered in an age-old plea for more of...him.

She registered him lifting her, then the cool table on her sweaty back when he lowered her onto its steel surface. Her legs hung off the edge at the knees.

He pulled away to gaze at her. "Give me two," he rasped.

"Huh?" She huffed, having thought enticing him might spare her. Doing any form of exercise this morning wasn't appealing after the way he'd worshipped her last night.

He gestured with his fingers for her to meet his mouth for a kiss. Without her feet flat on the mat, doing a sit-up was harder, but she tried anyway, using the backs of her knees to grip the table. Up she went, groaning as she did so, then an inch from his mouth, he offered her his cheek instead.

"Hey, that's cheating," she said.

"Is it?" He grinned. Tapping his pants, they opened, revealing an erection peeking out. He caught her calves and dragged her ass closer to the edge. With her legs spread around his hips, he freed his cock and positioned it at her entrance. Then he waited. "Another."

She obeyed, though her attention was on him, on what he might do. As she came up, he thrust into her. She clenched her teeth against a cry, and with extra effort, despite the exquisite torture of having him deep inside her, she finished the sit-up. When she tried to kiss him, he gave her his cheek again.

He withdrew his cock but didn't leave her. "One more, *ensa*."

"I swear, Aaro—"

"Another," he commanded, and damn, if his authoritative tone didn't shoot spasms of heat through her.

She leaned back, then lay there. He was teasing her with the promise of a fuck, all to get her to do her silly exercises. She met his gaze and tore off her sports bra, flinging it aside. Cupping her breasts, she sat up and, this time, didn't try to kiss him. His neon eyes glowed, showing her he wasn't unaffected. His nostrils flared, and he'd parted his lips.

He plunged into her, rewarding her. She bit her lip, swallowing her gasp. What she wanted to do was gyrate her hips and make some demands of her own. Instead, she released her breasts and locked her fingers behind her head. Down she went, biting her tongue when he slid his cock out of her. Those ridges were a marvel, rubbing along the most sensitive and nerve-rich part of her body. She didn't break eye contact when she lay back, needing him to see how much she ached for him. Her breathing labored. Her heartbeat thundered in her ears, and even though her abs pinged as if on the cusp of cramping, she sat up, more than eager for his plunge. Back and up she went until she reached the count of fifteen.

A tremor had taken up residence in her knees, but it had nothing to do with her sit-ups. Her core twanged, needing him to bring her relief. Each thrust made her desire climb until she simmered, close but not close enough to orgasm. And the man kept it up, unphased. Sure, his body was taut, yet his touch on her hips remained gentle.

"Another, Leona," he growled.

She shivered at his hoarse voice but didn't move. "I'm done. Thank you for the session, Aaro." She wiggled out from under his touch, vowing to never mention to him how much strength it had taken to pull away. Closing her legs drew a moan when all her senses were focused on her throbbing clit and core. "I'll just take a shower...and finish myself off." She staggered over the mat, trying to walk without whimpering.

From behind, he wrapped his arm around her, catching her across her cleavage, to pin her back against his front. "Without me? I think not, *ensa ra ensa*," he whispered, his breath hot on her ear.

His cock pressed at the juncture of her thighs when he hoisted her up. In mid-air, he spun her like she was a baton. She squeaked, throwing out her arms to catch herself. Instead, he caught her and lunged forward, capturing her against the wall. The cold of the steel mitigated the heat from his chest warming her breasts. She cried out at his velvety skin on hers. Then at the familiar pressure as he inched his cock into her. She groaned, throwing her head back. He released her, keeping her in place with his body, to cup her face.

"Look at me, *ensa*."

She obeyed, her mouth falling open when he pistoned into her. It was all too much, too fast and intense. She panted and clung to him in case he thought of abandoning her. A fiery flush of heat forged through her, tightening her core until she could do nothing but feel. If she made any cries or pleas, she couldn't say. Her world narrowed on Aaro, on his beautiful eyes, on his cock igniting her from within, and on that blossoming light in her soul. She splintered into a million prisms of color when at last the orgasm slammed into her. He kissed her as he shuddered his release.

A hint of wild desperation came with his kiss when he lingered, feathering his lips from cheek to cheek, then across her mouth again. She descended from her mind-shattering orgasm to his reverent kisses and caresses, almost as if he pleaded for forgiveness. It wasn't needed, not when he'd delivered on his unspoken promise. He hadn't pulled out yet, not that she minded with how complete he made her feel.

Sliding an arm between her back and the wall, he gathered her against him and spun to sprawl them on the mat. Then, on his knees, he leaned back to smile at her before saying, "Another, Leona?"

When he withdrew and thrust into her, snatching her breath, all her resistance melted. She hooked her legs around him, slid her arms over his shoulders, and let him have his way with her. This time, without any complaints or threats.

DAYS LATER, AARO PACED medical, guilt chewing up his insides. "The effects of the *Ethera* has subsided?" He cast a glance at Flad. Could the medic be wrong when the craving for Leona had not diminished? Would it ever? He didn't dare ask Flad, for how would the male know this?

"Yes, consummating your union was the key." The medic beamed as he skimmed through the med-E.D.'s results.

Aaro grimaced. She was still in the dark, and now he didn't know how to tell her. Worse, he loved her, which meant losing her would be a double-edged sword. Not only would the void revive, but he'd have his hearts broken, as Benedict had suffered.

Aaro could still recall the passage.

Benedict tightened his grip on the balustrade, his gaze fixed on the blue of Elizabeth's bonnet as she weaved through the crowded dock. He shouldn't have let her leave. But what choice did he have? To her, he was a rake, a scoundrel of a captain, a rogue. If she only knew... He grimaced. Would knowing have changed anything? Would she have looked at him differently? Seen his lineage and not the man before her?

He didn't know.

And now he never would.

A crack split his heart in two, forming a schism so wide there was no way to heal it. The agony was worse than being stabbed with a claymore. He rubbed his side where the scar still itched on cold nights.

Because of his cowardice, he'd loved and lost her. She deserved someone better.

Aaro released a shuddering breath. "Can you heal broken hearts, Flad?"

"What? There is no such condition." Flad flicked his hand then stilled. "What are your symptoms?"

"I am fine...for now."

"You anticipate such an illness?" Flad rose and tapped the med-E. D.'s display vid. He trawled through data, a scowl forming. "Nothing in our archives mentions such a thing. I could reach out to the medical board, perhaps one of our *lima kuu* would know."

"Do not bother the great teachers just yet, Flad." Aaro squared his shoulders. "My hearts breaking is not guaranteed."

Flad studied him, his gaze intense. "You have not told her, have you?"

Aaro clenched his jaw at his battle-bond's intuition. "No," he gritted out. "The *Ethera*—"

"Cannot be blamed for your lack of honor, Aaro."

"I know," Aaro whispered and slumped against the bulkhead. "I cannot bring myself to tell her. Let me have this time with her before I allow the void re-entry."

Flad's eyes widened. "You believe she will reject you?"

"Yes, for my lack of courage alone." Aaro straightened and grasped Flad's shoulder. "And she has the right to leave me."

Before Flad voiced his concern, Aaro left. He strode to his quarters, wishing he could think of a way to reveal his deception. More than a week had passed since Sarvis while the *Valiant* traveled to Yithia. He needed his mind clear and his focus on their upcoming session with King Urio. Any dealings with the Yithians were rife with danger, hence the battleships circling their planet and three suns.

He'd have to prep Leona as well. If she hadn't done her research, that is. Smiling at any Yithian was considered sexually aggressive. And if she triggered an intergalactic incident, King Xeus would expect Aaro to intervene. Something tight squeezed Aaro's chest. Every muscle tensed at the thought of Leona in danger. On the *Valiant*, she was safe. Here, she was all his, despite their tasks and responsibilities. For now, he could pretend she had chosen him, knew about the *Ethera*, accepted that she would never leave him...

He was such a fool.

A message buzzed up his arm. His breath caught at her name glowing in holographics. She wanted to snuggle this evening? He could agree to that. *Alodon's balls.* Anything she wanted she would receive, without hesitation. A fact she had yet to realize.

He glanced at his wall, lingering on her black garment, then faced the display vid. "Danic et Ynic."

It didn't take long for the screen to flicker, revealing Danic's face. "Aaro, what is it, my battle-bond?" Danic had yet to focus on Aaro, but when he did, he froze. "Is that...? You found your *Dar Eth*?"

Aaro winced then met Danic's matching ice-blue gaze. "In a way."

"Oh?" Danic smirked. "What have you done?"

"She does not know." Aaro rubbed a hand over his face.

Danic's humor faded. "Are you on medication? For the *Ethera* cannot be quelled."

"I know, and no, we have consummated the pairing."

Anger flicked over Danic's face, hardening his jaw. "You chose not to tell her."

"How?" Aaro roared. "How did you tell yours?"

"Izzy made it easy for me, revealing how she had known Supreme Commander Oyaz was hers. Although, Simone's blindness meant she could not see that she had triggered the *Ethera* in me. I told her the moment I hugged her naked form." Danic chuckled. "A story for another time."

"One I wish to hear." Aaro sagged. Danic could not offer him guidance. As usual, the male was more honorable than Aaro. But he could not give up hope that Danic might still assist. "Leona escaped a life where she had no say. She is strong and independent, and telling her the *Ethera* has locked her to me..." Aaro gritted his teeth, his mind conjuring images of her walking away.

"I understand but cannot condone your silence, Aaro. Tell her and live or die," Danic grimaced, "with the consequences."

"I know," Aaro whispered. "I expect death, which is why I will not tell her during the time we spend together. After her mission is complete, she is free to leave me." Pain scorched his hearts at what lay ahead for him. "Uncontested," he mumbled.

"You are a fool," Danic spat.

"I know," Aaro snapped.

"Have you spoken to Kanzo?"

"Of course not. As the king's adviser, the less he knows about my dishonor, the better."

Danic growled and shoved his face closer. "Fix this, Aaro. Be the male I know you are."

"I...cannot. I love her, Danic. I am not ready to lose her."

Danic settled back with a huff. "Let me know how it goes."

"I will," Aaro said. "End comm." He pressed his temple to the black display vid and sighed.

Chapter Sixteen

Leona stared at the blank canvas, not knowing what to paint. A glance at Soph showed her on her fourth galaxy, each stroke perfect. Leona had attempted a landscape, a bowl of fruit, a multi-tool, a self-portrait, and each time, she'd end up painting white over her disasterpiece. Gritting her teeth, she dabbed her brush in yellow and tapped the canvas off-center. Before her eyes, as if her hand had muscle memory, she drew a daisy like her father had shown her when she was a girl. A tear slipped free as the petals formed. Minutes flowed into hours while she feathered the disk flowers and added luminescent gray to the ray petals. She layered shades of blue across the background, then neatened around the flower, taking care along the green stem.

"That's stunning," Soph whispered from beside her.

"My dad taught me," she managed around the lump in her throat. "It's been decades since I last drew." She stepped back to admire her artwork. The strokes were sloppy in some areas, but overall, she was happy with it. "I'll put it on the wall in the 'kitchen.'"

"Nice," Soph called, leaping to the side to grab a fresh canvas. "Do one for me too, please."

"If you do a galaxy for me. I want it for my bedroom."

Soph beamed then cried out when Ranh filled the doorway. "Come. See."

He chuckled and entered, then took the time to admire their artwork. Humming and ahhing splashed pink across Soph's cheeks. "I am jealous, Lady Soph. This is something Etteria has lost over the centuries since we became war-driven."

"Want to try?" she asked, reaching for a canvas.

"I... I would not know where to start," he said.

"Try splashing paint on, then see how it feels. There's something addictive about the glide of the brush across canvas."

Ranh glanced at Leona. "Would I be in your way?"

"Of course not." Leona smiled. "I would suggest an apron though. Paint gets everywhere." She gestured to his uniform.

"I'll order one," Soph sang, darting for the replicator.

"Here, use my easel." Leona unhooked her painting and stepped aside. "I'll take this to my room and check on the dolls."

He stilled. "I do not want to chase—"

"Nonsense, Ranh. I was done already." She patted him on the shoulder and left. It was nearing the end of the shift anyway. What she felt like was a night cuddled up with Aaro, eating popcorn and watching a mindless movie. She giggled at the idea of watching a science fiction thriller. How would he react?

She balanced her painting against the wall behind the rehydrator then activated her O.D.I.

His response was swift. *Of course, ensa. Anything as long as I am with you.*

"Excellent," she squealed, ecstatic as if this was their first date.

A quick scan of the dolls in use showed them well cared for, so she returned to her cabin. She hopped into the shower, this time gargling instead of brushing her teeth over the basin. No mint flavor lingered, nor did the water taste strange. Still, she ran her tongue along her now squeaky-clean teeth. Out of the shower she darted, and while the air dryer did its thing, she spun on the spot, doing a few wiggles and jiggles to a random tune she hummed.

In a toweling robe, she flicked through the replicator choices. She wanted something pajama-like but easily removable. A nightgown or negligee was too blatant and going commando under the ordered baggy shirt even more so. She chose skimpy shorts and shimmied into them. Then with a tug to yank the shirt to the side to expose her shoulder, she laughed as she skipped to the display vid. Arranging the chairs took a moment. She tapped her chin and studied them. Soph was right. A couch would be better. Not that Leona would ask for one when her stay here was short.

She shoved that thought aside, willing sadness to remain at bay. Less than seven weeks was all she had with Aaro. She blinked, squared her shoulders, then skimmed through the rehydrator's menu, searching for popcorn, soda, and candy. Oh, a cherry slushy? He would love that with the amount of cherry soda he drank.

When the door chimed, she commanded it to open.

In waltzed Soph. "I know, I know, you're getting ready, bad timing and all that. I just came to tell you…" She glanced out the door before whispering, "Ranh's a damn natural. I could sell his paintings and make a fortune." Her gaze settled on the tubs of popcorn. "Oh, good idea. I wonder if Alien van Gogh would be interested in a movie." She waved as she left.

Leona glanced at her silly daisy painting. It was in no way up there with the masters, but it invoked memories of her dad, and time spent with him while her mom lounged on the pool deck, throwing out gems of wisdom. Dad had laughed. That was before he'd found out about her overspending, her lovers, or her painkiller addiction. One deceit he could have dealt with, but three?

Leona hadn't wanted to suffer through such a betrayal, which was probably why she hadn't dated anyone with marriage in mind. Aaro was different. He'd never lie to her, and she doubted he'd cheat on her either. Besides, in two months, he'd be a cherished memory. She couldn't see him giving up his career to stay with her on Callisto. And she did want him to find his *Dar Eth*. Ice coated her heart. Didn't she?

The chiming door meant it was time. When it opened, he strode in and scooped her into his arms for a crushing hug. He did nothing but hold her, his face buried in her unbound hair. She settled against him and waited, just like the first time he'd hugged her. Peace descended, and she succumbed, letting any negative thoughts fade.

"Thank you," she whispered. "I felt like a movie and company."

"A pleasure, *thamani*." He pinched her chin and raised her gaze to his. Then with infinite slowness, he lowered his lips to hers.

The kiss was sweet, not going past the heat threshold where she'd want to strip him for a good licking. Instead, he drew back, but only far enough for their breaths to merge.

"I have missed you," he said.

He is the sweetest man. She dipped her chin to kiss his fingers. "Come, sit. I hope you're hungry."

"It does smell good," he said.

As soon as he sat, she handed him his slushy. One sip widened his eyes, and he drank deeply among groans of delight.

"I chose a movie about aliens in space," she said. "I'm curious what you'll think about our overactive imaginations."

He arched a brow as a smile teased his cherry-pink lips.

She started the movie and handed him the popcorn as she settled beside him.

"They look like Gika," he whispered when the first alien appeared on screen. He glanced at her. "Their saliva is acidic."

"Like hydrochloric acid?" she gasped.

His eyelashes fluttered. "Yes. More popcorn?" he offered and crossed to the rehydrator.

"No thanks." She laughed.

He returned with a massive container. "I enjoy snuggling." He grinned.

"I see that," she said when the tub occupied his lap and the screen got his attention. Not that she minded. This was what she'd needed. No sex, no dinner and conversation, just relaxing.

By the time the lead female escaped with the cat, Aaro had finished his popcorn and fourth slushy. He held her hand resting in her lap while she cuddled against his shoulder.

"I like that she survived. She was smart." He pressed a kiss to Leona's temple. "Your men are not all this stupid?"

"No." She flicked a dismissive hand. "It's a story and not real. Like our porn movies."

He frowned. "Our instructional vids?"

"Yes, Aaro. What the women can do in those...*vids* isn't a true reflection of actual sex."

A slow delicious smirk curled his sexy-as-hell mouth. "All I have done to you is as shown."

"What?" she whispered.

"You are my first and only human, Leona."

"What are you saying, Aaro? You have had lovers before, right? Even if they're other species?"

"Yes, but Etterian females, though similar in biology, are not as easily pleased."

She blinked at him. "So you have to work harder to bring them to orgasm?"

"No, they have one position for the male's denit to rub along theirs."

Well, that sucked. "Ah."

He dragged her onto his lap. "Everything about you, Leona, is soft and sweet."

"Charmer," she teased, stretching up for a kiss.

He feathered his mouth across hers then ran his fingers through her hair. "A time has been reserved for your interview with King Urio tomorrow." A frown pursed his lips. "I cannot bring more males even though Yithia poses a greater threat. Only I will guard you, *ensa*."

"Just you is perfect, Aaro."

He stilled, and his eyes swirled a brighter blue. "No one shall harm you, my Leona."

Heat exploded inside her. He thought of her as his, just as she thought of him as hers. How could she feel this much so fast? She'd asked that question many times, but still, an answer eluded her.

"Should I wear your ceremonial gown?" she managed despite her thumping heart.

"Yes, and your hair in a braid."

"Gotcha." He wanted her to look as Etterian as possible.

His nostrils flared as he entangled then detangled his fingers from her hair. "Your hair is lifeless."

She jerked back. "It is keratin," she said then frowned. "Isn't your hair...lifeless?"

He grabbed his braid, sliding his fingers to the tail. There, he removed the clip and said, "*Malia pado.*"

Before her eyes, his braid unraveled then strands of hair swirled outward as if he was underwater. She gaped, not daring to blink. In a daze, she tried to capture a lock, only for it to coil around her finger. More joined in until a black snake wrapped around her arm. With a tug, it sprawled her across Aaro's chest.

"It likes you, *ensa,*" he said, his voice hoarse.

She nodded, her eyes no doubt as wide as saucers.

"*Malia pa,*" he said, his gaze fixed on her.

Like magic, his hair braided itself. No wonder hair care didn't take up hours of their day.

"Neat," she smiled, a little stunned.

"Do not smile this day. Yithians consider it an offer to mate."

"What?" she squeaked. "You can't be serious?"

Aaro met her gaze, no humor in his expression.

"Okay, acknowledged. No smiling."

"Tell me, *ensa,* what is that?" He pointed at her daisy painting.

"Art," she said. "I did it today."

"You did?" His mouth curled in awe. "It is beautiful. I do not know of such a flower." He stilled. "Is it real?"

She chuckled. "It's a daisy, Aaro."

His eyelashes fluttered again. "I see."

"It's Soph's idea to brighten the space. Could we order paint for the walls?"

"Paint?" He laughed, then stood, taking Leona with him. He lowered her feet to the floor, and with a hand at her elbow, ushered her to the nearest paneled wall. "Opacity: mirror."

She squealed when a mirror formed, showing her mussed reflection.

"Opacity: green," he said with a grin, his gaze fixed on her.

She didn't blink when the mirror switched to forest green. "Wow," she cried out. "Wait until I tell Soph."

"So, no to the paint." He looped his arms around her waist, forcing her to face him. "Now can we snuggle?"

She rose onto her toes to place a kiss on his chin. "Please."

He slid his hands under her shirt, captured her ass, and hoisted her against his chest. "Would it violate snuggling rules if I make you chant my name?"

Her heart thudded. "No," she rasped.

"Good to know, *ensa*."

Chapter Seventeen

Aaro woke up early and lay in Leona's bed, content to hold her. They would not train this morning for he needed to prepare his males. Porting wasn't allowed close to the royal court at the center of Mascroba. Which meant only by *kuta* could they reach the king. This opened many avenues for attack.

She mumbled something in her sleep. So he drew her closer, splaying his fingers across her back. He tapped his O.D.I. and organized a meeting with his males for later. Then he chose *Stolen Love* and continued where he'd left off.

> *Benedict snuck past waiting guests, uncaring that he was cravat-less and in muddied Hessians. At least his linen shirt was crisp and clean. Whispers trailed his passing. He should have taken the time to tie back his hair. But in his haste to find Elizabeth, his appearance hadn't been a consideration.*

He caught the familiar curve of a most beloved cheek. Attempting to reach her, he may have been a bit brutal in shoving guests aside. At last, she stood before him, looking more breathtaking than she had a right to. He'd hoped for a paler complexion and sadness in her eyes; some sort of indication that she'd missed him.

"What are you doing here?" she whispered and crowded him to usher him out.

"I came for you. Leave here, London, all this, with me."

"Why, Benedict?" She closed her eyes when her name carried across the conversations around them. "You are ruining my reputation," she hissed.

When he didn't budge, she spun on a heel, breezing her sweet fragrance over him.

"I love you," he squeezed past his constricted throat.

She stumbled but didn't peek at him. Her shoulders trembled, then she dipped her head as if she struggled with indecision.

"Bloody hell, woman, I love you. Did you not hear me?" he roared, silencing those gathered nearby. He didn't spare a glance at the guests, not when Elizabeth was all that mattered.

"And that means what? You are a smooth-tongued dev-il, no doubt claiming you love every woman you have ever known." She met his gaze. Pain, anger, and desire burned in her eyes.

"No," he whispered as he drew nearer. He captured her elbow to stop her from leaving him. "Only you."

"Lord Applethwaite, is that you?"

Benedict stiffened, but he didn't dare break away from Elizabeth. She arched a brow as if to say, answer the man. No realization flicked across her expression.

"Bennie, it is you!" A hand thumped Benedict across the shoulder.

He pasted on a smile and faced the intruder. "Jeremy, you haven't seen me. I'm just collecting what's mine."

When he gazed at Elizabeth, her brow had begun to wrinkle. Bloody hell.

"It is good to see you, ol' boy. We searched for you after that blasted accident, but alas, you were deuced hard to find."

"What accident?" Benedict asked but didn't glance at Jeremy.

"The death of your father, of course."

Benedict whipped his gaze up, ice chilling him from his ears to his toes. "What?"

"Left everything to you, ol' boy. Been running the estates in your stead." Jeremy puffed out his chest, straining his ill-fitted embroidered waistcoat.

Elizabeth's eyes widened.

Benedict's gaze was on her. He should have seen the slap coming. And even if he had, he wouldn't have ducked. She deserved vindication, for he had deceived her, in a way. It wasn't as if he'd known he was more titled than before he'd left England's shores.

"Bennie—"

"Not now, Jeremy. I'll stop by the manor tomor-row." He grabbed her by the elbow and dragged her through the crowds to the terrace.

She struggled, but he held firm. Once through the French doors, he snapped them shut.

"Lord?" She pursed her lips then folded her arms across her chest, thrusting her exquisite breasts up.

His gaze snagged for a moment before he clasped her by the shoulders. "I don't give a damn about my title, Elizabeth. I would leave London with you in an instant."

"You did not reveal a word of it to me, Benedict, of your history. Am I not trustworthy?"

Aaro deactivated his O.D.I. and gazed at Leona. Benedict's deceit was too close to his own.

"You are my *Dar Eth*," he whispered, his voice forlorn in the silence of the room. He should wake her and tell her. How hard could it be? "I love you, Leona," he said.

She mumbled again and rolled away from him. If this didn't stop both his hearts, he didn't know what would. That she might have heard him almost killed him while flooding him with a hopeful relief.

He released a shuddering breath and followed her, feathering kisses down her neck. She arched on a muted hum, spreading her thighs so his hips could sink between them.

"Morning," she moaned.

He cradled her face and savored the moment. "Morning, *thamani*."

She smiled, her gaze still sleepy. "What time is it?"

"Early. I need to prepare for today. I will collect you when it is time." He stole another sweet kiss before sliding off the bed.

As he dressed, he admired her with her hand tucked under her pillow. He'd stop at his quarters, cleanse, and change into clean armor. Her scent on his skin was his alone to cherish. It didn't take him long before he was striding through the comm room to the war room set to the side. His males waited: Ranh, Krist, and Flad included.

"Be prepared for anything," Aaro said, gripping the war table. "With the revolution in secret and the abduction of human women, we need to expect trouble."

"What do they want with sex-cybs?" Krist asked. "Surely not for mating?"

"I do not know," Aaro said. "These are machines, despite their feminine appeal. What the king does with them is none of our concern." He met each male's gaze. "My focus is keeping Leona safe."

"I am pleased that Lady Soph is remaining on board," Ranh said.

"Agreed," Flad said. "I would prefer that you each carry a spare med-gun."

All nodded at his request.

"As you requested, I have ensured the rehydrators and replicators of the *kuta* are fully stocked. In addition, extra sol reserves have been added as well as a location beacon," Ranh said. "The last time Etterians were planetside, Supreme Commander Ulriq and Xan had to mount a rescue."

Sogair. Aaro suppressed a shiver. Ulriq's *Dar Eth* Jack had to battle one, her human weapon tiny in her hands. Of all the creatures in the universe, a sogair was Aaro's least favorite. It was their combined speed, strength, and stealth, but more than this was their growls that reverberated through flesh and bone.

Helpless, Ulriq had watched when Jack had fallen beneath the creature.

Xan and Lady Quin had faced wilanegy—those blue, spiked beasts hunted by smell, going berserk at the scent of blood. Not to mention the underground gracc that had nearly swallowed Xan, with the hope of digesting him over ten days. Thankfully Lysara wasn't on Leona's route, and if it had been, Aaro would ensure no blue-spiked animal or massive worm came near her.

"As you know, only I will escort Leona to King Urio. Stay with the *kuta*, and be vigilant." Aaro rolled his shoulders. "This delivery should not take long." He hoped.

"We reach planetary orbit in less than an hour. The time on Yithia is nearing the magnus sunset," Krist called from the comm console with a clear line of sight to the males around the war table.

Aaro grimaced. Their 'night' wasn't ideal, but royals weren't always logical.

"I will assist Lady Soph in loading the sex-cybs," Ranh said on his way out of the comm room.

"Leona and I will meet you there." Aaro veered around Saan, who squeezed Krist's forearm then assumed the pilot's seat.

Aaro strode along the passages to Leona's quarters. This time tomorrow, Yithia would be behind them and Maloid in their sights. Queen Alllero was a sweetheart. He smiled. He'd met her once and he doubted she'd remember, but still, a trip to the royal city of Argaxx would be a pleasure.

"Leona?" he called as he entered her quarters unannounced. He'd assumed she'd still be asleep.

"What do you think?" She stepped out of the cleansing room with her ceremonial gown gaping.

He stilled, not wanting to blink. "What is that?" he rasped. The top piece was half-a-corset, ending at her waist and sheer enough to show her skin beneath. From the black belt were straps attaching mid-thigh to where sheer leggings began.

She snapped the ceremonial gown closed and paused beside him to slip on her footwear. "Bustier with a garter belt." From her forefinger, she swirled a strip of cloth similar to the one he'd mounted in polycarbonate. "With or without panties?"

"Panties?" His O.D.I. hurried to update him, flooding his mind with images. "Female, I prefer for you to be in armor, head to toe." He caught her wrist and tugged her into his arms. "And I would love nothing more than to bury myself in you, to have your fulfillment trigger mine." He snatched a quick kiss. "But we do not have time for that." He gritted his teeth. "With panties."

She shimmied into the delicate strip, straightened the gown, then flicked out her hair. "Ready."

After she left her quarters, he rested his temple on the cool bulkhead while he adjusted his temperature, praying his armor would cool his ardor. "Later," he whispered.

When they entered the bay, Soph offered a tablet then stepped back to let Leona and Aaro pass. "Good luck," she called.

"Thanks." Leona smiled and strolled up the ramp. She paused beside the two sex-cybs strapped to the rear wall, along with the usual crate. After shoving the tablet into her pocket, she sank into a seat and let him strap her in.

As he bent over her, she ran her tongue along his earlobe.

He stiffened, his nostrils flaring. "Leona," he groaned.

"I'm...nervous. Please distract me, Aaro," she said, trailing a trembling finger over his armored chest.

What did she expect from him? He glanced at his males boarding the *kuta*. "Etterians have excellent hearing, and your cries of fulfillment are for me alone."

She pouted, looking far more adorable than she should. "As long as you make me scream later, I suppose I could behave."

"*Ensa*, I need to keep you safe. Already, with what is beneath your gown, focusing will be difficult."

"You're right." She slumped. "I'm sorry, Aaro, I don't know what I was thinking." With her hands clasped on her lap, she curled into herself. "I've just heard terrible things about Yithia."

He cupped her cheeks to meet her gaze. "No one would dare attack Etterians, not if they value their life. I plan for danger but do not expect it, *thamani.*"

"I should change. Can we make time?" She gestured to the replicator mounted to a bulkhead.

He hesitated, torn between wanting her to remain in her daring garments and having the temptation removed. As an Etterian warrior, he could bear it a little longer. "No, stay as you are. This delivery should be swift." He dipped his gaze to where her breasts strained the gown. "Soon," he promised, meeting her gaze.

Sinking into the seat beside her, he fixed his gaze on the door sliding shut. His males assumed military stances, spreading their legs for balance while clasping their hands behind their backs. Flad remained on the battleship but on standby should he be needed.

"King Urio's liaison has confirmed the appointment. He will meet us at the landing pad to the south of the court." Ranh deactivated his O.D.I. and gazed at the display vids as Krist swung the *kuta* through the bay doors. A glimpse showed them closing before the view filled with Yithia.

Leona gasped. "It's pretty. I expected something to reflect the species."

"Not all Yithians are bad. They are greedy, though, and that drives their behavior." Aaro captured her hand and pinned it to his thigh.

"True for humans too, I guess," she said with a shrug.

The green globe speckled with white clouds could be considered beautiful. Their black continents were few, bold against green seas so deep Etteria couldn't penetrate them. "Their cities are miles underwater. With three suns, the temperature can be scorching on the surface."

"Wow, I'd love to see one of these cities."

"We have images," he offered.

"No, in person, silly." She nibbled her lip. "But from afar. Let's not invite danger."

"Why—" He paused. "Ah, I understand. Izzy calls it tourism."

She chuckled. "Yes, something like that."

"Alas, we cannot. Males have died trying to reach those depths, which is why your Earth is helping us build submarines."

"Oh?" Her eyebrows leaped. "Makes sense."

When the *kuta* penetrated the atmosphere, the inside warmed a few degrees. Then the flames cleared onto the pale-yellow skies where the planet switched from day three suns to night one sun. Down they traveled. Mascroba, the royal city of Yithia, came into view, sprawled across a patch of land defying the number of occupants living there. As far as Aaro knew, their buildings went underground to best avoid the midday suns.

"Scout the area for possible hiding places," he said to Ranh. "If trouble hits, I need to know we have planned accordingly."

"Acknowledged, Sub-Commander Aaro," Ranh said, flicking through the holographic maps on his O.D.I.

"It all feels so espionage-ish," Leona said.

"Whatever it takes to keep you safe," Aaro said, running his thumb along her jawline.

Black stone buildings grew taller the closer they traveled. They housed the ambassadors and visiting dignitaries. Underground was Urio's domain. Krist touched the *kuta* down with the barest of bumps. The door opened and out marched Ranh and Krist, taking the time to check the waiting Yithian. They fell into formation on the edge of the platform, their backs to the *kuta*.

Hot air flooded the compartment, whipping curls off Leona's temple. "Wow," she whispered and fanned herself as he unbuckled her.

"Welcome to Mascroba, the Royal City of Yithia," he said, offering her a hand to lift her to her feet. "Remember, you are Etterian."

She splayed her fingers across his chest and rose on her toes to kiss his chin. Then with a deep sigh, she gathered the cybs and glided down the ramp toward the waiting Yithian. His black sleeveless tunic over matching leggings clung to his silver-gray body. Black bands circled his bare arms. His solid black gaze fixed on Leona, and he bowed his head in welcome.

"Lady Leona, a pleasure," he hissed in greeting.

"The pleasure is all mine." She snuck a wide-eyed glance at Aaro. "I speak Yithian?" she mouthed.

He grinned then picked up the crate.

"Great Illustrious King Urio is most excited to meet you," the liaison said. "I am Emissary Deroj. Please, follow me."

Along narrow stone bridges they walked, a glance off the side revealing a crevice with fading lights showing how deep it went. They stepped on a floating platform which descended the moment Aaro's heel cleared the edge. He said nothing, just assumed a position behind Leona as if he was nothing more than her escort.

"Is this your first time to Mascroba, Lady Leona?" Deroj asked.

"It is. We were at Sarvis a week ago. A pity I didn't get to visit planetside."

The emissary studied the sex-cybs changing positions with perfect synchronicity. "They are unusual," he said. "Though they appear soft."

"They are meant to be," Leona said. "Mating something hard wouldn't be comfortable, I'm sure."

"Mating?" Deroj snorted. "These are not gladiators?"

"No." Leona almost smiled but stopped herself in time. Aaro released a breath. "Mating is preferable to fighting, is it not?"

"Indeed, though not the typical Etterian mentality," Deroj said as he stepped off the platform and onto another bridge. He hurried toward massive doors that opened as they approached. "Please." He slid to the side, and with a sweep of his hand, gestured to the throne room where crowds gathered.

Leona strolled ahead, her head held high. Silence settled over the massive room. The walls were solid black stone, engraved with green veins of Ferusi gems. The air was chilled, not that it bothered Aaro, though he should have anticipated it. Yithians didn't like the heat.

He flicked his gaze from side to side, trying to assess levels of danger with so many in attendance. Ahead, King Urio loomed. He pushed off his throne and thundered toward Leona. Not once did her stride falter when an impressively large Yithian barreled down on her.

"Your majesty." She dipped into a low bow. "I come bearing two sex-cybs as gifts."

Deroj scurried passed and whispered something in Urio's ear. Aaro strained to hear but couldn't catch a word, not when conversations resumed around him.

"Mating?" Urio straightened and circled Leona, his gaze on her. "I have met a half-breed Etterian female, Lady Leona." He ran his gaze over her, his teeth dimpling his bottom lip. "You are as unusual as she was."

Leona didn't respond, though what could she have said when she knew nothing about Ava.

"Come, bring your...mating machines." Urio caught a length of Leona's hair in his meaty three-fingered grip.

Aaro stiffened. Fire burned along his nerves and vision, that a male would dare to touch what was his.

The king stomped from the room through a door to the rear. Deroj danced on his feet, trying to get Leona and her cybs to follow. When she did, he relaxed then scowled at Aaro for daring to join her.

"I go nowhere without my guard," she said, coming to a standstill. "Do you wish to tell the king why I will not obey him?" Her tone was imperious, her words clipped.

The emissary bobbed. "This way, please."

As a unit, they proceeded to where Urio waited in a bedroom of sorts. A massive mattress sat in the middle of a two-stepped dais. A variety of fabrics and colors served as linen, with no blanket in sight. The room was a little chilly, made more so by carved stone murals as the walls. It was dark-toned, cold, unwelcome, and through an opening in the ceiling flickered gray geometric shapes across the floor.

"Bring a machine," he demanded, flicking open his robe to reveal a naked Yithian, a sight Aaro wished he could scrub from his memory. Their bodies were like Etterians, as in big chests, wide shoulders, into two legs and arms. But there the familiarities ended. Silver-gray skin that was heat sensitive and slimy to the touch. Wide-set eyes and black above two nostrils, and a thick neck joining at the edges of their shoulders. But what made them impressive were their long teeth dripping venom.

Leona tapped her O.D.I., paused in front of a cyb, then said in Galactic, "Showtime." Grabbing the hand, she led the cyb to the strange wobbling bed.

"Where is its sex?" Urio ran his hands along the cyb's sides.

Leona touched the cyb between the thighs. "Here, your majesty." She handled this odd incident better than Aaro could have. Though, with how she and Soph discussed mating, he doubted anything could phase her. "Would you mind if I watched?"

Aaro stilled, struggling to keep his jaw from dropping.

"You are the first Yithian to mate a sex-cyb. I would like to know how to improve her performance for your maximum pleasure."

Urio's gaze warmed. "You have courage, little one. Show me where and how."

What followed would forever haunt Aaro. He wished he'd looked away, studied his boots, or stayed in the throne room. Leona took the king through the mating positions and what holes were available for 'thrusting' as she'd termed it.

When Urio bent over the cyb, his ass as bare as the rest of him, Aaro struggled to keep from flinching. A glance at the emissary showed the male staring ahead, unbothered by this scene. Wise. For sanity's sake, Aaro fixed his gaze on Leona, loving her focus and eagerness to improve her craft. She was breathtaking as she adjusted the cyb's performance.

"Calzantu, spare me," Urio roared as he rammed his malehood into the poor cyb and stilled.

No. Aaro refused to look. He shuddered, swallowing bile.

"I see," Urio panted, slipping into the robe the emissary offered. The king's skin glistened under the lighting. Venom dripped from his fangs onto his chest. "That...was incredible." He paused beside the other cyb, stroking her cheek. "How many do we have?"

"Two, my king," Deroj muttered. "I assumed they were intended for the arena."

"No, they are ill-suited for such endeavors. Leave them in my chambers."

"May I hand them over to their carer, your majesty?" Leona asked.

Urio stared at her, then at the cybs. "Deroj, see to it."

"But, my illustrious king, we have no one in mind."

"What sort of care is needed, Lady Leona?" Urio held up a jar of green liquid, offering it to Leona.

She didn't notice with her gaze on Deroj. "Someone technical. I have a crate with spare parts, just in case. They don't require much maintenance since they can create their own lubrication—"

"Spare me the details. Deroj, if you do not choose someone, these machines will be your responsibility."

The poor male bobbed, his gaze on the cybs. "Ah, yes, my king."

Urio strode from the room, a goblet in hand. Deroj scurried after him, leaving Leona and Aaro to follow.

"That was weird," she whispered. "Enlightening, though."

"Horrifying," he grumbled.

She laughed and snuck a kiss, pulling away from him before he could wrap his arms around her. "I'll position them by the wall. Leave the crate at their feet."

She hurried away to do just that, commanding the cybs to sleep with a 'goodnight.'

"Can we go now?" she asked, glancing over her shoulder when she left for the throne room.

The crowd was abuzz while a Maloidian spoke to King Urio. "A gift from a lower grade species? Can it be trusted?"

"I do not see why not." Urio scowled, his slicked forehead furrowing. "Why do you distrust this, Barro?"

"I have never heard of such machines, my king. Why now?" He dipped his speckled head, his tentacled hair tranquil. "Too much is happening for this to be a coincidence."

"Then we shall place them in a well-guarded room." Urio waved at Deroj.

Barro pursed his lips but nodded. "Are you Earthian, Lady Leona?" he asked, his voice carrying across the room.

Leona stiffened. "I am Etterian."

His black eyes narrowed. "I have been fooled before." His gaze flickered to Aaro. "Are you her *Eth*?"

Aaro paused. He'd meant to claim her if needed, but Barro would know about the eye-color change. Leona's eyes hadn't altered to ice-blue; therefore she couldn't be his *Dar Eth* if she was Etterian.

"No, Ambassador Barro."

"Why would Etteria endanger a female?" Barro folded his arms and circled Leona. "Her skin is not dark enough."

"I'm a half-breed." Leona met the male's gaze. "I haven't met my *Eth* yet." She glanced down as if the topic was hurtful.

Barro grimaced. "My apologies, Lady Leona. I meant no offense."

"None taken, Ambassador Barro. Your majesty, I thank you for agreeing to see me. If I may conclude the handing over..."

"Yes, of course. Deroj, see to it, then escort them out." Urio caught Leona's hand and gazed at her upturned face. "You are most welcome to return, Lady Leona."

"Thank you, your majesty." She bowed, handed the tablet to Deroj, and left.

Aaro trailed her, his shoulders refusing to relax. Something could still happen. Without a word, she stepped onto the hovering platform. He assumed a position behind her. Together they waited for Deroj to join them. When he did, his walk was brisk, his posture tense.

"Again, I apologize, Lady Leona. I see the missive stipulated a technician should be on standby. I shall choose someone worthy."

"Thank you, Deroj. It is hard to release my charges to the care of another. I do worry," she said and again almost smiled.

Up they climbed, the hot wind tossing her curls wild. Aaro clasped his hands behind his back and stared ahead.

"Should you have any concerns, please, contact me. My details are on the tablet." She glided off the platform when it reached their landing pad then strode across to the waiting *kuta* as if she had all the time in the world. When she climbed up the ramp, Aaro's males retracted, walking backward.

Krist powered up the *kuta* as Ranh shut the door on Deroj standing alone on the edge.

"It went well?" Ranh asked.

Aaro winced then kneeled to buckle Leona in her seat.

"I think so," she said. "Learned a few new things, and that's always good." She grinned. "Did you know I can speak Yithian?" She waved her wrist at Ranh. "Sure, Aaro said I could but to hear it coming out of my mouth... Unbelievable." She arched a brow at Aaro. "Why didn't you claim that I'm yours when you said you would?"

Aaro grimaced. "Your dark blue eyes announce to all that you are unclaimed."

"Oh?" Her eyes widened.

His Leona wasn't stupid. She'd figure it out without him having to tell her. His hearts paused. Good or bad, he'd have to face her reaction. "I thought it wiser to not have them doubt your gift."

"That makes sense..." She frowned, narrowing her focus on his eyes. "Does that mean you're claimed?"

He blinked at her, words lodging in his throat. "A discussion for another time, *ensa*." Before she asked him anything else, he sat next to her but didn't strap in, not when his males didn't either. He'd only done so before because she'd been concerned. He released a slow breath. *Maker*. He was glad they were done with Yithia.

Perhaps he should not have thought that, for a thump slammed him against the bulkhead. The *kuta* sputtered, dipped, and plummeted.

Chapter Eighteen

Leona studied the men in the shuttle, finding that none of them had the same eye color as Aaro. Claimed he'd called it. She bit her lip, trying to remember if she'd seen anyone on the battleship who matched. No memories came to the fore. Shit. She peeked at Aaro, at the tightness of his jaw. A pulse ticked at the base. Okay, so discussing it now was O.U.T.

The shuttle's backside swung out.

She gasped and gripped Aaro's knee. Even through his thick armor, the muscular definition of his leg was a delight. She blinked that thought aside. Had something struck them? Like hail?

She opened her mouth to ask.

The shuttle lurched and threw her to the side, banging her temple against Aaro's shoulder.

"Alodon's balls," he roared. "Krist, stabilize. Ranh, track whatever hit us, find its source, and notify the *Valiant*."

"Yes, Sub-Commander Aaro," Ranh called, his fingers flying over his O.D.I. His stance held him in place despite the shuttle spinning out of control.

"I knew it was too good to be true," Aaro growled and settled his gaze on her.

"Maybe the lingerie wasn't wise," she said, forcing humor in her voice when fear constricted her throat.

"Perhaps full armor as per my suggestion?" Aaro smirked and leaped to his feet a second before the shuttle dipped. He flew toward the front but caught himself on a seat.

Leona swallowed a squeal, her line of sight now the shadowy crevice far below. Krist fought the controls, typing across the console. The shuttle shuddered then plummeted.

This time, she screamed.

"This makes no sense," Ranh was saying, one hand holding onto a strap hanging from the shuttle's ceiling. "Nothing on the buzz indicated the king was displeased with the gift." His brow furrowed. "Anyone else have an issue—"

"The Maloidian Ambassador Barro?" Leona said through her clenched teeth while tightening her grip on her knees. The strap around her waist held firm, but she hung upside-down. Her cheeks burned from the blood rush. "He wasn't happy."

"We have good relations with Maloid," Aaro said.

"You said it yourself, not all Yithians are bad. Maybe not all Maloidians like Etteria?" Leona threw out her arm to right herself. She peeked at the display vids. Flying past them were walls, lights, and bridges in solid black.

Krist cried out and punched the console.

The shuttle halted its descent so fast her stomach hit the top of her throat. She swallowed past the lump, closed her eyes, and offered up a prayer. When she gathered the courage, she opened her eyes to a silver-green river flowing at the base of the crevice meters below them.

Sweat coated her temple. They'd been so close to dying.

An explosion propelled them forward, and the shuttle shot along the rushing water.

"Krist?" Aaro clambered to his feet and gripped the back of the pilot seat.

"It is not me, Sub-Commander." He held up his hands.

"We are being controlled," Ranh called, the colors of his holographic buttons flickering like a rainbow. "I cannot... It is..." With wide eyes, he raised his gaze to Aaro's. "Durn."

Aaro stilled. "Are you certain?"

Leona frowned. "But you said—?"

"An estimated few hundred live, *ensa*." Aaro gripped Ranh's wrist and read off his O.D.I. "Alodon's balls, who could convince a Durn to serve him?"

"Well, if we just wait, we'll soon find out," Leona said, folding her arms across her chest. "I don't even know why sex-cybs are garnering this much attention. It isn't as if they're like...new tech."

"It could be something unrelated," Aaro said.

Shit. She rubbed her face, hoping to calm the burn along her nerves. "What's this about a revolution in secret?" She had heard that, right?

"A small faction is hoping to overthrow Urio," Ranh said.

"They have allied with King Xeus, so no, they cannot be behind this," Aaro said without looking at her. He peered into the display vids. "There. A lit landing pad."

"They await our arrival," Krist said, pushing out of the seat to unholster his gun. The thing was solid black with four buttons on the side.

She glanced at Aaro, half-expecting him to do the same. Instead, he flipped open a panel and withdrew a greatsword. She tried not to gape. But damn, when he sheathed the weapon down his back, her stomach muscles tightened. That was sexy as hell.

Still, what could a sword do? She tried not to giggle as the hysteria lashed at her senses. He was bringing a damned big knife to a gun fight. Ranh and Krist also chose swords then crowded the shuttle's door as it landed.

Aaro unstrapped her from the seat, then shoved her behind him. He stood with his nose to the door. Ranh nudged her back. Then Krist edged her into a corner until the only thing in her line of sight was a wall of broad shoulders covered in black armor.

Then again, she didn't want to be fired upon. They were far more prepared for whatever the hell this was. She focused on calming her breathing. For the first time since arriving on this unwelcoming planet, she felt naked...exposed under her gown. *Dammit.* A glance at her dirty slippers highlighted the sorry state of her attire.

She flinched when the door opened to that oppressive heat.

"Sub-Commander Aaro, welcome," someone said. The hiss in his voice identified him as Yithian. "My apologies for the intervention. My Durn friend, Zucis, intercepted an instruction to destroy your shuttle in an 'accident,' hence the explosion. Deceiving your enemy and saving you was the best we could do at such short notice."

"You have me at a disadvantage," Aaro said, his voice husky.

She trembled for another reason and shifted from foot to foot. After all this time, she still found his sexual appeal devastating.

Ranh glanced at her, his intense gaze enflaming her cheeks. He couldn't sense her desire, could he? *Quit being silly, Leona.*

"I am Kbal, and I serve Commander Pyo," the Yithian continued.

"As suspected, Kbal. To what end are we here?" Aaro's voice hardened. "That you endangered a female does not paint you in a favorable light."

"*We* did not bring a female to Yithia, Sub-Commander."

She winced. The man wasn't wrong. Although, her presence here hadn't been up to Aaro. She had no doubt, that if he'd had a say, she'd have remained on the *Valiant*.

"They will monitor the skies, searching for evidence of your deaths. We invite you to spend the night with us as our guests."

"If your data officer will assist me?" another man with a cultured, smooth-as-silk voice asked.

She strained to see who had spoken but alas, even at her five-foot-seven, she wasn't tall enough to peer above Etterians.

"With?" Ranh stepped out of the shuttle, creating a gap.

A blue-skinned man stood before them, his figure athletic. A 'V'-necked sleeveless beige shirt over matching yoga pants did nothing to detract from his striking features: angular cheekbones and jawline, and white hair and eyes.

"We must mask the *kuta*'s markings," he said, confirming the smooth voice was his.

Aaro gestured to his men to file out. "Very well. We thank you for the invitation, Kbal." With a glance at Leona, he stretched out his hand to her.

She clasped his warm fingers and allowed him to draw her closer. Once he looped his arm around her, she leaned into the curve of his body.

"Lady Leona, may I introduce Kbal?" He swept an arm out to the Yithian dressed like the blue man.

"A pleasure to meet you," she said. What she wanted to scream was, 'why the hell did you scared the shit out of me?'

The blue alien studied her then gazed into Aaro's eyes. A smirk curled his pale blue lips. "Kbal, she is not Etterian."

"Are you certain?" Kbal focused on Leona, and the urge to squirm gripped her. He was shorter and not as broad in the shoulders as their megalodon king, but he was more imposing than Deroj. Authority poured off him, made noticeable by the deference his soldiers gave him.

"Etterian females measure their honor as the males do. If she was truly as claimed, her hair would be to her heels. Also, her skin tone is unusual." The Durn approached Leona with his hand thrust out. "Human?"

Aaro stiffened, then he shoved her behind him again. "Mine," he gritted out.

The blue man laughed, his teeth bright in his dark face. "I merely greet a human as is customary, Sub Commander Aaro. I do not wish harm to your—"

"If you must," Aaro snapped and clasped her arm. He urged her around him but kept her near. "Leona, he is a Durn."

"Zucis." The man held out his hand again.

She accepted it for a shake, but he didn't release her. Instead, he cupped her hand and forced her to step away from Aaro.

"A pleasure to meet you, Leona."

Aaro broke the contact, snatching her hand from Zucis's grip. "I suggest we get out of the open. Tell me more about this instruction. Who issued it?"

"A discussion best not embarked on now," Kbal said over his shoulder as he entered a rock-hewn passage.

Aaro followed, his hold on Leona making her jog behind him to keep up. The walls narrowing forced him to release her.

With the uncertainty of their situation, she tucked her fingers between his belt and armor, the contact with his warm skin calming. His back muscles spasmed beneath her touch, and the look he tossed over his shoulder shot bolts of tingling excitement to her extremities.

Damp heat coated her skin the deeper they traveled. A dripping added to the stomping of military boots. Water saturated her slippers. She wiggled to rub her forehead across her shoulder, grimacing at ruining the delicate fabric if it was silk. A single stone the size of her palm illuminated their path every few meters. She hesitated when she passed one resting on the floor of an alcove, tempted to inspect it for a power source. But Aaro didn't notice, and Krist behind her didn't let her linger.

She sucked in deep breaths, struggling to get the thick air into her lungs. An organic smell along with wet rock dominated her nose, and a spinach-like flavor coated the back of her throat. From darkness, they burst into light. A cavern opened out, its ceiling high above and filled with veins of that glowing rock. Smoothed sections also added light with more alcoves glowing even brighter.

On the flattened floor were tables and benches. A rehydrator and a replicator sat to one side. Another surface held bubbling cauldrons, blue flickering flames beneath them. Whispering Yithians lined up, bowls in hand. Some sat and ate, scooping orange and purple leaves with their fingers. The low hum of conversation added a humanity she'd strangely expected to find. They said that people viewed the universe through their experiences and perceptions. So too had she, painting all species with human traits like the need for companionship and the appreciation of a good meal.

"Areemi," Aaro whispered, his gaze on her. Something in his eyes snagged her focus, and she allowed herself to drown in those neon-blue depths.

What fascinated her, though, was the lights. "What are these illuminating stones?"

He scooped one from the nearest alcove and showed her. Its light bathed his face in warmth. "*Lumnari*, a Yithian export."

She rose onto her tiptoes to study it from all angles. "How are they powered?"

He chuckled, then with the gentlest of touches, gathered her hand in his and placed it on her palm. She gasped. It was cool, giving off no heat, but it glowed. She raised it to eye-level to peer into its opaque-yet-pulsing light.

"How long does it last?"

"Decades." He shrugged.

"Help yourself to something to eat," Kbal said. "Or would you prefer I show you to your rooms first?"

A cold shower would be lovely now, but she hesitated, not wanting to make demands when Aaro might have other plans.

"Our room please," he said, then dragged his gaze from hers to meet Kbal's. "My males can decide as they see fit."

"Very well." Kbal strolled down another passage, past a mini waterfall with stones shimmering from the pool's depths. Already the air cooled. At last, through many turns, he paused outside a metal door set into the rock. "Your room, Lady Leona."

"And mine, or do you think I would leave her unguarded, Kbal?" Aaro glared.

Leona leaped in front of Aaro and placed her hand on his chest. "Thank you, Kbal." She bowed her head in thanks. Not smiling was damned hard, but there was no way on this planet-from-hell that she would 'come on' to a Yithian by being polite.

The Yithian studied her a moment, then pressed a white button to the right of the door. It swished open. By the time she peeled her gaze off a fuming Aaro, Kbal had gone. With a sigh, she slipped around Aaro into the cooler confines of the room. A five-by-five-meter space was cut into the rock, with a bed carved like a hole in the rear wall. An open-air shower drew her closer. The way the gown stuck to her skin had started to irritate her. She tapped the magnets and flicked off the garment, letting it fall where it may. A step and she toed off one slipper. Another step, and off went the other.

"If you remove that bustier, Leona..."

She froze, her fingers at the ribbon to untie it. "Aaro, I'm hot, sticky, and—"

"Beautiful," he said, his voice like gravel.

She shivered, allowing desire to blur her senses. With a shrug and still in the lingerie, she stepped under the spray. As expected, the water activated, and she moaned, raising her face.

The muted thuds of armor dropping to the floor reached her, so she spun to feast on Aaro in his glorious nudity. *Shit, I will never get tired of looking at him.* He crowded her, forcing her to retreat until her ass hit the wall. A sharp tug at her waist and the silky slither of water between her thighs told her that he'd torn her panties off.

She gasped. He gripped her under her arms and lifted her as if she weighed nothing. With her back pressed to the wall, he slipped his hands to her waist while kneeling. No, he wasn't—

The brush of his lips across her sex drew a whimper. Delicate swipes of his tongue spiraled heat, need, and tingles outward, enhancing the craving for him to thrust into her. She wanted him kissing her but needed his mouth to be exactly where he had it now. A cry escaped her when he sucked on her clit, increasing the ache in her core. The yearning intensified.

An orgasm barreled toward her, too fast, too soon. She sank her nails into his hair, holding him in place when she tumbled off the cliff. Her hips gyrated, riding his mouth and tongue in a dance as old as time.

"Maker," he rasped against the inside of her thigh.

She wiggled her legs, asking him to lower her. But he didn't. Instead, he stepped between her splayed thighs, nudged at her sex, then slid into her an inch at a time. Too close to her orgasm, all her nerve endings were on hyper-alert. His denit rubbed along the top of her channel, then he hit her G-spot, and she splintered on a scream.

He cupped the back of her head then pounded into her, slamming her against the wall.

"Oh," she whispered, overwhelmed by this much intensity. Like a supernova in reverse, her world went from normal to focused on his every move. The soft grunts from his wide and sensual mouth sent a shiver down her spine. The way his gaze locked on hers and what the meaning was behind his eyes caught her breath. But her heartbeat faltered when he protected her even from the wall as he made love to her.

Yes, she'd read that right. Sure, he owned her with his long, strong, and purposeful thrusts, but there was tenderness in his touches, kisses, and fleeting expressions. Her heart swelled, her soul expanded, and that alien warmth unraveled, like a ribbon caught in a breeze. A sense of freedom, of peace, swept over her. She slipped her hands over his shoulders and clung to him, letting him take her wherever he wanted, letting him lead her. She trusted him not to harm her.

Another orgasm snuck up on her, knotting her stomach. She froze, threw back her head, then cried out his name.

He pressed an open-mouthed kiss to her throat, his grunts and muted roars reverberating through her. Time slowed. He stilled, his breathing ragged, his heartbeat thrumming against her chest. His touch gentled further as he stroked her from under her corseted breast to her bare hip then up again, past her collarbone to cup her cheek for a sweet, lingering kiss.

Tears pressed at the backs of her eyes. How did she get so lucky? He could've chosen Soph to be his lover for these two months. She tried not to dwell on that thought. Her teeth itched at the idea of any other woman having him. Not that she had him either, but her silly heart didn't want to listen.

"I'm hungry," she said between feathering kisses across his jaw.

He laughed, grabbed her ass, and lifted her off the wall. "I am too, *thamani.*" A single step took them out of the water's spray, but she didn't see any blue or gray buttons. A small alcove held thick cloths that looked like towels.

"Is *areemi* edible?"

He lowered her until her feet touched the cool floor, then fiddled with the ribbon to her bustier. "They have a rehydrator." He stripped her of the lingerie, then grabbed a towel to rub all over her body. "Choose what you want, if they have your human food."

"I can eat *kreso*," she said past the lump in her throat. 'I love you' had formed on her tongue, but she couldn't do that to him. Loving him might trap him. He was such an honorable man, that her loving him might make him think he had to love her back. No, she wanted his love to be freely given, not out of some sort of obligation.

He straightened, hooked the towel around her neck, and tugged her closer. "I want you again," he whispered, his gaze searching hers. "I crave you, Leona, with every cell of my being. Your taste, scent, and touch are addictive."

"I feel the same," she managed, despite the tightness in her chest.

He grimaced. "We are not safe here, not truly. I must get to the truth behind this incident."

"Do you think Kbal lied?" She stepped away from Aaro to grab a fresh towel. With long strokes, she dried his shoulders to his fingertips, then his pecs to his rigid cock to his toes. She swallowed when his erection bounced. Oh to run her tongue along that length, to hear his breath catch in his throat, to have him roar her name... There was power and satisfaction in bringing this virile man to his knees.

"I do not know. It could be a ruse." He said no more while she wrapped the towel around his waist and tucked it in the corner.

She took her towel from him and did the same, knotting it at her cleavage. A glance at her forlorn and limp gown made her wince. The room had no replicator, so she couldn't order something better.

Wetting her underwear, in hindsight, had been stupid. Now she'd have to wear the gown and be even more exposed beneath it.

He could at least wear his armor again.

She sighed. If he could do it, then so could she. No one would dare to claim humans weren't made of sterner stuff. She scooped the gown off the floor and slipped it on.

"Let's go find out." She snapped the gown closed and wiggled into her ruined slippers. "Also, how the hell did a Durn land here if they're so scarce?"

"My thoughts exactly."

She rubbed her hair while watching him pull on his pants, snapping them closed at the waist. It hung low, exposing a little of his Adonis belt. Would she get a chance to run her lips over those sinfully delicious indents? On went his chest armor, locking in place above his sternum. With one thump, she could release it as quickly. His boots were next, large, black, and military. They were too clunky, no doubt hiding tech she didn't know about.

"I do like it when your gaze is upon me, *ensa ra ensa*," he said, a smile twitching his lip. "And when you run your tongue along your plump bottom lip, it makes me ache for you."

She hummed, torn between another round of sex and hearing him call her by his endearments. No doubt they meant 'sweetheart' in his language, but still, she liked the tenderness softening his voice and making her insides like gooey caramel.

"Come." He held out his hand, and she slipped her fingers across his wide palm. When he closed his grip around her, something sealed shut in her chest, like whatever it was had completed its task. *Shit, I should talk to Flad about this.* But how to explain it without sounding like an idiot? It's why she hadn't spoken to the older man yet.

She trailed Aaro along the passages, grateful he'd at least paid attention when Kbal led them through the maze. When they reached the cavern, the strained silence stiffened Aaro's shoulders.

Ranh had Kbal pinned to the floor, his gun pressed to the Yithian's temple.

Chapter Nineteen

"Ｗʜᴀᴛ ɪs ᴛʜᴇ ᴍᴇᴀɴɪɴɢ of this?" Aaro demanded while nudging Leona behind him.

"Kbal is insisting we spend days here," Ranh gritted out, then climbed off the Yithian to allow him to clamber to his feet.

"I merely suggested it, if Zucis and Ranh cannot hide your shuttle's signature."

"Data Officer Ranh et Mavanh, explain this." Aaro strode closer, one hand held behind him to ensure Leona stayed out of the line of fire. Attacking anyone, no matter their species, was uncalled for. And by the looks of things, Ranh's actions hadn't been justified.

"I do not trust this...Yithian. How could he have convinced a Durn to serve him? How could they have taken control of the *kuta* from us? How did they know we were en route to begin with? Why have they not revealed who they claim is behind the 'attack' on us?"

"I asked Kbal to await my return," an older Yithian said, weaving through those gathered to reach Ranh. "My apologies for the delay. I had to ensure my information was accurate."

With his gaze fixed on the approaching male, Aaro whispered to Ranh, "Take a moment."

Ranh hesitated. "Sub-Commander—"

Aaro flicked a glance at him. "Now."

When Ranh fell back, coming to stand beside Krist, they both holstered their blasters but kept their fingers on the grip.

"You command with ease," the older Yithian said, switching his attention between Ranh and Aaro.

Kbal straightened his garments and bowed. "My apologies, my lord."

Aaro frowned. The only male Kbal would obey had to be...

"Commander Pyo." Aaro thumped his chest as a sign of respect. Ostracizing the male King Xeus had allied with wouldn't do well for Aaro's career or help in getting them off this damned planet.

"Sub-Commander Aaro, please, join me." Pyo gestured to the nearest table. His black gaze settled on Leona for a moment. "Lady Leona, please, choose something to eat. "In your absence, Zucis added human foods to the menu."

"Oh, thank you," she said, then crossed to the rehydrator. "Aaro, would you like *kreso*?"

"Choose for me, *ensa*," he said, trying not to grin like an idiot. That she'd thought of him shone bright joy in his chest.

"All right."

He stared after her then settled onto the bench. "I do not know the full details, but if Kbal was correct in his claims, you have my gratitude for saving us."

"It has been a while since Etterians visited Yithia, not since Lady Ava fooled King Urio." Pyo ran a clawed finger from his temple to the bridge of his nose. "She was free to leave with her *Eth*, though why you were not, this concerns me." Again he stroked his forehead. "I have watched the footage from the throne room, and King Urio seems in good spirits."

"He was most accommodating." Aaro swallowed a grimace when images of Urio and the sex-cyb rose to the fore.

"Indeed. Which meant someone other than the king wanted you dead. He has the authority to kill you where you sit, no excuses needed. And he is not a male who likes subterfuge." Pyo sounded as if he respected the male. "Your attacker had to be lurking in that throne room."

"Deroj didn't seem too happy with the way things ended," Leona said, sliding a wide plate onto the table before Aaro. A flat bread covered in yellow, orange, red bits, brown circles, and green leaves offered up a most tantalizing aroma. "Can I get you anything, Commander Pyo?" she asked, hitching her thumb at the rehydrator. "Some *areemi*?"

Pyo jerked back as if punched. "That...that would be appreciated, Lady Leona."

She scurried off, leaving Aaro to gaze after her. Somehow, she managed to surprise and delight him when he least expected it.

"A worthy *Dar Eth*," Pyo said.

Aaro snapped his focus to the Yithian. "Thank you. Do you think Deroj could be behind the attack?" Not that he believed the 'attack' happened, not fully. If he pretended to be certain, perhaps Pyo would reveal more than he had planned to.

"No, Deroj serves me."

The air seized in Aaro's lungs. "He plays his role well."

"Indeed. He was most animated about these mating machines you delivered."

Aaro nodded. "Those he must now care for."

Pyo hiss-laughed. "The need for a technician allowed me to insert another of my spies. My thanks. King Urio took well to the machines. We are weakest when we seek our pleasures, are we not?"

Aaro snuck a glance at Leona hurrying back with a bowl in hand. She placed it in front of Pyo then sank onto the bench beside Aaro.

"You don't like pizza?" she asked, tearing off a slice of her own before biting into it.

Images from his O.D.I. fluttered across Aaro's mind, and he tore off a piece. Rich flavors coated his tongue, and he groaned, popping the slice into his mouth.

"Good?" She arched a delicate brow. "I chose the meatiest one on the menu." After licking her thumb, she gazed at Pyo. "Could Barro be a problem? He claimed I wasn't trustworthy. It *was* a close call when he asked if I was Earthian. Aaro said being considered Etterian would be safer."

"And wiser," Pyo said around a mouthful of *areemi*. "To harm a female, especially an Etterian, is to instigate war with Etteria. All know of the thousands of battleships at King Xeus's command, the military might in so many warriors, the planet-destroying machines in his arsenal. But Maloid has a treaty with Etteria. For Barro to show his distrust intrigues me. Why and why now? What is the male up to?"

"I know a little more," Ranh said, standing at the end of the table with a cup in hand. "Prince Citus bartered Lady Ava from Barro and at too low a price to appease a Maloidian. Barro's niece stole Operations Commander Malo's *Dar Eth* and was shipped to Fuyra as penance.

Lady Izzy had a hand in convincing Prince Balllio to return to Maloid and assume the role of heir-apparent when the next ruler of Maloid was unknown."

"Queen Alllero has not died yet," Aaro growled.

"She is not well," Pyo said with a wince. "The G.C. believes her death will be sooner than expected."

Ranh sank onto the bench beside Leona. "And with no heir, the fate of Maloid would belong to the most cunning."

"Still, killing us would garner what?" Aaro asked, glancing between Pyo and Ranh.

"A chance to rattle King Xeus, to shake Etteria off their pedestal?" Pyo settled his black gaze on Leona. "Perhaps revenge for losing one female to Etteria? Vengeance for the treatment of his beloved niece?"

"You think Barro ordered the strike?" Aaro bit into another slice and hummed. He shoved the plate across to Ranh, offering him some. The male hesitated then took a slice. "How certain are you, Commander Pyo?" Aaro couldn't go to King Xeus with rumors. He needed facts and evidence.

Pyo paused with a handful of *areemi* halfway to his mouth. "I am not. The instruction came from the throne room. That is as far as Zucis could trace the signal."

"Alodon's balls," Aaro muttered.

"Though, it does look like it was planned tri-sun days before your arrival." Pyo activated his O.D.I. and flicked his finger across the holographics.

A buzz rippled up Aaro's forearm to his elbow. With a greasy finger, he skimmed through the vid Pyo had sent. A chokaar had fired at their *kuta*, the heat signature undeniable. The date indicated today.

The footage showed them jerking and swerving, then plummeting and exploding. He'd have Ranh test the authenticity of the file, for anything could be fabricated.

"I have other transport on standby should Zucis fail his task. He has managed to communicate with your battleship. They will meet you on the dark side of our moon. A cargo shuttle flying to the mining colonies on Tecus would not be unusual." Pyo finished his meal then shoved the bowl aside. "Keep the shuttle in exchange for yours."

"I thank you again," Aaro said, unsure what else he could say.

"I hope this proves my willingness to assist Etteria. When the time comes, I expect the same."

"As decreed by King Xeus," Aaro said, not about to make promises outside his authority.

"Fair enough, Sub-Commander." Pyo gestured to Leona who'd slumped with her temple on his upper arm. "Perhaps it is time to rest?"

Aaro looped an arm around her and drew her into the curve of his body. She offered a weak smile then yawned. "Ranh, try not to kill anyone." Aaro met his gaze. "And aid Zucis where you can."

"Acknowledged," Ranh said, having ordered his own pizza.

Krist sat opposite him, a slice in hand. "I will guard him."

Ranh scowled but said nothing.

Aaro rose, scooping Leona to her feet. "Come, *ensa*."

"Thank you for dinner," she said to Pyo then let Aaro lead her away. Once inside their room, she sat on the bed and slumped. "I could sleep for days," she mumbled.

"Indeed." He chuckled, stripped off his boots and chest armor, then sprawled beside her.

She rolled onto her side and threw a leg over his. With her cheek on his shoulder, she fell asleep. He hugged her closer, gripping her hip in an act of ownership. He pressed a kiss to her temple then stared at the ceiling. If Pyo was true to his word, Aaro would have Leona back on the *Valiant* in the morning and traveling away from Yithia. He'd convey all he'd learned to King Xeus, and let the older wiser male handle this.

As long as nothing else endangered his *Dar Eth*.

"*THAMANI?*" AARO CALLED AS if from a distance.

Leona mumbled and buried her nose against his skin, inhaling deeply while doing so. He smelled *so* good. She wished she could bottle his cologne, and when cold, lonely nights back in Callisto turned out to be too much for her, she could whip out that bottle and sniff it.

She was being silly, insane even. How could she explain to Soph what was in that bottle? The woman would think her crazy.

"Leona, the *kuta* is ready," Aaro said, his touch burning her from temple to chin. "Come, *ensa*, we must leave."

She forced her eyes open and gazed at his gorgeous face. The man was too perfect. He had the kind of handsomeness that would make a fortune in modeling. Careful not to bump her head on the low ceiling above the bed, she climbed onto him to place a kiss where his jaw met the strong column of his neck. He slid his hands under the gown to grip her ass for a lust-inducing knead. A solid bulge pressed at her sex, stripping the fog of sleep from her mind. She gyrated her hips, rubbing herself across that firm length.

"Leona," he rasped in that sexy-smooth voice of his.

"Just a quickie, babe," she said while licking her way to his right nipple.

She hummed at the taste of his hot-velvet skin. The huffs and soft grunts he made empowered her. When she sucked a nipple into her mouth then swirled her tongue around it, he groaned. His fingers dug into her ass, so close to where she throbbed for him.

She squirmed down as much as he would let her and tapped his belt. It gaped, revealing the round head of his erection. Without hesitation, she dipped and laved the tip.

"*Ensa*," he said, his tone warning.

"What, Aaro?" She met his gaze while she opened his pants wider.

"Do that thing with your tongue."

She grinned then fluttered her eyelashes 'innocently.' "This?" She wrapped her mouth around the head of his cock and sucked.

He arched, his eyes closing as his mouth parted.

When she ran her tongue over those ridges, he cried out, his body stiffening like too-tight elastic. He caught her under her arms and dragged her to his mouth for a scorching kiss. She melted against him, trying to gather her thoughts. She had a mission. What was it?

When he broke the kiss to nibble on her bottom lip, the sensation of his cock at her entrance registered. *Oh, yes, that.* With a wiggle, she lowered herself onto him, relishing his growl. The length of him rubbed along her channel so well she struggled to breathe. *So good.*

Then she sat up, almost bumping her head on the rock. He stilled, concern furrowing his brow. She ducked a little and started to grind. His expression hardened with need. He lowered his hands to her hips and kneaded her with every slide forward of her hips. His cock penetrated so deeply she could do nothing but experience the primal sensation of being filled.

"*Thamani*," he whispered.

She shivered and kept a steady pace even though his hands urged her to go faster.

"Leona," he gritted out.

She smirked. "What do you want, babe?" Without waiting for his response, she rode him harder, then her looming orgasm shifted her focus from him to internal. Tingles started at her core, and a shimmer of addictive heat followed. Her hip movements stuttered as her need ramped up a notch.

Joy, fire, and color slammed into her, and she arched, his name on her tongue. She tried to keep riding him, to focus, but she couldn't, not when he gripped her hips and pounded upward into her. Sensations exploded, blurring her vision and seizing her breathing.

"Leona," he rumbled. He stiffened, every muscle straining.

She took over, sliding her hips back and forth, hoping to extend his orgasm.

His eyes widened, then narrowed on her. "Maker," he graveled.

She found herself staring at the rock ceiling, Aaro pinning her to the bed. He slanted his mouth across hers, delving his tongue in before she could react. She moaned and looped her legs around his hips, sinking his still-hard cock deeper. He broke the kiss and pressed his temple to hers.

"Good morning." She chuckled, trying to wrap her arms around him.

"Indeed," he said, pulling back to meet her gaze. He held himself off her in a push-up, bulging his arms and shoulders. His braid dipped across his chest. She caught the thick rope and ran her hands along the length she could reach.

"You think Pyo is...honorable?"

"We shall find out soon enough, *ensa*," Aaro said, switching all his weight to one arm to brush the hair off her temple. His touch was gentle and elicited a flood of warmth that started in her chest and circled her heart. He slid out of her and off the bed in one smooth motion.

The loss of him filling her and the heat pouring off his body drew a shiver. She dipped her head to hide a pout. What would it be like to spend the day in bed with him? They could pig out on fast food while watching movies. She wanted him all to herself. That wasn't so hard to admit.

"Leona?" He offered her his hand which she accepted.

As soon as her fingers slid across his palm, he tugged her off the bed. Okay, so she ogled him as he dressed. Although, she hid that she did so by finger-combing her hair then braiding it loosely. All she had to do was put on her slippers, but he had his armored vest and boots.

"If you keep looking at me like that—"

"Oh," she gasped, the tips of her ears burning. A little flustered, she hurried to the door as if to say she was ready when he was.

He laughed, caught her wrist, and spun her into his arms. A swift kiss distracted her as did his solid body against her.

"Come, *ensa*." He led her along the narrow passages, and when they stepped into the vast cavern, all were waiting for them.

"Good." Pyo slapped the table and stood. "The cargo shuttle awaits." He strode toward the first tunnel he'd led them through.

The Durn tapping Aaro halted their departure. He gestured with a blue finger for her to carry on. She hesitated, then Aaro nodded to Krist who waited for her.

She cast a glance at Aaro then left him, alone, with the strange blue alien.

Chapter Twenty

Zucis waited until they were alone before he drew Aaro toward the waterfall. Its hush might smother any conversation if anyone listening wasn't Etterian. "I did not get a chance to speak with you last night. I wish to ask Etteria for asylum." He met Aaro's gaze, his white eyes unblinking. "I understand King Xeus has already offered sanctuary to two of my brethren."

Aaro sank onto the bench. "He has."

"I serve the lesser of two evils, for Pyo is attempting to be honorable. That is a rare trait, but without guidance, his honor falls short. Those who fight for the monarchy make me do—unspeakable things." Zucis stiffened. "Please convey my earnestness to your king. If he doubts it, mention 'death trigger.' I am certain Operations Commander Malo et Dalo has encountered them by now." He pushed off and held out his arm.

"I will do as asked, Zucis." Aaro swung his O.D.I. across the Durn's.

"You have my gratitude," he managed. "And may I wish you eternal bliss with your *Dar Eth*."

Aaro bowed his head, then hurried along the passage. He had planned to comm King Xeus upon their return. This incident should not be kept secret. Besides, Ranh and Krist would record it in the daily annals.

A death trigger?

He climbed into the elongated cargo shuttle and nestled between crates, next to a strapped-in Leona.

"What did he want?" she asked.

He shook his head. Sharing that information with her before he'd told his king? No, this was something he couldn't discuss with so many in hearing range. He captured her hand and squeezed it, hoping to convey he'd share soon enough.

'Death trigger' wasn't something he heard often. They were organic implants undetectable by med-guns or O.D.I. scanners and found in the carrier's brain. When the password was uttered by the carrier or an interrogator, it could trigger a kill switch or spill the information. Either could happen with no outward indications which one could occur.

How could he explain this to Leona? Given her intelligence, she would understand. That Yithia was forcing Zucis to do this was the real concern. Why? What were they hiding? Aaro slumped. He'd convey all this to King Xeus and Operations Commander Malo, and let them deal with it.

Leona was Aaro's mission, and after this Yithian trip, he needed to be more cautious.

True to Pyo's word, a cargo shuttle had been prepped for them. On the platform stood a few Yithians. Aaro paused before Pyo and thumped his chest.

Leona waited at the ramp, Krist and Ranh beside her. Aaro offered her his hand, and when she accepted, he led her into the shuttle's compartment. Not like a *kuta*, it held no seats, so he pinned her between him and the bulkhead. Krist sank into the pilot's seat while Ranh sealed the door.

The engine was slow to start, arching Aaro's brow. He cast a glance at Ranh. Maker, he prayed nothing else went wrong.

Within seconds, Krist launched them upward, veering the shuttle along strips of black coasts, around the island of Iphara, then up, breaching the atmosphere amid shudders and jerks. Leona crushed his hand in hers, but she said nothing. The vast expanse of space filled the forevids, the edges illuminated by weak sunlight. They shot around Tecus, the darkness like a solid line across the moon. There, as promised, waited the *Valiant*.

Relief threatened to dip Aaro's shoulders, but he held firm. Until they docked, he wouldn't relax his guard.

"Pilot Saan, request docking in bay 'A1.'" Krist tapped the console then grabbed the lever.

"Docking confirmed, Pilot Krist. Do you require medical?"

"No, all are well." Krist swung the shuttle to 'slide' into the bay sideways. He touched down with a solid thump. In the shuttle's forevids, the massive doors of the docking bay sealed.

Ranh smacked a button and the shuttle's door opened. The ramp extracted.

Aaro drew Leona into his arms and buried his face in the curve of her neck. They were home and safe. He took her hand and led her out of the shuttle, the bay, and toward the common.

"Welcome, Sub-Commander Aaro." Saan thumped his chest. "We were most concerned when we lost the *kuta*'s signal."

Soph barreled in and hugged Leona, taking her away from Aaro. "Damnit, Leona, I damn near died," she said, crushing, releasing, then crushing Leona again. "Saan said you went missing. What happened?"

"It's a long story," Leona said, winked at Aaro, then ushered Soph out the door. "But first, I need a shower and clean clothes. Maybe a cocoa too."

Aaro faced the comm room and the males who'd run the *Valiant* in his stead. "My thanks," he said. "Get some rest. We have two days before we reach Maloid." He waited until only Saan remained. "Comm the king, Saan."

"As you wish, Sub-Commander." His fingers flew across the console.

The display vid flickered, revealing Adviser Kanzo.

Aaro grinned at seeing his old friend's face. "Adviser, thank you for taking my comm."

"Adviser, like we were not battle-bonds first, Aaro." Kanzo laughed. "How fare's things?" He stilled, stepped closer to the display vid, and both eyebrows shot up to his hairline. "You found your *Dar Eth*?"

"Yes," Aaro said, his chest expanding with uncontrollable warmth, dampened only by the knowledge that he had yet to tell Leona the truth.

"Congratulations. You were the last of our battle-bonds to be paired." Kanzo glanced at his O.D.I. "Why do you seek an audience with King Xeus?"

"A Durn on Yithia revealed something most alarming."

"Another Durn?" Kanzo met Aaro's gaze.

"Yes, and I need Operations Commander Malo to join the comm." Aaro curled his fingers into fists. Energy coursed through him, making him irritable. "Zucis asked for asylum. He offers information on 'death triggers.'"

Kanzo stiffened, flicked a finger across the screen, and it split into three. King Xeus blinked at Aaro. Malo took longer to answer.

"What is it, Sub-Commander Aaro?" Xeus frowned. "Has anything happened to the women?"

"They are well, my king. I met another Durn." Aaro glanced at Malo when he appeared. "He mentioned death triggers and asked for a rescue. He implied he is a Yithian prisoner and serves Pyo." Aaro went on to explain the fake crash and his doubts it was truly a rescue.

"Perhaps Zucis instigated the farce to meet you." Malo scowled.

"Indeed." Aaro's instincts were validated.

"Operative Cylo is en route on a mission near Mascroba. I shall have the two 'meet.'" Malo smirked. "Another Durn? We suspected only someone with that level of intelligence could implant organic death triggers but had yet to find the male. Well done, Sub-Commander, and congratulations on your *Dar Eth*. I trust we will meet her soon?"

Aaro smothered a grimace. Which meant he needed to tell her before they visited Etteria. "Of course, Operations Commander."

"Excellent. Malo, keep me informed on your operative's progress." The display vid blinked off on the king. Malo followed shortly after.

"Thank you, Adviser," Aaro said. If he didn't tell Leona soon, he might as well prepare to meet Lady Ava again. As a hairstylist, she meted out their judgment, slicing off a Foot of Honor.

"See you soon, Aaro."

Aaro slumped into the comfy the moment the comm ended. He tapped his fingers on his tablet resting on the table. Leona was right: a cleanse, a meal, and maybe the next chapter of *Stolen Love* would be a second good start to his day.

WHEN LEONA STEPPED OUT of the ceremonial gown, now stained at its hem, collar, and sleeves, it thumped as it hit the floor. She stared at the pooled garment for a minute, trying to figure out why alien silk could make a noise. Flicking it up, she tested its weight then grimaced at finding a pocket heavy. Shoving her hand inside, her fingers closed over something cool and smooth.

She gaped at the glowing *lumnari* stone on her palm. *Shit.* When had she stolen it? Chewing on her lip, she swung between telling Aaro and keeping it a secret, not wanting him to think her a thief.

"Well, you are one," she said, flipping the stone over.

She placed it on the closed toilet seat and stepped into the shower. What would Aaro say if she added it to his collection? No, she should start her own. She chuckled. *Sure, my first item is stolen? What a conversational piece.*

She groaned, relishing the warm spray easing the tension between her shoulders. Yithia had not been fun. And the thought of three more deliveries drained her. Would they be as eventful? Had John known about the Yithian-Etterian hostilities? She doubted it.

While the air-dryer did its thing, she studied the stone. Jagged veins had glowed in the rock-hewn walls like bioluminescent fungi. She hadn't thought to take a picture. No, all that she'd recorded of her time on Yithia was the king testing out a doll. She snorted. *Sure, tourism at its finest.*

At least she'd met a Durn. Sort of.

Once dressed, she snapped on her boots while browsing the many options on the rehydrator, not sure what to order. She started with something to drink, then hurried from her cabin. With her hot cocoa clasped to her chest, she stepped into the workshop. Her hair had yet to fully dry, but donning her uniform was like wrapping a warm blanket around her. Soph stood before another painting, this time of oranges.

"What did I miss?" Leona asked and chose a chair, settling into it as it cupped her ass.

"Nothing much." Soph shrugged. "I figured something bad had happened when you didn't return by shift end."

"Well, I did get to watch the Yithian king do a doll." Leona grinned.

"Wait, he wasn't repulsed by it?" Soph dabbed the canvas. "I thought they would take our dolls and toss them in the arena."

"Nope." Leona flicked her finger to the nearest display vid. King Urio pounding the poor cyb filled the screen. "Look at his cock, Soph."

"Oh, wow." Soph gaped and inched closer, dripping paint across the floor. "I hadn't thought they were humanlike with their sharklike skin and face. But he's got a chest, pecs, bulging biceps, and an ass

I could bounce my...paintbrush on." She waved her brush for good measure.

"Soph, quit looking at his ass. Check out his cock." Leona tapped the vid. "So thick and strong, and with such a bulbous head." She paused the vid, managing to catch Urio between thrusts.

Soph split her fingers to zoom in. "I didn't expect it to be such a pretty pink on the tip. And those ridges?" She stroked the vid, smearing a little paint.

Leona pursed her lips. She couldn't confirm it was their denit. But she suspected it did the same. Since the ridges circled the alien's member all over, she had to assume, for it was on the side facing the vid as well as on the top.

"And who would think a massive shark is that...um...fit." Soph's cheeks burned bright.

"Ew, Soph." Leona wiggled her eyebrows.

"It's been a while since I've had a man between my sheets," she huffed. "And who knows how long before I find one willing."

"True. Go ahead, drool away." Leona flicked a hand at her paintings of planets. "Did you do these?"

"Nope, those are Ranh's." Soph returned her brush to the palette then crouched to wipe up the paint droplets. "I tell you what, being in space is boring as hell. Especially when you took my new art buddy with you." She leveled a scowl on Leona.

"Sorry, babe, we kind of needed him." Leona gripped the empty mug between her knees. "I just want to gorge myself on popcorn and ice cream. My mood's all over the place. Oh, and pizza, loads of pizza."

Soph jerked back. "But you hate pizza? Said if you see another slice, you'll launch yourself out the nearest airlock."

Leona grimaced. She had said that after Soph had ordered pizza four days in a row. "Well, I'm craving it. Cheese, pepperoni, tons of garlic on a crispy wood-smoked base?" She hummed, her stomach gurgling.

"Sounds delicious." Soph grinned, but her amused tone said she didn't believe Leona.

"And I could sleep for hours." Leona swiveled on the chair and ordered a pizza from the rehydrator—with all the toppings. "Maloid is in two days, Soph," she said around a mouthful. "I can't go through another 'adventure.'"

Soph stiffened, then helped herself to a slice. "Does Aaro think it's going to be tough?"

"What does it matter?" Leona smothered a yawn. "I'm tired already, and we still have Maloid, Kulai, and Etteria to go."

"How about I do Maloid?" Soph winced, but she met and held Leona's gaze.

"You'd do that for me?" A tear slipped free. Leona sniffed, leaped to her feet, and hugged her.

"Sure." Soph held her hand high, keeping the pizza out of Leona's hair. "If Aaro won't mind."

"No, I must do it." Leona leaned back and sighed.

"Fine, then I'll make sure pizza and ice cream await your return."

A tremulous giggle slipped past Leona's defenses. "Thanks, Soph."

They chewed in silence, their focus on the grunting men occupying parts of the screens around the stilled image of Urio's sculpted ass.

After shoving the last slice at Soph, Leona slapped her thighs. "Let me get to work. A little bit of monotony is just what I need."

She slid the tablet closer and increased the volume on all the vids. Grunts and moans filled the air. Cyb malfunctions were still a concern. Resuming her seat, she let her mind wander. She had much to think about, especially where it concerned her emotions and Aaro. None of which she was ready to speak to Soph about.

Her friend snuck a narrowed glance at Leona then returned to her too-red oranges.

Chapter Twenty-One

Two days wasn't long enough for Leona to fall into her routine again. Nor could she forget the unpleasant trip to Yithia. So, being on a shuttle breaching Maloid's atmosphere had her on edge. Aaro had gone a little overboard this time. Two shuttles were traveling to Argaxx, both housing four soldiers plus Ranh and Flad.

Aaro had seated her to the right of him, giving her a clear line of sight. The vids spanned the front of the shuttle, or *kuta*, whatever that meant. Dark purple-black skies illuminated with each strike of lilac lighting. Hazardous crevices marred the surface of Maloid. No cities, villages, or seas were visible.

"The planet's solid rock?" she asked Aaro, who'd rested his hand on her thigh.

"Yes, underground rivers and seas provide water."

"And the food? Do they farm?" She frowned.

"Watch," he said, humor drenching his voice.

She snuck a glance at him, wishing she could steal a kiss. The shuttle dipped. She clung to him, her breath in her throat.

"We're fine, *ensa*. We must travel into a crevice to reach the queen's hall." He caught her chin and urged her to look ahead.

Her eyes widened. On the steep walls grew fungi, glowing red, orange, and blue. Maloidians hung off harnesses, gathering the plants or scooping yellow jelly into floating crates.

"They sing while they work. Krist?" Aaro called to the pilot, who flicked a switch on the console. A haunting melody echoing with a thousand voices filled the shuttle's compartment. No words were sung, but the tune held such emotion—of longing, of family, of legacy—that it summoned tears.

"It saddens you?" Ranh asked, his eyebrows brushing his hairline.

"Oh, no, it's so beautiful," she managed, clasped Aaro's hand on her thigh, and squeezed it. "Thank you for sharing this with me."

The purple walls gleamed with moisture, and with the fungi, it was far brighter and more colorful than Yithia. Danger didn't taint the trip, and for the first time since stepping into the shuttle in a fresh ceremonial gown, she could breathe.

Still, she wore black leggings and a tight tank top under the gown, not wanting to be vulnerable again. And she'd French braided her hair for that authentic Etterian look.

The shuttle touched down, jarring her from her thoughts. The door opened to a sweet organic scent. Warmth smacked her, but also, the air...was thin as if not enough of it circulated this far down.

The singing grew in volume, and she stepped off the ramp to gaze up, circling and smiling.

"They do not sing all the time," Aaro said, grabbed the crate, then faced a Maloidian awaiting them on the platform set into the cliff.

"Greetings, Sub-Commander Aaro et Zaro and Lady Leona," the man said in Galactic, then bowed, his tentacles swaying as if he was underwater. Black markings merged from his temple into his scalp. He wore a long tunic over harem-style pants and pointy bejeweled slippers—all in shades of green. "I am Eeezo."

"I can smile?" she asked Aaro, leaning against him to whisper.

"Yes." He grinned.

"Oh, good." She slumped then gathered the dolls.

Eeezo led them into a well-lit tunnel, rock-hewn like on Yithia, but it had an exotic air, like a museum, with strange ornaments nestled in various tall alcoves lining the sides. If she had time, she would have lingered and read the plaques at the base of each display. One or two looked like the fertility statues Aaro had on his shelves.

How had he bagged one? They seemed...precious. She huffed. More importantly, where could she find one? Shoving a statue inside her gown and running was O.U.T. She giggled at the thought of the expression on Aaro's face if she tried it.

The wide passage expanded into a cavern. Wall-mounted lights illuminated the purple rock in bold circles of lilac. Pockets of space held cushioned chairs mimicking the colored fungi they harvested. A long counter housed a rehydrator and replicator, with all manner of species crossing between with cups or plates in hand. A range of aromas assaulted her nose, and she struggled to identify them, in search of the familiar. One almost smelled like roast chicken.

No one paid her any attention until the dolls paused behind her. People froze in mid-chat or with utensils halfway to their mouths. Maloidian was a given, and she recognized Yithian and algri. One man stood out, his hair the flamboyancy of autumn. Gold beading shone in his braids, and his skin was more gold than bronze. He smiled at her, revealing vampiric teeth.

Damn if her heart didn't flutter in her chest. He was gorgeous.

She snuck a glance at Aaro and sigh-hummed. Nope, her man was sinfully delicious. *Her man?* She snorted. For now. Aaro gripped her elbow, snapping her out of her erotic daze. His hot fingers scorching her through the silk was enough to curl her toes in her silly slippers.

"Come, Queen Alllero awaits," he said, his voice thick and husky.

Heat burned the tips of her ears, and she hurried forward to where Eeezo waited at fifteen-foot-tall gilded doors. They swung open on silent hinges, surprising when they were a forearm thick. She was tempted to rap on them with her knuckles to test whether they were solid.

A forest-green marble floor glimmered in the golden chandelier's light. Impressive pillars wider than her arm span reached to a ceiling mimicking an unfamiliar galaxy. The room was empty, and her footsteps thumped, echoing off the walls. Cushions were stacked to one side on the empty stone throne.

Eeezo hurried past to a carved mural behind the dais. He tapped a round fruit and the door opened inward. "My prince awaits," he said and flicked his hand, urging them to hurry.

The narrow door only allowed single file. Aaro went first, then Leona with her dolls. Eeezo trailed them.

She gasped. The green flooring continued to a patio. The view was spectacular, of a molten-silver waterfall tumbling into a garden that would have rivaled Eden. Strange birds and insects flittered from fungi to plants. Petal-shaped chairs, overstuffed and bright pink, took up the space. Eeezo weaved through them and out into the garden.

"Your majesty?" he called.

From behind the bark of an upside-down tree stepped a Maloidian man. He wore tight leggings and a shirt that crisscrossed, clinging to every indent.

"Ah, Lady Leona." He smiled and held out his hand. "I am Prince Balllio."

She stumbled forward, catching her toe on a clump of grass. *Way to go, Leona. Destroy a plant while you're at it.* "Thank you for meeting with us, your majesty."

He shook her hand while peering into her eyes. "You are the third human woman I've met, Lady Leona. It delights me you are all so different." He gestured to the swaying fronds of the gray tree. "This is a *tewaa*. It is considered...moody." He rose onto his toes and plucked a white blossom, then with it cupped in both hands, he offered it to her. "It will never die, this flower."

She accepted the gift, for it was just that.

"Sub-Commander Aaro, I must apologize on behalf of Queen Alllero. My aunt is not well." He cast a glance at another mural, no doubt hiding a door. "It is best if you inform King Xeus, for her time with us draws to an end." Sadness drenched the man's features, yet his tentacles drifted, at peace. "My aunt was most adamant that I receive this gift of sex-cybs." He raised his gaze to the dolls then at Eeezo. "Maloidians do love things we have not paid for."

Eeezo chuckled. "My prince speaks the truth."

"Wonderful," Leona said. "I need to hand them over to a technician. We will support you from afar. They have been pre-conditioned so they will not need additional maintenance."

"Of course, Neeruu is on standby. Eeezo, do fetch the girl." The prince gestured to the chairs.

Leona wanted to explore the garden but didn't know how to ask. And with the blossom still in her palm, she didn't have a spare hand anyway. So she sank into a chair and almost pouted when it didn't adjust to her backside.

"Miri insisted I return and assume my responsibility. She did not compel me too, but that woman is about loyalty, honor, and the importance of family." Balllio glanced outside as a drizzle started. When he refocused on Leona, a smile tugged at his wide lips. "My time with my battle-bond Madyx has taught me how to deal with...politics. This next phase in Maloid's history promises to be an interesting one." He approached a doll to stroke her collarbone exposed by the deep 'V' of the kimono. "So lifelike. And," he chuckled, "modeled after you?"

Leona jerked back then flicked a wide-eyed gaze at Aaro. He'd implied the same. "No, your majesty. They are all the same height with a set amount of curves. I would say they're modeled after a typical human woman."

"I doubt that, Lady Leona. Miri and Izzy are in no way similar. However, these sex-cybs resemble your form." His touch was reverent when he caught up a ribbon of red hair and tested the texture between his fingers.

Leona chose to go with humor rather than sit there stunned. "I do believe you just called me typical." She pursed her lips to smother a grin. "As in average. I should be deeply offended."

Balllio laughed. "Indeed."

A petite Maloidian female scurried behind Eeezo, then dipped into a bow before Balllio. "My prince."

"Neeruu, your charges have arrived."

Her head whipped up. She gaped at the dolls then approached them, her steps short and bouncy, like Soph's. "Oh, yes, incredible." She circled one doll, then the other, rising on her toes to peer into an ear, or kneeling to touch a bare knee. When she faced Leona, her cheeks had paled. "I had heard of such things, but to have these here..." She broke into an alien rendition of jazz hands. "Thank you, Prince Balllio for entrusting these to my care."

Leona placed the blossom on the arm of the chair then pushed to her feet. She dug the tablet out of her pocket and handed it to Neeruu. "Everything you need to know is on this. And my contact details should you have any concerns or ideas. We are always improving on the cybs' performance for maximum pleasure." Leona leaned in to whisper, "If their mechanics interest you, I can organize a factory visit. I find their inner works fascinating. Their design is simply...ingenious."

"Oh, that would be amazing," Neeruu exclaimed with more jazz hands.

Leona offered her wrist, and with a bright smile from Neeruu, swiped her O.D.I. across the woman's. "I will answer any correspondence you send me."

"Thank you." Neeruu activated her O.D.I., selected a command, and as one, the dolls followed her out of the room.

"Excellent. Would you like to stay for a meal?" Eeezo asked.

"Unfortunately, we embark for Kulai next. And as you must know, it is a long journey." Aaro dumped the crate in the poor Maloidian's arms. "May Alllero shine upon you."

Leona frowned at that off sentence, but when Balllio pumped her hand again, she assumed they were allowed to leave.

"A pleasure, Lady Leona, and I wish you great success in your endeavors," he said.

With a hasty curtsey, she scooped up the blossom and trailed Aaro out. He waited for her in the throne room, then with a hand at her elbow, ushered her gawking self back to the shuttle.

"It went well?" Ranh asked the moment they stepped into the clearing.

"I am pleased," Aaro said as he guided her to a seat.

She clasped the blossom while feathering her thumb over the delicate petals. "Babe, how can this not die?

"The *tewaa* in that garden is purported to be ancient, *ensa*. It is said they do not blossom until they reach at least a thousand years of age. Such a gift from the prince is to be treasured."

"But it doesn't die? That's what he said."

He shrugged. "Many things in the universe defy belief, *thamani*."

She held the flower up to the weak light within the compartment. To put a sliver of a petal under a microscope was to destroy it. Anyone who could do that was a monster.

Aaro strapped her in. She raised her arms to aid him then flashed him a smile in thanks. Maloid done. That hadn't been so bad. "How far is Kulai?"

"About eleven days." He pressed a kiss to her temple and settled in the seat beside her. "Do not worry, *ensa*. I shall keep your mind occupied."

"Oh?" She smirked. "I believe we have a misunderstanding here, Sub-Commander Aaro, for it'll be me distracting you."

He chuckled and draped his arm around her as Krist shot the *kuta* upward. The other shuttle darted past the front vids as it too returned to the *Valiant*.

"Challenge accepted, Leona," Aaro rasped.

Chapter Twenty-Two

THE DAYS BLURRED FOR Aaro in a mixture of bliss and guilt. Every night with Leona beside him, he opened his mouth to reveal the truth and failed. He caught up his braid and brushed his palm across the tip. Cutting it now would serve him right. He hadn't commed Danic or Kanzo. Danzo knew, and his judgmental expressions were like a serrated dagger to Aaro's hearts. Kanzo had no idea and gazed at Aaro with respect he didn't deserve.

They were six days in the eleven-day journey. Time was running out. Leona couldn't step onto Etterian soil without knowing her place was with him. Aaro grimaced. He lay awake at night, plagued by the thought that had Etteria not been on the itinerary, would he tell her at all?

King Xeus, Kanzo, and any *Dar Eth* would reveal to Leona what the change in Aaro's eye color meant. No, he had to be the one to tell her, to convince her to stay...with him.

"Sub-Commander?" Pilot Saan hovered his hands over the console. "I am picking up a strange signal. Data Officer Ranh, can you confer?"

Aaro stiffened, pushing the deactivated tablet aside, and crossed the comm room to stand behind Saan. "What is it?"

"I cannot say. I have not been trained to read such a signal." Saan raised an expectant gaze to Ranh, who flicked through the galactic hologram above the war table.

He zoomed past the debris field—of what used to be Durn—to an unchartered planet beyond it. Etteria had no call to venture there often. "It is originating from Vora." He gaped, double-tapped the planet, and zoomed in farther. "And the signal is Durn."

Aaro's eyes widened. "I have not spoken the word 'Durn' for years of my life, and now, I have met a Durn, *and* we have found a lost signal? If I was superstitious, I would suspect subterfuge."

"Same, Sub-Commander. This is most unusual." Ranh tapped and flicked data to the side. "I shall gather what I can and send it to Adviser Kanzo. I do believe the Durns we shelter in Issneen would find this discovery intriguing."

"Agreed." Aaro activated his tablet and drew it closer with a fingertip. He'd sifted through all messages, reports, and graphs on their stock levels, all in an attempt to avoid finishing Benedict and Elizabeth's story.

He hesitated now, still unsure if he could deal with Elizabeth's censure.

"I don't give a damn about my title, Elizabeth. I would leave London with you in an instant."

"You did not reveal a word of it to me, Benedict, of your history. Am I not trustworthy?"

Aaro paused. No, he'd read that part.

The pain in her lovely eyes skewered him. Aye, not sharing his darkest secret had made her doubt her worth. What a fool he was.

Aaro stared at 'doubt,' wondering if his silence would do the same to Leona. Just last night, he'd gaped like an *omeika*, flapping his lips as he fought for words. Likening himself to those carnivorous fish made no sense, but the only memory he had was when one had lain on the beach, gasping for air.

She'd cupped his jaw, gazing into his eyes. "What is it, Aaro?"

"I need..." *to tell you something.* Opening and closing his mouth, his mind blanked. His focus shifted away from her face to the strange painting she had mounted above the rehydrator. "May I have a flower?"

Her gaze had whipped to the artwork, missing him slumping in the chair. "Of course. I'll do one for you tomorrow."

He'd slunk away from her quarters, heading for the nearest common to vent his frustrations.

She hadn't been feeling well but had declined to summon Flad. "We ate too much, that's all," she'd said, clasping her stomach while offering him a weak smile.

He hadn't seen her for a few hours. Perhaps she was still not well. He typed a message to her via his O.D.I.

Her response was immediate. "Of course. Same time tonight?"

He twitched at her question. Why would this night be different? Why would she ask?

"I look forward to seeing you, *ensa*." He sent the message and settled back to read on. Perhaps Benedict had a way of resolving his situation without losing Elizabeth? Aaro could apply the same strategy if it made sense.

"My title is my past, Elizabeth. You are my future." He caught a curl and tugged on it, as gently as he could, then he released it, allowing it to bounce into place. "You must know how much you mean to me. Watching you leave nearly killed me. I—" He cleared his throat. "I tried to tell myself that not being in your life was the best for you. That you deserve happiness. As a privateer, I can only offer you...me."

She said nothing, simply stared at him. A tear slipped down her cheek, pulling at his heartstrings.

He caught the droplet with the pad of his thumb. "I am sorry, my love. I did not mean to hurt you."

"*I love you too, Benedict,*" she whispered.

"Yes," Aaro roared, then winced. His males gaped at his uncharacteristic outburst. "Um, just something good," he mumbled.

She cupped his jaw, running her thumb along his bottom lip. "Your lack of title never bothered me, just that you hid this from me."

He caught her fingers and led her deeper into the garden, choosing the shadows of a tree to hide in. "My father and I argued, my love. Still, the pain of our last encounter torments me." He drew her into his arms, relishing her softness against his body. "I felt like a stubborn fool. I should not have reacted to his jibes. Leaving the way I did, I carried regret and guilt. I still do."

"I understand why you couldn't share this with me, and," she leaned in for a kiss, "I forgive you."

"I do not deserve you, my love."

"That is true." She laughed. "Now, you need to face whatever obligations the death of your father thrust upon you."

"Indeed," Benedict said, dipping to run kisses up her neck.

"And post the banns," she said.

"If I don't attain a marriage license first. I cannot wait the three weeks to have you, my love."

She tutted. "So impatient. I need to appease my family and ensure my reputation remains spotless. In addition, my mother will never forgive you if I wed without the extravagance she so desires."

He grimaced. "I best ask for your hand in marriage too."

She chuckled and looped her arms around his neck. "You shall have me, never you fear, my dearest. For I cannot wait either."

Post the banns? Without speaking the word 'banns,' his O.D.I . wouldn't inform him of its meaning. And after his outburst, he wouldn't dare whisper it. He typed it into the archives on his O.D.I. and waited.

Banns of Marriage: A notice read out on three successive Sundays in a parish church, announcing an intended marriage and giving the opportunity for objections.

He switched off the tablet and stared at it, discarded on the table. Leona was his future, that was true. But his lying wasn't his past. That was his present. So, he couldn't use those words to aid him. And leaving her *would* kill him. If it was for her happiness, then as her *Eth*, he had to comply. Whatever gave her a long and fulfilled life was his honor to provide.

He would find out that night if being with him made her happy. Her answer would determine the path he chose.

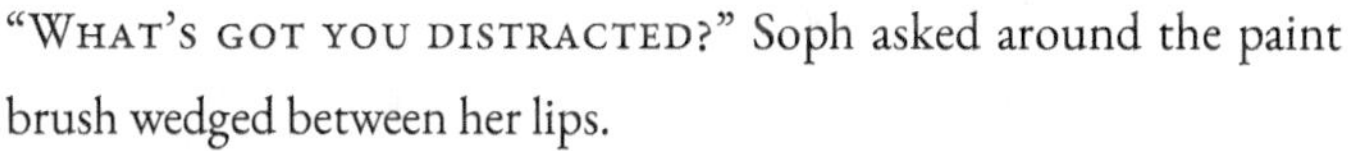

"WHAT'S GOT YOU DISTRACTED?" Soph asked around the paint brush wedged between her lips.

"Aaro, of course." Leona added the finishing touch to the painting of a daisy he'd asked for. She couldn't shake the thought he meant to say something else. "He's been acting...strange."

"Well, looks like the honeymoon period is over," Soph mumbled.

Leona stilled. Could that be it? Their affair drawing to an end? The sex was still amazing, his passion as phenomenal as their first time. Maybe something had happened at work? Or was it the Yithian incident that bothered him?

She'd only know if she asked him.

Picking up the painting, she placed it on the table and positioned the next canvas. This one would be quick and hopefully, both would be dry by dinner time. She glanced at the time stamp on the bottom right of the display vids.

"Leona, how are things?"

She yelped and whipped her gaze to the screen. Soph ducked low, pulling down her canvas with her.

John blinked at Leona, humor twisting his lips.

"Shit," she whispered, flicking a glance at her easel. She placed the brush on the palette and stood in front of the display vid, a little too close to 'naturally' hide their goofing off. "All is well, except for the trip to Yithia. We had a bit of an incident."

"Oh?" He raised his coffee cup to his lips for a sip.

"It was something not related to the cybs or my presence. Aaro...I mean, Sub-Commander Aaro handled it well. We delivered the gifts to Prince Balllio of Maloid about a week ago. We are now en route to Kulai."

"I'm glad you two are safe. I find it odd, though, that something happened on Yithia and yet they've ordered a dozen cybs. Well done. You and Sugar will receive a sales bonus."

While Soph smothered her squeal, Leona faked a cough. "Um, thank you, John."

"The addition of vanilla to the cyb's skin was a stroke of brilliance. Sales have skyrocketed across all markets. Extra bonuses will be added to your payroll."

"It was Sophia's idea," Leona said. Bonuses would pay for Thea's education or living expenses.

"Because you're a team, you shall both receive the compensation. Continue the good work." The screen flickered onto the six-paneled display vids. The volume reverted to default, filling the room with grunts and groans.

"Bonus?" Soph leaped to her feet to dance and bounce about the room. She paused when she reached Leona, then threw her arms around her. "Thanks for trying to give me the accolades."

Leona managed an awkward shrug. "I don't need the tokens. Thea does."

Soph giggled and stepped back, wiping her damp cheeks with trembling fingers. "Might be a good idea to give my sister a call anyway."

Leona slumped against the wall after Soph left the workshop. John hadn't said anything about their painting. Would he at a later stage? She hoped not. But he didn't strike her as a vindictive man, nor did he gain anything by mentioning it.

"Leona?"

She yelped, then sighed, recognizing Aaro's husky voice a second after her heartbeat thumped out of control. "Aaro," she said, offering him a smile.

"You alone?" He leaned back from where he filled the doorway, no doubt checking for Soph.

"I am."

He stepped into the workshop and swiped his wrist over the access pad. The door clicked shut, thunking as the deadbolt sank home. She straightened then pushed off to face him. He circled the table, tossing a glance at his painting resting on top. His strides were forceful, long, and eager. His eyes narrowed, and his intense focus was on her.

Butterflies fluttered in her stomach, swirled, then dove, pummeling her core until liquid heat exploded, traveling outward in waves. *Wow. What a man.*

"I need to talk to you," he said, stopping an inch from his chest touching hers.

"Oh?" she said, her voice barely above a rasp.

"Aye... I mean, yes." His nostrils flared, and he trembled. "Why are you aroused?"

She blinked at him, torn between hiding her burning cheeks or meeting his gaze head-on.

He groaned and layered his body over hers, pinning her against the wall. His lips on her neck, along her jaw, then across her mouth emboldened her. She clung to him, wrapping one leg around his hip. Something incredibly hard rubbed against her sex.

"Maker," he whispered, gripping her broken overalls and shoving them down. He hoisted her up high with his hands gripping her ass.

In black panties, she wiggled, trying to get him to bring her down. The ceiling touched her head, so she threw out a hand, hoping to grab ahold of something. "Aaro," she managed, but it came out like a moan.

Cool air brushed across her sex a second later as her panties flaked off her. He'd ripped them off to run his tongue across her clit. She cried out, struggling to not fall while an overwhelming heat swamped her core. His tongue mastery was on another level. A mewl lodged in her throat when he juggled her to dip his thumb into her channel. The double assault was beyond her ability to handle, and she screamed, splintering into a thousand fireworks and flares. Her vision blurred while her heartbeat bombarded her ears. Her clit throbbed, greedy for more.

He lowered her, sliding her down the wall until she slid onto his cock. She looped her arms around his neck and gripped him close. As he pounded into her, he pressed his open mouth to her neck. She shuddered when he licked across her pulse while his denit rubbed along her G-spot. Another orgasm burst through her, trembling her knees where they gripped his torso. She arched and rode the ripples, relishing each rise and fall of explosive joy.

"*Thamani*," and "*ensa ra ensa*" spilled from his lips. The endearments swelled her heart and pressed tears behind her eyes.

"Aaro," she said, wishing she could call him something else that wouldn't sound trite. Sweetheart, honey, babe couldn't convey what he invoked in her.

Instead of roaring when he orgasmed, he grunted with each thrust, his gaze locked on hers. Emotion swirled in their depths, something unsaid. Hope burst like a supernova, filling every inch of her soul, and that warm ribbon unfurled, touching the far reaches of her heart.

Could he be falling in love with her? Was that what was bothering him?

Calling herself all kinds of a fool, she tried to swat down that hope. She wasn't his soulmate. And loving him would only bring her pain. They had Kulai, then Etteria, before the long trip back to Callisto. She still had time with him.

He didn't pull out but stepped back, his arms around her keeping her crushed against his chest. "Not what I came here to say." He chuckled.

"I'm not complaining," she said while burying her face in the curve of his neck. Damn, he smelled so good. His cinnamon cologne somehow reminded her of Christmas and happier times spent with family.

"Tonight, *minus susa*," he said as he withdrew and set her on her feet. He righted her uniform with her torn panties in his large hand. One tap of his pants and his erect cock disappeared from sight. *What a pity.*

She stared after him, her mind tormented by the reason behind his visit. Quickies weren't to be disregarded. She'd loved it and the way he gazed into her eyes as if she was the most precious 'female' in the universe. Still, what had he meant to tell her?

Tonight? Yes, she'd find out what was going on later. If he didn't distract her again.

FULFILLING HIS VISION HADN'T been Aaro's intention when he'd found Leona alone. But her uniform, her hair in a high tail, and the way she'd leaned against the wall had reminded him of the images that had bombarded him mid-Ethera strike. With his painting on the table, against the wall had been his only option.

Loving Leona came with such surprises. No matter where or how they made love, she was exquisite. And the *Ethera* expanding between them gave him much hope.

Now he would have to tell her the truth over dinner. It was his turn to visit her quarters. He'd have preferred to wait for her, needing time to gather his thoughts and find the right words.

When he entered her quarters, the aroma of pizza greeted him. His painting leaned against the wall, a miniature beside it. One wall had newly mounted shelves upon which sat the *zeeda* blossom Prince Balllio had given her. She hadn't understood how precious such a gift was. Maloidian ambassadors would be sent to Earth to forge a human-Maloidian treaty. A *lumnari* stone sat beside the *zeeda*, giving off a warm glow.

She wore a dress that clung to her shoulders with thin straps and fell to her bare toes. The fabric hugged her curves as she moved. She hummed a birdsong and swung her backside in a swirl. Her hair cascaded around her, falling in shining waves.

She is beautiful.

He'd never get tired of looking at her.

"*Ensa.*" He came up behind her, slid his hands along her hips, and cupped her belly.

She placed the plates on the counter and wrapped her arms over his. "How was your day?"

"Perfect with you near," he whispered then snatched a quick kiss.

Her cheeks bloomed a lovely coral color, then she gestured to the table. "Let's eat. I assume you want to go over what to expect on Kulai tomorrow?"

"Yes, among other things." He settled into a comfy and stared at the cherry soda she placed before him. She knew him well.

"I can't tell you how starving I am. My appetite's exploded." She laughed as she tore off two slices of pizza to dump on her plate. "I'm sorry it's pizza again, but I've been having this odd craving." She shook her head. "Anyway, I've read the archives on Kulai, what type of planet it is, what kind of weather, but, Aaro, after a while, all that information just blurs."

He chuckled. "It is better to see and learn than to read and guess."

"True," she said around a mouthful.

He bit into his piece and hummed. "I like this one more."

"It's meatier," she said while licking her thumb. "So, tomorrow, first thing in the morning?"

"Yes, for a short trip to the Kulaian Council. Since they do not interest themselves in off-worlders, the Tokauri chieftains should not be present. They can make things...difficult."

"What? Why?" She rested her elbow on the table with a pizza slice draping over her hand.

"They have antiquated ideas on females and their place in their world."

"Oh, I remember this part. There are no girl Tokauri. Their genetics prohibit the birth of that gender. Did the Durn interfere here as well?"

"No, it is only the Tokauri who suffer so. The Kulaians have no such limitations."

"Well, it's like Etteria where only boys are born. And to have children, they kidnap women for that specific purpose. Once they're impregnated, they return the women to their families, who, like trained dogs, deliver the day-old babies to the Tokauri tribes. To keep a boy will start a war with all the tribes combined." She harrumphed. "I must say, this pissed me off. It's barbaric; that's what it is."

"Regardless, we do not wish to draw their attention to you, Leona. Because you are female, they might consider you property."

She squeaked then gulped her drink—a milky beverage that had an intriguing aroma. "And not the dolls?"

"They will not find your sex-cybs interesting for they cannot bear sons." Aaro grimaced. "Kulai shouldn't even be on the list. It is far too dangerous a place for any female, no matter the species. We can still cancel this delivery."

"I doubt John knew about the Tokauri, after all, the Kulaians are peaceful. And besides, you said it yourself, the chance of seeing the chieftains is slim. As much as I want this to end, Aaro, I agreed to this mission. Dad made me a woman of my word." She picked at the cheese, gathering it together before popping it into her mouth.

He rolled his shoulders. By Etterian law and as her *Eth*, he could refuse to put her in harm's way. But he doubted she'd change her mind even knowing she was his *Dar Eth*. He took a long pull from his cold soda. "The council is easily discerned. Their skin has paled, become grayer and less...silver."

"Silver?" She widened her beautiful eyes.

He looked away, needing to break their allure. "The Tokauri adhere to the old ways and, as such, are more silver. Each chieftain, no matter what garments they wear, sports a thick necklace of gold and precious stones. The color of the center stone denotes their tribe. The Kulaians refrain from jewelry of any kind. To them, it means devotion to the archaic ways."

"Ah, so there's a rift between the Kulaians and the tribes?"

"Yes. I share their differences so that you are not deceived. As usual, I will be at your side." He cradled his soda and watched her eat another slice.

"You're not hungry?" She frowned.

"Not this night." What could he say? That his stomach was a twisted, roiling knot?

She stilled, placed the unfinished pizza on the table, and rubbed her fingers with a paper square. "What's wrong, Aaro? You haven't been yourself since Maloid." She gestured between them. "Do you want to end this?"

His breath hitched, and a shudder tore through him. "No, never."

"Oh," she whispered. "Are you angry with me then? Or has work been hard on you?" She clasped his hand and squeezed. "You know you can tell me anything, right?"

Could he? Would she not just leave him for his deception? Trust was hard to restore once lost.

She burped, then cupped her hand over her mouth. "Sorry," she mumbled. Her face flushed red, and she bolted for the cleansing room.

"You are not well," he growled as he hurried after her. What food she'd eaten, she purged.

He kneeled on the floor beside her and drew her hair to the side.

"I think I'm lactose intolerant," she mumbled between gags.

"Lactose?" The O.D.I. hurried to update him. How was this possible? How could the body reject a known food substance after years of consumption? It made no sense. He raised his chin to the ceiling and said, "Emergency. Pilot Saan, send Medic Flad to Lady Leona's quarters."

"Acknowledged, Sub-Commander."

Aaro returned his attention to his *Dar Eth*. That she suffered so burned his chest like hot shards of metal skewering his flesh. No, whatever she needed to heal, he'd get it for her. She was his joy, his future, and he wanted her to live a long and contented life.

"I don't need Flad," she mumbled as she wiped her mouth across the back of her wrist.

"Please, *ensa*, for my peace of mind."

She slumped and curled into him. "Okay. But whatever is wrong, he tells me first."

Aaro jerked back. "Why?"

"It's called patient-doctor confidentiality."

He blinked, disbelieving what the O.D.I. told him. As someone in medical, Flad could hide information from his commanding officer? "I am his sub-commander. He *must* obey the chain of command."

"Then don't ask him to break his oath to me." She pushed out of Aaro's embrace and clambered to her feet. Her face paled, but she steadied herself with a hand on the wall, before leaning over the basin to gargle. She straightened and met his gaze in the mirror. "It's my body, Aaro. I decide when, how, or if I tell you."

He scowled, not liking this one bit.

She splayed her fingers across his right pec and dipped to meet his gaze. "If whatever I have endangers anyone else on this battleship, or if it's a matter of life or death, then Flad can tell you."

He cupped her hand, pinning it in place. "This does not please me, *ensa*, but I suppose I can allow it."

"Good, anything wrong with me, especially if it's my womanly bits, isn't something I'm comfortable sharing."

He forced a smile, but the reflection showed it as unnatural. "Fair enough."

"What is the matter?" Flad called from the common room.

"Aaro?" She arched a brow and nudged her chin at the front door. "Give me and Flad some privacy, please. I need to explain to him the purpose of patient confidentiality."

Aaro gritted his teeth. He was being banished? Squaring his shoulders, he strode past Flad. "Then I bid you good night." No way would he stay around when neither would tell him what was wrong with her. He'd have to trust Flad to do everything Etterian possible to heal her.

When the door closed on his backside, he roared, venting his fury. No one had ever mentioned how difficult it would be to deal with a *Dar Eth*. Alodon's balls, he was finding out the hard way.

Chapter Twenty-Three

Chasing Aaro out had felt like kicking a puppy. Leona winced, shifted, then rolled onto her side, careful not to harm...the baby. Her mind reeled from that bit of information, which she'd only gotten *after* she'd argued with Flad about not sharing her medical details with the entire universe. He'd scanned her, then beamed like a proud grandfather.

"You are pregnant. That is your term for it, yes?" His voice was hoarse and thick with emotion.

She'd stumbled back and sank into the chair. "What?" she'd whispered. "But I have a birth control implant."

"Which is untested against Etterian sperm."

She shook her head. "The implant stops the creation of eggs by modulating—"

"Your hormones, yes. But Etterian sperm releases a chemical that counters that."

"Oh," she mumbled. *Shit*. "I'm pregnant?"

"I am delighted for you and Aaro, Leona."

"Don't you dare tell him, Flad." She leaped to her feet and gripped her hips. "I'll tell him as is my right. It's…good news." She gaped then cupped her stomach which hadn't expanded yet. "It's a boy? Can you tell? Or is it too soon?" She bounced on her toes while ignoring the tears spilling free.

"It is a female." Tears glimmered in Flad's eyes. If he cried, she'd join him. They'd be a sobbing mess together.

"But…Aaro said girls are rare."

"Not when an Etterian and human have mated." Flad grinned. "The Maker has blessed us indeed."

Mated? What an odd way to say they'd had sex…a lot.

"When will you share this with Aaro?" Flad demanded, shoving his medical device into his military pants pocket.

"Before we reach Etteria. He'll want to tell his family."

"Very well." Flad headed for the door. "I shall scan you weekly for the archives and for safety."

"Thank you," she said, then on impulse hugged the man, who stiffened like a slab of marble.

After the flustered medic left her alone, she paced, too excited to sit or sleep. A girl. Dad would have been so happy. She sniffed. And she would have to tell Soph too, maybe even John. How would this impact her time at Cyb Ent? Was her career over before it had begun? Would Aaro fight over custody? Or would he offer to marry her to 'make her an honorable woman?'

Her heart swelled even as pain squeezed it like a fist had broken through her ribcage. Oh, how she loved him. But if he chose to stay near her because of the baby and not because he loved her, where was her happiness in that?

He'd left as she'd asked; that act in itself had shredded her emotions when she'd wanted to call him back, to keep him near. Her fear had been something personal was wrong with her like a bladder or yeast infection.

But a baby girl?

Tears spilled, dripping off her chin and onto her knees she clasped against her chest. Oh, she was a fool. She knew better than to hope for fairy tales of princes and weddings. Independent her had run from any chance of that, especially when her suitors were of her mom's choosing. But here, Leona had chosen Aaro, let him into her bed and heart, all while acting as if what they had was fleeting with no consequences.

She giggled, a little hysterical. "Not to worry, little one. I want you no matter what."

Patting her belly, she prepared for bed. Reaching out to Aaro plagued her, but she set the urge aside. Tonight, it was just her and her daughter.

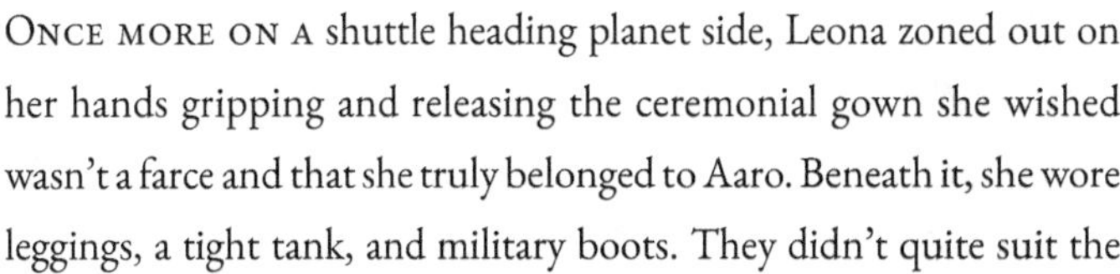

ONCE MORE ON A shuttle heading planet side, Leona zoned out on her hands gripping and releasing the ceremonial gown she wished wasn't a farce and that she truly belonged to Aaro. Beneath it, she wore leggings, a tight tank, and military boots. They didn't quite suit the kimono-style garment, but she wasn't sure what surprises Kulai would bring.

When Aaro had strapped her in, she'd wanted to tell him about their daughter. She had no doubt this news would make him ecstatic. Even more so because it was a girl. The gender shouldn't matter, though. When she did tell him, she'd leave off that little bit until the end.

She cupped her stomach and gazed ahead, not once glancing at the front vids to see what Kulai looked like. It didn't matter. Finishing this journey was all she ached to do.

Last night, before bedtime, she'd succumbed and ordered a pair of booties from the replicator. She'd tucked them inside the bedroom closet. Leaving them lying around before she told Aaro was in poor taste. Yet she'd opened that closet this morning, more times than she could remember. Breakfast had been healthier than she'd eaten in years. Coffee was swapped for herbal tea, which made her gag, so she opted for a diluted fruit juice.

Pregnancy explained the weird cravings, hunger, and exhaustion. And with her birth control implant, she'd never know if she missed a period. Well, no more. Flad had deactivated the device for the baby's safety.

"*Ensa*?" Aaro clasped her hand to pin to his thigh. "Are you well?"

"Oh, so well, Aaro. Flad gave me a clean bill of health." She flashed him a smile. "I've never been this...well."

He slumped with relief.

A twinge of guilt made her wince. She hadn't meant to worry him. "Sorry, I should've told you last night, but I went straight to sleep."

She leaned her temple on his upper bicep. "I meant to give you your painting, and the little one I did for your shelf."

"Tonight, *thamani*." He kissed the crown of her head.

The shuttle shuddered, no doubt breaching the atmosphere. The dolls stood against the wall, a crate at their feet. *Please, Lord, let this trip be uneventful.*

"Does the council have a form of address?" she asked, twisting to face Aaro.

"Councilmale and if you know his name, add it to the end."

"Simple enough to remember," she said. "Where are we going? A visitor station?"

"In a way. Their great hall is where they gather to discuss matters of Kulaian importance."

"I hope we can be in and out with little for them to want to talk about."

"Agreed." Aaro leaned in to whisper, "Your scent has changed. Why is that, *thamani*?"

She grimaced. After the vanilla incident, she'd stopped using any deodorant. Not once had Aaro mentioned she stank. Had he kept quiet to be polite? "How do I smell normally?"

"Addictive, sweet, and exotic, like I described to you before. Now your scent is sharper, stronger, and more intoxicating." He sucked in a breath so hard it flared his nostrils. "I love it, *ensa*," he rasped in his drenched-in-sex voice.

"Um, thanks," she mumbled. His olfactive skills were off the charts, but she doubted he was an anomaly.

The door opening snapped her from her thoughts. Distracted, she hadn't noticed Krist landing the shuttle. Mustard yellow to olive green plants reached up to the skies. They looked like banana trees left to grow unhindered. The color of the rocks and soil ranged between ochre and butterscotch, the latter making her mouth salivate. Chunks of sand looked like fudge crumbs. The sky was an exquisite gray-green, the roiling clouds in turquoise.

"So pretty," she whispered.

Along a stoned path to a domed building peeking through the banana leaves waited three men. Before facing them, she ducked inside the shuttle to collect the dolls. Maybe she could hand them over to these men and leave. She'd be here for five minutes, tops.

As per protocol, Aaro's soldiers circled the shuttle, their gazes outward. Swords gleamed down their backs, their hands inches from their guns. She strode down the ramp, her dolls on her tail. Aaro would bring the box, acting more like an assistant than her lover-cum-sub-commander.

Only then did she focus on the Kulaians waiting for her. Their skin was a pale iron color, their eyes a matching gray, startling against white hair slicked to their scalps. Their button-up shirts to their knees weren't unusual. But their bell-bottom pants didn't hide their two-toed feet—one human-like big toe alongside a toe the width of their feet. She pursed her lips, trying not to react to this oddity.

"Welcome to Kulai. I am Councilmale Naio," the middle Kulaian said in galactic. "I must say this is unprecedented. The G.C. and the Kulaian Council decreed that no technology shall be introduced without approval."

Leona stiffened. *Wait? What? Didn't John sell them two dolls? A little heads-up would've been nice.* A glance at Aaro showed him just as stunned. When he said nothing, she closed her eyes for a second to gather her thoughts.

"I understand, Councilmale Naio. Which is why I've brought two for you to sample." She gestured to the sex-cybs behind her, drawing the man's gaze to them. "If their presence offends you, Councilmale, I'm more than prepared to take them somewhere else." Like she'd hoped, they could be returning to the *Valiant* within minutes.

"These are the devices?" Naio hesitated, then strode around Leona. "I thought these were your companions." He raised a hand then halted. "May I?"

"Of course," Leona said, bowing her head.

What followed was akin to a viewing at a horse auction. The dolls were stroked, prodded, squeezed, and their mouths pried open. Naio sniffed a doll then stepped back. "She only has two breasts. Is she defective?"

Leona blinked then swallowed a giggle. "They are modeled after humans, Councilmale."

His frown was ferocious, furrowing his brow and narrowing his eyes. What chased away her fear was his bushy eyebrows wiggling like massive caterpillars. "I am not familiar with that species."

"I'm human." She swept a hand down her front.

He stared at her, and inch by inch, his eyebrows rose until they touched his hairline. "I see the resemblance. How silly of me not to have noticed."

She bristled. *Enough with the comparison. I'm not a doll.* "I'm certain their creator could add as many breasts as you want," she gritted out.

Naio gaped. "That is possible?" He ducked his head to confer with his men.

She tried not to tap her foot as time passed. Instead, she studied the foliage, the strange blue blossoms the size of her thumb nail, the odd squeaks and calls of what she had to assume were birds, and the peeking in and out of two moons behind the clouds. Only one sun warmed this world. She closed her eyes and relished the rays on her face.

"We shall keep this gift, and our thanks to their creator for their generosity."

"Excellent." She grinned. "I will need to hand them over to a technician or someone who can care for them."

"Why? Are they like pets or children?"

"No, but they can break, and they do require rest between...sexual sessions."

Naio took a step back. "Sexual? I assumed they served as slaves. Can they bare offspring?"

"No," she said.

More fervent whispering followed.

"Indeed, these gifts are well received," the councilmale said.

"Excellent." She pointed to her feet, her gaze on Aaro. He placed the crate there and fell into position behind her. "Here are extra parts *should* you need them." She whipped out the tablet. "All the information to maintain them is on here."

Naio didn't attempt to take the tablet, so she placed it on top of the crate.

"If that will be—"

"Why was I not invited to this council meeting, Naio?" A man the size of a gorilla stepped from behind the trees to the left of the clearing.

Holy cow.

He was bare-chested in dark harem pants that cinched in at his narrow waist and sculpted calves. Handmade shoes, looking more like masculine ballet slippers, hugged his feet. Underneath a thick gold chain, he wore no shirt to hide his ripped chest, his dark gray nipples striking against his silvery-gray skin. He was like that all over, except for his blinding white hair that fell down his back.

Shit, are his eyes molten silver? They're stunning.

The semi-naked man roared something that raised the hairs at the back of her neck. Aaro stepped in front of her, blocking her view. She dug her fingers between Aaro's armor and belt, needing his warm skin to keep her from running.

"Do not be rude to our guests, Jazu. Kulaian, please," Naio said.

"Why was I not invited, Naio? As the nearest chieftain, I have a right to be here."

"I intended to chase them away if you must know." Naio scooped up a lock of a doll's hair and tested the texture against his cheek. "Come, see for yourself why I changed my mind."

Jazu crossed the clearing, approaching with long, forceful strides. When he paused beside Aaro, he peered down at him from an additional foot of height. This close, a sliver of ice trickled down her spine. This man was huge and glowered like an instinct Grizzly.

"Etterian," he spat, his upper lip curling.

In a blink, he grabbed Leona by the elbow and crushed her against his chest.

She cried out and threw up her hands while his body-odor-meets-something-organic assaulted her nose.

"She is my *Dar Eth*. How dare you touch her," Aaro said in a low voice, made more intimidating by the anger clipping each word. His men had drawn their guns, half-raised in warning.

"*Dar Eth*? Your *kassu*?" Jazu sniffed her like he had all the time in the world.

Since her O.D.I. didn't translate that word, she had to assume it was Tokauri. Regardless, she understood its meaning.

So did Aaro when he crowded the chieftain. "Yes. Now release her."

"And what if I choose not to?"

Naio tried to intervene, grabbing the chieftain's shoulder. "Jazu—"

"By touching my female, you start a war with Etteria. You cannot be so foolish as to chance it." Aaro rested his hand on his gun, his intention clear.

"Attack me and you risk harming her." Jazu smirked, twitching a faded scar that ran from his eyebrow to dimple his cheek.

"She can be healed. You, I would leave to die."

"Jazu, release the female," Naio snapped.

In an instant, she was free. Aaro snatched her and shoved her behind him.

"You would go to war over a female?" Jazu studied Leona again. Then he drew in a deep inhale. "Ah, her scent is rich, promising." He flicked a dismissive hand at the dolls. "They smell...wrong."

"Regardless, they will serve as *pagsu* do," Naio said. "Bring the gifts. The council will be most interested. Jazu, since you are here, join us."

The three councilmales headed up the path to the domed building in deep greens and mustard yellows, no doubt made from natural resources found locally. Aaro squeezed her hand then released it to pick up the crate. She eyed the chieftain, not sure the situation had been resolved. When Aaro glanced at her, she commanded the dolls to follow her.

The Etterian soldiers circled back to the shuttle, and in all this activity, Jazu didn't move. Every sense told her where he stood, quiet, like he waited for something. By the time more silver-gray men stepped from the foliage, it was too late for anyone to react.

Aaro crumbled. The crate fell and landed at his side with a thud.

Krist bolted into the shuttle, the engines coming on a moment later.

Ranh lunged for, his fingers brushing her arm.

She'd stood there, frozen, her gaze fixed on Aaro. With a cry, she knelt beside him, only then spotting what had knocked him out. "Someone, give me a med thingy," she called, pulling a dart from his neck. "What the hell?" she muttered, staring at the befeathered needle.

When a hand clamped on her shoulder, she thought it was Ranh. But up she went, hoisted off the ground with ease. Her vision spun then filled with the chaos in the clearing as Jazu sprinted for cover. The dolls raced after her, narrowly dodging silver men in the process.

"Goodnight," Leona screamed, not wanting them damaged.

Since Jazu pinned her to his shoulder in a firm hold, she wasn't worried about the baby. But with every step he took, Aaro's sprawled body got smaller. She pummeled Jazu's broad back. Had the asshole killed Aaro? Was he dead? Her heart cracked and splintered. Darkness seeped out from the depths of despair. Uncaring as thick and wide banana leaves smacked her, she wiggled to beat Jazu with her fists and elbows, as Aaro had taught her.

Jazu grunted and almost dropped her. He slammed her across his shoulder, knocking the wind out of her. Gasping, she stopped fighting to suck in great gulps of air. She clung to the silver gorilla, accepting that she was well and truly kidnapped. For now, she would go quietly and at the first opportunity, she'd make her escape. All while praying Aaro came for her...

If he lived.

Chapter Twenty-Four

"Sub-Commander Aaro, how do you feel?" Flad peered into Aaro's eyes then blinded him with the med-gun.

"Fine," he croaked and pushed to a sitting position. Agony pulsed outward. He cupped his neck and triggered a fresh sweep of fire.

"Good. Now, get up. We need to find Leona."

Aaro stiffened. "What...do you mean?" Visions of a Tokauri chieftain flashed across his mind, and he leaped to his feet, already reaching for his greatsword.

"I have her location." Ranh grabbed Aaro's wrist and swiped across it. A buzz ran up his arm, and a holographic marker popped up.

"For this slight, mete out what justice you see fit, Sub-Commander Aaro." Naio clasped his hands in front of his chest and bowed. "We, the Kulaian Council, do not want a war with Etteria."

"Your offer is accepted, Councilmale Naio," Aaro gritted out. His jaw clenched shut. A Tokauri chieftain had his Leona. That could mean only one thing; the winter storms were near, and they needed females for procreation.

"I shall trail you with the shuttle," Krist said. "All the warriors will travel with you."

"It is quicker if we fly there," Aaro snarled.

Krist frowned. "The jungle's too dense to land."

"Alodon's balls." Aaro stiffened further, his body now taut enough to ache. "Pilot Saan," he said into his O.D.I.

"Yes, Sub-Commander Aaro."

He focused on his wrist, trying to calm his breathing. "Can you track Lady Leona's O.D.I.?"

"One moment... Yes."

"Port us all to her now." Aaro gripped Flad's shoulder, and in a ripple, his males touched each other seconds before they ported.

"No," Jazu yelled when they appeared in front of him with Leona draped over his shoulder. "I claim her as mine."

A scan confirmed a dense jungle surrounded them with hip-high plants obscuring their feet. It would've taken hours to hack a path through it. Muted light sifted through the thick canopy, toying with the shadows between the tree trunks.

"Why should I accept your claim when you did not acknowledge mine?" Aaro glowered. "She is *my Dar Eth*, Jazu. You know damn well what that means. You forget the old ways, Chieftain."

"Aaro?" Leona called, hope and joy in her voice. She started to struggle, punching the Tokauri in the head and on his back, just as Aaro had taught her.

"You can have one of the others," Jazu growled as he jiggled her.

"*Dar Eth*," Aaro thundered, raising the tip of his greatsword to tap the underside of Jazu's chin. His Tokauri males emerged from the shadows and shifted closer. So did Aaro's warriors. "I can kill you where you stand. Etteria, the Kulaian Council, and the G.C. will find your death justified." Aaro didn't glance at Jazu's tribe. "Your males will be unfortunate casualties. What a pity."

Jazu glanced at his males. He lowered Leona, letting her dart to Aaro, who threw out an arm to catch and tug her behind him.

"Warrior to warrior, I challenge you for her." Jazu unsheathed his twin *sulacs*. The dagger blades gleamed silver in the meager forest lighting.

Aaro smirked. They weren't Maloidian steel, unlike his greatsword. "She *is* a prize but not intended for you."

"Any female on Kulai can serve Tokauri." Jazu thumped his chest. "Scared you will die at my hands?"

"No, Aaro, don't fight him. Let's just leave this hellhole." She pressed herself to his back and kissed his shoulder blade. "Please. I can't bear you getting hurt."

"Ranh," Aaro called. Plants rustled, and Leona cried out when Ranh dragged her to the side.

"A challenge has been made. A warrior must accept, Lady Leona. It is the code." Ranh whispered.

"Well, it's stupid," she snapped.

Jazu struck first, swinging his daggers so fast Aaro barely managed to leap away. Matching stings registered where Jazu had drawn blood. Leona gasped, so Aaro drowned her out, not needing her to distract him.

He sidled to the left, then to the right, testing Jazu's reaction time. His right side was the slowest, no doubt caused by whatever had scarred his face. Aaro feinted then struck from the right, landing a firm punch to Jazu's jaw. The male stumbled, then caught himself. He wiped dark gray blood from his split lip.

"You aim to toy with me, thinking it will return some of your wounded pride. After all, a chieftain and not a male from your precious Etteria stole your female from under your nose."

Roaring, Aaro swung his greatsword and sliced through the *sulacs* Jazu had crisscrossed in front of him. As expected, the blades were no match against Maloidian steel. The tips landed at Jazu's feet.

The male gaped, then gurgled. Blood trickled from the thin slice across his neck. He dropped his *sulacs* and fell to his knees. With his fingers, he tried to stop the bleeding.

Aaro glanced at the closest Tokauri male. "I can heal him—"

"That is not our way," the younger male said. "Our chieftain challenged you to a fight to the death, Etterian. To lose one's life this way is noble." He crossed to Aaro and collected the discarded *sulacs*. On his flattened palms, he offered both to Aaro. "As is honorable, you will accept Chieftain Jazu's prized *ukog sulacs*."

Aaro sheathed his greatsword and palmed the bone-handled daggers. "Thank you."

The male bowed and gathered Jazu's lifeless body. Once he joined the tribe, they faded into the foliage.

Leona shook off Ranh's hold and ran to Aaro, throwing her arms around him. "That was a thousand kinds of stupid. Flad, heal him...please." She crushed Aaro in a hug and buried her nose in the curve of his neck.

He chuckled and hugged her back, relishing her softness he'd been so close to losing. "Shall we go home, *ensa*?"

"No, I can't. I have to hand over the dolls to someone. Besides, shouldn't we tell the councilmales we killed a chieftain?" She leaned back to meet his gaze.

"I am sure the tribe's new chieftain will inform them, but we can, just to ensure we leave on a good note." He tried to reach around her to tap his wrist.

Flad huffed, activated his O.D.I., and said, "Pilot Saan, please return us to the shuttle."

As per the previous port, his males gripped each other's shoulders. Since Aaro held Leona, Flad touched her back. When they materialized on the stone path, Councilmale Naio was ordering his males around, waving his arms in flamboyant gestures.

He gawked at Aaro, then hurried across to him. "Where is Chieftain Jazu?"

"Dead," Aaro said. That male's death had been too swift to appease the anger that still lingered.

Leona slapped his upper arm. "Chieftain Jazu challenged Sub-Commander Aaro to a death match."

"*Mugbu*," Naio gasped, his cheeks darkening. "It is their way, and honor dictates that you accept." He clasped his hands at his chest and bowed. "I, on behalf of the Kulaian Council, do not hold you accountable." He faced Leona. "May we now take our gifts?"

Leona gasped and whipped around. Her shoulders sagged at finding her sex-cybs where she'd halted them. "Of course, Councilmale Naio. I'll need a technician." She frowned. "Didn't I mention that?"

Naio raised his hand. A skinny youngin rushed toward him. "This is Heelu."

Relief summoned Leona's smile. "They don't need much maintenance, and everything you need to know is on the tablet in the crate holding spare parts. If you have any questions, I'm a message away."

The male bowed and hurried to the crate.

She trailed him. "For now, you can control them using these commands…" She activated her O.D.I. and offered her wrist, asking him if she could scan it across his.

He blinked at her then at her arm.

Her gaze flicked to Aaro. "He doesn't have an O.D.I?"

Aaro laughed. "Seems so."

She squared her shoulders. "Heelu, to get them to follow you, say 'direction.' All the other commands are on the tablet. 'Showtime' for when they need to perform…sexually. 'Curtain call' when it's time to end their sessions. And 'goodnight' to put them into power saving mode."

She waited until the youngin repeated the commands. Hesitating, she left him and strode to Naio. Clasping her hands in front of her chest, she bowed her head. "It was a pleasure meeting you, Councilmale Naio. My apologies for the…incident." She hid her grimace at having to apologize for something she hadn't instigated. Diplomacy was what it was.

The irritable male beamed.

Aaro cupped Leona's elbow and ushered her onto the *kuta*. Only once he had her strapped in and Krist launched the shuttle toward the *Valiant* did Aaro release a long breath.

"Not how I'd hoped this would go," she said.

"Same." He gazed at her upturned face, taking the time to memorize every magnificent inch of her. "I will need to comm my king. It would not be wise for him to learn of this through non-Etterian buzz."

She hummed, closed her eyes, and settled back.

He captured her hand and pinned it to his thigh. The heat of her through his military pants went a long way to calm his erratic heartbeats. He could have lost her.

"I suggest a full scan when we return, Sub-Commander," Flad said in a low voice, his gaze on Leona. "We need to make sure whatever poison was in that dart has left your body."

Aaro frowned. "I thought the med-gun—"

"It woke you, but I did not check if the drug was eradicated."

Aaro wanted to groan like a petulant *damu*, instead, he asked, "Can you not do it now?"

Flad glowered. "You know the limitations of a med-gun."

"I feel fine, Flad."

This went nowhere in minimizing Flad's stare.

"I will visit you after I have spoken to the king." When all Aaro wanted was to hold his *Dar Eth*.

After they docked in the bay and while the doors still sealed, he ushered Leona to the comm room. "Comm King Xeus, Pilot Saan," Aaro commanded. A second later, the forevids flickered to Kanzo's face. "Greetings, Adviser Kanzo. Is the king available?"

Kanzo's good humor faded at Aaro's serious tone. "Is this urgent, Sub-Commander Aaro?"

"We have just returned from Kulai."

Kanzo winced and tapped on his O.D.I. "The king will be a moment."

Aaro waited.

"Sub-Commander Aaro, what seems to be the matter?" King Xeus filled the display vids, his ice-blue eyes almost made Aaro smile.

"Chieftain Jazu attempted to steal my Leona. Of course, the male is dead. Councilmale Naio has absolved me and Etteria of this. I simply wish to keep you informed."

"Is your *Dar Eth* well?" Xeus asked, shifting his gaze to Leona hovering behind Aaro. "Milady?"

She hesitated, sliding glances between the vids and Aaro. "The chieftain didn't hurt me, your majesty," she said, her voice cold.

Aaro scowled at the anger in her eyes. *What is this?*

"Thank you for notifying me," King Xeus said. "I will liaise with Naio to ensure all is well between Kulai and Etteria."

"We need to inform the G.C. as well."

Kanzo received a glare for that intrusion, but when Xeus faced the screen, no emotion flickered in his eyes except joy. "Congratulations on finding your *Dar Eth*. Welcome to the Etterian family, Lady Leona. I insist you dine with me when you arrive in Issneen."

The forevids returned to the surrounding space and a last glimpse of Kulai.

"Aaro, what did he mean? *Dar Eth*?"

Chapter Twenty-Five

Aaro flinched. "I can explain, *ensa*." He grabbed Leona by the elbow, then ushered her out of the comm room.

"You've been using me?" she asked, trailing him. "Or are we lying to your king now?"

He closed his eyes against the pain in her voice. "Never. Just..." He stepped to the side to let males pass in the narrow passage. "Let us find somewhere private."

The moment he stepped onto the viewing deck, he spun and drew her into his arms. She struggled, but he held firm. "I did not know how to tell you, *thamani*."

"Tell me now," she demanded, her voice muffled where he pressed her face to his chest.

"You are my *Dar Eth*."

She squeaked, "What?" She pummeled his chest until he released her. Once free, she staggered back, but her gaze stayed fixed on him. "How do you know? Is it tied to the color of your eyes?" She stiffened. "No, tell me how long have you known?"

"From the day we met."

Her eyes widened, then narrowed as red flushed her cheeks. "You've lied—" She spun, giving him her back.

"How could I tell you that according to Etterian law, we are paired...um, married?"

She faced him, gaping. "We're *what*?"

"Paired. I hoped time spent together would deepen our affection, and it has."

"I told you why I ran away from Earth, Aaro, to steer my own life. If I wanted someone to decide my fate, I would've stayed with Bradley." She cupped her belly and sniffed. "I thought I knew you, could trust you, an honorable man. Now..." She met his gaze. "I don't know who you are."

The pain sliced through his chest like a greatsword through prey. He curled his fingers into fists and willed himself not to reach for her. She had it right. He'd known this would happen. Still, the agony was beyond compare.

"I understand," he croaked.

When she abandoned him, his world crumbled. The dormant void rose like a wave of black ichor, consuming him where Leona's light had once burned so brightly. He slid down the closest bulkhead, unable to quell the roaring in his ears.

He could do and say nothing to make her choose him. It had to be her decision. He'd known that, and yet fear had driven him to take her free will. Now, he'd never grow old with her. *Oh, what a fool I have been.*

Flad had tried to warn him. Danic too. Aaro wiped his face and stared at his damp fingers. "Ranh," he rasped into his O.D.I. "I relinquish command to you. Note it as such in the annals."

How Aaro reached his quarters he couldn't say. He snatched her garment off the shelf and curled on his bed with the thing clutched to his chest. Its hard edges dug into him, but he didn't care. He'd gambled and lost. She hadn't loved him as he'd hoped. Maybe she never would have.

Misery circled his thoughts, of a future without her.

Time ticked by as he relived every moment spent with her. Visions tormented him, of her returning to him, holding and kissing him. It was so real that the void's constant bombardment eased as if the darkness retreated from the blinding light Leona's presence created. Then he would reach for her, his hands finding nothing but air. He'd slump, and the cycle would start again: despair, longing, visions, and grief.

Someone pounded on his door. Flad visited him in his room. Words were spoken, slowed as if underwater. Medication was administered, and at last, Aaro succumbed to the bliss of darkness.

"How did the delivery go?" Soph asked as she leaned against the open doorway to Leona's cabin.

Leona growled, words tumbling up her throat and lodging there.

"Whoa." Soph threw up her hands. "What the hell happened?"

"Turns out," Leona gritted, "I'm Aaro's *wife*."

"Huh," Soph whispered in a that-makes-sense tone.

"That's all you can say? Like the ass hasn't been lying to me since we met?" Leona whipped back and forth, trying to ignore the growing darkness deep inside her. The warm fuzziness was somehow...gone.

"Well, you two act like a married couple, so it's not a long stretch of the imagination you could permanently be together-together. Why didn't he tell you?"

Tears stung behind Leona's eyes, but she willed them to stay away. "He said he didn't know how."

"Lame," Soph sang. "Wait, what do you mean wife? When did you say 'I do?'"

Leona's hysterical laughter thickened the lump in her throat. "Doesn't work like that, apparently. According to Etterian law, once paired, the marriage is official."

"Shit. Just like that." Soph sank into a chair while Leona paced. "What are you going to do?"

"I don't know, Soph. I love the idiot, but this?"

Soph hummed. "Come to think of it, whether he told you or not took away your ability to choose."

"Say again?" Leona frowned.

"Yup, this *Ethera* thing soulmates you, or so you said, right? And Aaro not telling you was his decision to make. Both times, your fate was decided for you. Either way, he stood to lose you."

Leona harrumphed. "Whose side are you on?"

"My godchild's?" Soph wiggled her brows. "When were you going to tell me about the baby? After your seventeenth pizza? Cravings, mood swings, exhaustion?" She ticked off on each finger. "I'm blonde but not blind."

Leona winced. "I found out yesterday. Was going to share the news today. Then the incident on Kulai and this. I have a right to be pissed."

"You do," Soph said. "And how long are you going to hide the baby from him?"

Leona scowled. "Hey, no fair."

Soph folded her arms across her chest. "You stand at the edge of a cliff. Do you leap toward a life of love, adoration, mindless sex, and children, or do you creep down the mountain to your safe and lonely hut?"

"Shit," Leona muttered. "Way to sum up my choices."

Her door chimed.

"That could be Aaro now, here to sweep you off your stubborn feet."

"Pushing it, Soph," Leona called and opened the door. "Flad?"

The older man dominated the doorway but made no

"Sub-Commander Aaro has resigned his post, so I came to you, Lady Leona."

She stiffened, chilled fear slithering down her spine. "What?" She *shouldn't* care. The man had lied to her for two months. What else didn't she know? "Is he sick?"

"It is as he feared. You have rejected him."

She glared at Flad. "He lied to me. What kind of a relationship can be built on distrust?"

Flad settled into a military stance as if he were at ease. It was so incongruent with the pleading note in his voice. "Did he tell you the void will return?"

"The void?" What the hell did that have to do with this? "I thought the *Ethera* eradicated it."

"Only if you, his light, remain in his life."

She stumbled to the side and sank into the closest chair. "It's back?" she whispered.

"Yes, and it is killing him. He is not even fighting it, Leona. I have removed the final traces of the Tokauri toxin then had to sedate him. There is nothing more I can do."

"Why didn't he tell me?"

"He wanted you to choose to stay with him not because of the *Ethera*, but because you love him." Flad grimaced. "I did not understand his motivations when he first revealed his deception. I do now. He feared you would reject him, and he expected to die for it."

Fire coursed through her veins. She was so furious that she could punch something. "Where is he?"

"In his quarters. As I said, I medicated him." Flad hesitated. "I can bring him out of it, but not if you mean to do him further harm."

"Me?" she screamed, her cheeks burning.

"Yes, save him if you love him."

"Argh," she cried out and, with Flad trailing her, stomped to Aaro's quarters.

Darkness met her entry, but she knew his home as well as her own and headed to his bedroom. A low light illuminated him sprawled on the bed, her panties clutched to his chest in a white-knuckled grip. Pain twisted his features. His breathing was ragged, and sweat coated his skin. *Shit, this Ethera thing is real?* She'd half-expected this to be a farce, an attempt to manipulate her.

As she stared at him, her anger splintered to reveal the hurt beneath. He'd lied to her, but that didn't mean he didn't love her. Every action, word, and look had proven his affection for her ran deep. And with their daughter on the way, he'd be even more protective. How could she stay away from him? Not when the *Ethera* blossomed inside her just standing in the same room as him. This was genuine, her love too.

"Wake him, Flad," she commanded and settled on the bed beside Aaro.

The medic held a device to Aaro's neck, a hiss followed, then he stepped back. "I will be outside should you need me."

Leona nodded, her gaze fixed on Aaro's fluttering eyelashes. When he settled his ice-blue gaze on her, her chest swelled, and heat unfurled in her stomach. Tears pressed at the backs of her eyes.

"How are you feeling?" she managed past the lump stinging her throat.

"Good," he mumbled.

She sighed. "Do you want to continue to lie to me, or do you want to try for honesty?"

He squeezed his eyes shut. "I am in agony. Never have I known such pain."

"I'm sorry," she said, not liking that he suffered, even due to his own stubbornness. "Are you up for a conversation?"

He sat up and rested her encased panties on her pillow. When he faced her, dread had darkened his eyes. "I am ready."

"I'm so angry with you I can't see straight." She winced and curled her bottom lip under the top one. "Sorry. Let me try again. I can't make informed decisions when you don't share all the facts. At the core of freedom are choices, Aaro. I choose to wake up late, to eat chocolate cake for breakfast, to love you." She clasped his hands then hugged him. His trembling ceased, and a deep sigh escaped him. "Oh, Aaro, why didn't you tell me?"

"I should have told you everything, *thamani*. This is my...penance." He buried his face in her hair, even as his ragged breathing eased. "I vow to never hide anything from you. Just...please...stay."

"For as long as you need, babe."

He grumbled at being called a child.

She chuckled and rubbed her nose across his right pec. "How about a shower, hm?" Not that he stank. His usual cinnamon scent had intensified into a deep musk.

His arms tightened. "No, if I lose sight of you—"

"I'll be in the bathroom with you."

He leaned back to cradle her face. "Is it truly you, Leona?" He offered a tremulous smile. "Am I not dreaming?" A frown knitted his brows. "Did you say you love me?" He shoved her back and clambered off the bed. "Be gone, you wicked tormentor." He staggered, gripping his temple as if his world spun.

"Dammit, Aaro. You're not dreaming. It's me." She snatched his hand and held it to her chest. "See. Real." Raising her face, she peered into his beloved ice-blue eyes. She filled her lungs with a deep breath. Her heart fluttered. Had she taken any longer to choose him, he might have died.

"*Thamani*?" He cupped her cheek, his touch infinitely tender.

Her heart melted. "Yes, Aaro."

"You love me?" His voice hitched on 'love.'

She swallowed and jumped off Soph's metaphorical cliff. "I do."

"Maker," he rasped and kissed her, his lips hot against hers. "I hoped," he whispered before kissing her again.

As soon as he broke away, she gathered her courage. She couldn't be furious with him when she withheld information as vitally important. "I have some news." She pulled away, but not out of his embrace.

He stiffened, fear darkening his neon eyes.

"I'm pregnant." She cupped his cheek. "I found out yesterday."

He paled, then sank onto his bed. "A *damu*?" He raised his glistening gaze to her. "We are having a son." He roared, leaped to his feet, and swept her into his arms. Around and around he spun her, laughing and crying as he gingerly held her against him.

Love bubbled over, and she cried with him. Once the tears had subsided, he hugged her as if he had no intention of letting her go. "Um, Aaro, my love, we're having a daughter."

The muscles under her fingers stiffened. He drew back an inch at a time. Shock contorted his eyes and mouth, his jaw slack. "Truly?"

She nodded.

Again, he held her, and she doubted he'd ever release her. "I never thought such happiness existed," he mumbled into her hair. "Thank you, *thamani*. I shall forever be truthful with you, *ensa ra ensa*. I am sorry for not being open with you. Can you forgive me, Leona?"

"I can and do. I understand why, Aaro, and I suppose, I would've run away at finding myself married the minute we met." She placed her palms on his temples to stare into his exquisite eyes. Offering him a wide smile, she whispered, "I love you, Aaro et Zaro."

His breath hitched, and he trembled. "And I you, Leona et Aaro."

She laughed. "I see. How about Aaro et Leona?"

"Whatever you wish, *thamani*." He kissed her and thoughts of names and plans fell to the wayside as he gathered her close to show her just how much he adored her.

Epilogue

A SPRAWLING RANCH-STYLE HOUSE wasn't what Leona had expected. Sure, the sky was pink... She giggled at that, but the white-stone building was picturesque against the blue-green grass of Etteria's farmlands. Aaro strode down the shuttle's ramp, his hand holding hers. She hurried to follow him, trying to match his long strides. A winding path in gray gravel met a solid-looking door. It opened and out ran a lithe woman with a thick braid trailing her.

Leona's stomach twisted as butterflies exploded outward. Her heart thundered in her ears, and her steps faltered. Would his family like her? She'd been tormented for weeks by this irrational fear. True, her relationship with her mother was her only benchmark, but she was adult enough to know not all mothers were the same.

"Oh, it is true," the woman gasped and crushed Leona in a hug. The scent of floral cinnamon swamped her. "I have a daughter." She sniffed.

Aaro chuckled. "Don't you mean *another* daughter?"

She released Leona to smack her son on the upper arm, then dabbed at her eyes with her silk sleeve.

"Mother, this is Leona."

"It is a pleasure to meet you," Leona said, then on impulse, squeezed her mother-in-law's hand.

"You are so pretty, and your pale skin is softer than an Eiltur's fur."

Leona glanced at Aaro, not sure how to respond to that. "Um, thank you. How would you like me to address you?"

The woman's dark blue eyes widened. "Mother or Idda." She stepped back and swept out her arm. "My home is yours. Zaro has gone hunting for fresh *kreso*, in celebration of your arrival and pairing."

Leona's stomach gurgled in eagerness. Pizza and *kreso* were the only foods her daughter craved.

"And Taro?" Aaro gestured with his thumb at the shuttle. "Leona insisted we get her a gift when we were on Sarvis."

"Oh, how thoughtful." Idda smiled. "She will join us with too much enthusiasm as per usual."

"Good. Once Father arrives, we have news."

Idda stiffened, cast her gaze between them, then hurried inside. "I will ensure he does not tarry."

Aaro ushered Leona into the foyer. Light flooded the house from all angles. Not a single wall was solid, except above the replicator. Well, with views like this, she could understand the appeal. The floor was gray stone, the chairs bigger and more colorful versions of those in her cabin. A fireplace occupied one corner, and a counter housed a replicator and rehydrator. No fridge, stove, kettle, or even a bowl of fruit added to the homey feel. The décor was quite clinical.

She worried her lip, now not sure if her new family would like her pathetic daisy painting. Aaro has assured her they would love it, but he might be trying to comfort her. As expected, he'd been beyond overprotective. Just yesterday, she'd handed over the dolls to a *lima kuu*—their term for a great teacher. In this case, Jarg taught engineering. For once, she was at peace leaving her dolls with him.

She still had to tell John how her circumstances had changed, but Aaro insisted she do so in person. Despite her being tired of traveling, what other choice did she have? Stay here on Etteria? Aaro was a sub-commander. And as his wife, she went where he did. Soph was also nervous about the future.

If Leona had a say, she'd set up a Cyb-Ent branch here. Etteria was far more central to the other planets. She grinned. Right, decision made. If John valued her, where she worked wouldn't matter. Of course, Soph would stay here too. And maybe Thea could move closer?

"Leona?"

She snapped her head up. "Sorry, my love, just lost in my thoughts."

He tapped a chair. "Come, sit, *thamani.*"

Like an obedient wife, she settled and rubbed her hands along the wider armrests. These chairs were overstuffed and far more comfortable. "Love the colors," she said, casting a glance at him.

"So would Soph. Ranh says her quarters are a clash of every color imaginable."

Leona laughed. "Yup, since she discovered the large replicator in the bowels of the *Valiant.*"

"May I offer you something to drink?" Idda swept a hand at the rehydrator. "Aaro instructed me to add your Earthian menu."

Leona beamed at Aaro for his thoughtfulness. "You raised an amazing man, Idda."

He sank into the chair beside her, then grabbed her hand and pinned it to his thigh. "Do not make my mother blush, *ensa*."

The woman waved, and with a bright smile, crossed to the rehydrator.

"I'd love a glass of orange juice, please," Leona called.

"I shall try it, too."

Leona twisted in her seat at the new arrival. Just like her mother, Taro was lithe and beautiful. Dark blue eyes matched Aaro's in shape, along with those slashing eyebrows. Her braid was almost to her knees.

"Do not get up," she said and hugged Leona, almost crushing her. "She is soft, like a dead *omeika*," Taro said.

Idda winced.

Taro was so like a teenager to state her mind. Leona chuckled. "And you're like solid rock. I'd rather hug a *kreso*." Which she assumed looked like an extinct buffalo.

Taro's eyes widened, then she cackled, slapping her leg just above the knee. "I like you, new sister."

"Good, or else I'll have to keep the present Aaro brought for you."

"A gift? Is this true, brother?" She bounced around Aaro who grudgingly headed to the shuttle with Taro peppering him with questions.

"I have never seen him this happy, Leona." Idda offered Leona a tall glass of orange juice.

She took the cold fruit juice and sipped it while staring at the front door. "He's stubborn, thinks he can bear the world's troubles, but he's also affectionate, kind, thoughtful, and now overbearing."

"I suspect he would be with a *damu* on the way."

Leona gasped. "Please pretend to be surprised when he tells you."

Idda chortled. "I shall play the perfectly delighted grandmother." She beamed. "That is your Earthian term, right? I must say, I love the sound and feel of *grand*mother."

That Idda had taken the time to add Galactic to her O.D.I., said much about Leona's welcome. "You shall be the best grandmother ever."

Idda sniffed again and dabbed at her eyes. "I am curious—"

"Idda, am I too late?" a man boomed, charging in through another door. Blue stained his shirt and yoga pants. He stomped his booted feet, splattering dirt everywhere. Before her stood an older version of Aaro, no less handsome with wrinkles at his eyes and mouth. He stilled and stared at her, his eyes narrowing. "I *am* too late. I only now told my males to cook the *kreso*."

"Zaro, come, meet Leona."

He hesitated, glancing at his clothing. So Leona leaped to her feet and hugged him.

He wrapped his arms around her and laughed. "Ah, a daughter not afraid of a little blood? I like that. Taro screams louder than a mating *kreso*—"

"Zaro," Idda gasped.

Leona stepped back while cupping her mouth to smother a grin. "I forgot you bleed blue." She shrugged.

"What color do you bleed?" Taro asked, skipping into the room.

Aaro trailed her, Leona's painting in hand. "As bold a red as our oceans."

"Truly?" Taro asked, then showed her mother the pink stone Aaro had found at Sarvis' visiting station.

"And this is for you, Mother. Leona paints these."

Idda twitched then raised her hands to accept the canvas. She gaped at it, turning it one way then another. "Paints?"

"It's a painting of a daisy—my father's favorite flower." Leona resisted the urge to wring her hands. Idda liked it, or she didn't. There was nothing Leona could do to convince her either way.

"It is stunning. What do I do with it?"

Burn it? Leona bit her lip.

"You hang it on a wall." Aaro took it from his mother and leaned it against the wall above the replicator.

"Yes, I see now." Idda hummed. "Oh, that *is* pretty."

"You painted this?" Zaro asked in a serious tone. "Such skills have been lost over time."

Leona nodded. "Human children start with these, igniting their creative minds."

Aaro drew her to his side. "And so will our...daughter."

Idda squealed, throwing her arms around Aaro then Leona. "You did not say... I assumed..."

"Trust you to guess, Mother," Aaro said before his father hugged him.

Since Idda had yet to release Leona, she waved Taro over and added her to the hug. Leona's tears threatened to spill at their jubilance. She had finally found her family.

GLOSSARY

Etterians worship one God, one Maker since the universes have only His fingerprint on all of it, a single golden thread through all of creation.

Tokens: an intergalactic form of currency

Kliks: predetermined length of distance.

Hatimaye – To bring an end (Hutt-ee-my-ee)

Etterian

Alodon (A-low-donn): who accidentally shot his balls off with his own blaster.

Teacher: lima (lee-ma)

Great teacher: lima kuu: (lee-ma koo)

Directions: semit (semm-it)

Lemon: giyua (gee-you-a)

Young one: damu (daa-moo)

Heart: ensa (enn-sa)

Heart of my heart: ensa ra ensa (enn-sa raa enn-sa)

Beloved: thamani (ta-mar-nee)

Little joy: minus susa (mee-nas soo-sa)

Little cat: minus cesu (mee-nas sess-oo)

Large: magnus (mag-nis)

Orgasm: fulfillment/deite asteri (see stars) / released (day-ta ass-tare-ree)

Starfighter: asteri peju (ass-tare-ree pear-joo)

Collection of glass vials: virak (vee-ruck)

Scum of the galaxies: xemi (ze-mee)

Hair up: malia pa (Mar-lee-a par)

Hair down: malia pado (Mar-lee-a par-dow)

Lysaran

Visitor: kashi (Kaa-shee)

God: Kaiha (Kigh-haa)

King: Kuna (Koo-na)

Orange fleshy fruit: Lemte (Lem-ta)

White flowers: Myameru (My-a-me-roo)

Precious: Delica (Dell-ee-ka)

Sweetheart: Sali (Saa-lee)

Arum Lily-type flower: D'nastu (D-nass-too)

Love Blossom: aroa loulu (A-row-a low-loo)

Maloidian

Title of respect: lommia (Lomm-ee-a)

Stubborn, lethal tree: tewaa (Tee-wah)

Tokauri/Kulai

Blade – Sulac (soo-lack)

Bone – Ukog (you-cog) - bone from some dumb animal, probably an ukog.

Braided – Gisul (gee-sool)

Father – Danno (dan-no)

Heart – Kassu (cass-soo)

Maker – Mugbu (Mug-boo)

Mother – Manno (man-no)

Sapphires – Buha (boo-ha)

Shit – Saho (sa-ho)

Star - stuon (stoo-on)

Stupid – Ungog (oon-gog)

Vessel/ship - sakay (sa-kay)

Pronunciations

Names

Aaro - Ah-row

Aldur - Al-durr

Alllero - A-le-row

Balllio – Bah-leee-oh

Bos - Boss

Bry-dar - Brigh-darr

Brynr - Brin-ner

Cales - Cale-es

Cento - Sen-tow

Citus - Sigh-tuss

Coldar - Coal-daar

Cria - Kree-ah

Danic - Dan-eek

Der - Durr

Diso - Dee-sow

Diyo - Die-oh

Eeezo – Eee-zoh

Eira - Eye-raa

Enyl - E-neel

Eriz - E-rizz

Garix - Ga-ricks

Gayn – Gain

Heelu – Hee-loo

Idda – Ee-dah

Iddan - Ee-dann

Idon - Eye-donn

Illan - Ee-lann

Jarg – Jar-g

Jazu – Jah-zoo

Jokta - Jock-tar

Kanzo - Can-zow

Keryr – Kerr-eer

Ksal - Ka-sell

Lurz - Lurr-z

Malo - Mail-oh

Matir - Mat-teer

Myan - My-ann

Myn-ras - Min-russ

Naio – Nay-oh

Nerx - Nurcks

Nuos - New-oss

Oyaz - Oh-yaz

Prex – Precks

Ranh - Rann

Ronin - Row-nin

Saan - Sarn

Sena - See-na

Siio – See-ooo

Sy'mar - Sigh-marr

Syna - Sigh-na

Tamra – Tum-rah

Taro - Tah-row

Tenu - Ten-oo

Trav - Trahv

Tinh - Tin

Vytus - Vie-tuss

Vodin - Vo-din

Ulriq - Yule-rick

Vorn - Vawn

Vyar - Vie-arr

Xan - Zan

Xeus – Zeus

Zaro - Zah-row

Ziot - Zye-ott

Places

Argaxx – Are-jax

Crustiiu – Criss-tee-oo

Dyuqa - Dee-you-ka

Etteria – E-tare-rea

Galaza – Gah-Lar-Zah

Gikaet – Gee-ka-ett

Iphara = Ee-far-ra

Kulai – koo-ligh

Lysara – Liss-saa-ra

Mascroba – Mus-crow-ba

Sarvis – Sarr-viss

Sosu – Sow-soo

Tokauri – Too-cow-ree

Yithia – Yith-ee-a

Battleships

Chikara – Chee-kar-a - Force

Gladio – Glad-ee-oh - Sword

Kushin – Cush-shin - To Pierce

Surata – Soo-ra-tah – Beginning

Usaha – Oo-saa-hah - Endeavor

Shuttles

Celeeri – See-lee-ree - swift

    Denessi – Denn-ess-ee - sodge

    Eshima – Ee-shee-ma - respect

    Kevol – Kev-oll - agony

    Kuta – Koo-tah - modular shuttle.

    Liri-ny – Lee-ree-nye – freedom

    Misaia – Miss-aye-a - memory

    Sasay – Sass-ay - whispers

    Yakin – Yuck-kin - belief

Creatures

Asnu – Ass-Noo – buffalo/donkey

    Eiltur – Ale-turr

    Gracc – Grrr-ack

    Ilag – Ee-Lug– leggy slugs that feast on sol.

    Kreso – Kreh-soo

    Omeika – Oh-may-ka

    Pagsu – Pug-Soo - cocksuckers

    Reshy – Resh-Ee - huge, like the size of a *kuta* shuttle, with massive jaws and rows of sharp teeth.

    Sogair – Sow-gare

    Wilanegy – Will-anna-jee

About the Author

Sevannah Storm is a fiction writer who immerses herself in fantastical worlds both magical and science fiction. She has a flare for the creative, having studied art and interior architecture, and spends her time drawing, oil painting, and writing. An avid reader from an early age, Sevannah finds her inspiration from various sources: games, novels, music, and the land of make-believe. The unique versus the practical has brought on numerous debates.

In her spare time, she does Pilates and rereads novels that snatch her breath away. Having embraced the social media world, you can find her on most platforms.

Her home is a land south of Wakanda, where animals roam free. Born in Zimbabwe, she grew up in South Africa. The crisp blue skies with cotton-candy sunsets expand her heart and soul, encapsulating a sense of freedom.

Words she lives by: "Know your pothole and dodge it. Don't work in a pencil factory if you're a vampire."

Sevannah loves to hear from her readers. You can find and connect with her at the links below.

Website/Newsletter:

https://www.sevannahstorm.com/

Facebook:

https://www.facebook.com/sevannah.storm

Instagram:

https://www.instagram.com/sevannah.storm/

Twitter:

https://twitter.com/sevannah_storm

Thank you for taking the time to read Lust Forged. If you enjoyed the story, please tell your friends and leave a review. Reviews support authors and ensure they continue to bring readers books to love and enjoy.

SOUL FORGED

THE GIFTING SERIES #1

Know-it-all Oriana agreed to travel with aliens who need women. But she didn't agree to abduction, life/death battles, and escaping with a bossy, arrogant man. She was sabotaged, attacked, and kidnapped, but she is far from beaten. Forced to participate in an alien battle arena with no promise of freedom, she has to forget the loss of her family and focus on surviving.

Enyl has given up hope. His people are dying due to a genetic modification gone awry. Darkness is consuming his warriors, and his world, as he knows it, will end. His father, the king, has rolled out a plan to save them all. But Enyl doubts a solution will be found in time.

And when a compatible female is found...and lost, he must rescue her, a human female capable of surviving despite all odds. However, freeing Oriana serves to anger the aliens holding her captive. Ensuring she is cared for—as per Etterian protocol—he is stunned by the strong connection between the two of them. Such a bond was only experienced between Etterian mates.

Is she his salvation or is that wishful thinking on his part?

Read it here:

https://books2read.com/u/mlAWr9

FATE FORGED

THE GIFTING SERIES #2

Jacqueline (Jack) Dunois struggles to find a man not intimidated by her career as a law enforcement instructor, especially in the small town she calls home. She would sacrifice a kidney to find someone who would make her ovaries clap and didn't live with his mother. Then she meets a supreme commander from another world who thinks the stars in the galaxies shine in her eyes... What's not to love about that?

Supreme Commander Ulriq doesn't believe in love, an archaic term for a volatile and untrustworthy emotion that Etterians were no longer subjected to. Until he meets Jack who triggers the *Ethera*, the soulmate force that irrevocably changes a male when he finds his ideal female. At that moment, his world, his focus, his very loyalty shifts. But when she is taken from him, it is too much to bear. Under the influence of the *Ethera*, he launches a rescue. He'll start a war and kill anyone who dares stop him, just to have her back in his arms.

Read it here:

https://books2read.com/u/bMY09v

SUN FORGED

The Gifting Series #3

Meeting a drop-dead gorgeous man, who falls onto a knee the first time they meet, sounded too good to be true for Ava. Of course, with her luck, he had to be an alien. Thrust into an unknown alien world, meeting weird and scary creatures, and fearing for her life, Ava tries to survive as best as a hairstylist can.

Kanzo never expected to find a life mate, a *Dar Eth*. Since he was young, he was taught that pairings were rare with fewer females born. The statistics on finding his *Dar Eth* would be slim to none. Instead of dreaming and longing for companionship, he focused on being the best male possible, to end his life on a battlefield with honor. But when he experiences the *Ethera*—the life mate force, and is blessed with his female, he isn't prepared for the level of pain, pleasure, and need she invokes within him.

Unable to save her as she's teleported from him, the dark consuming pain in his chest drives him into a blinding rage. With no idea who stole her or where to begin the search, he will scour the known universe to find her, to hold the female he never wanted.

Read it here:

https://books2read.com/u/3n5vaB

WAR FORGED

Being kidnapped by aliens does not sit well with Quinlan. Not only would her seven guardians give her hell if she doesn't attempt some sort of escape, but she refuses to be at anybody's mercy. With her practiced military skills, the help of an underground lounge singer and a personal assistant, she takes over the alien slave ship. Not knowing how to fly the damn thing, she sends a distress signal. ...The rescue comes swiftly in the form of a bronzed man with exquisite ice-blue eyes. Leaving her to ask the true question: has she just given up her newfound freedom for a gorgeous man who seems determined to have her for eternity?

As Elite Supreme Commander of the Etterian Forces, Xan answers a distress call in Earth English. That is all he did. The female who captured the slave ship shows remarkable skill, making her a warrior in her own right. Said skills should be respected and honored. Except she is his *Dar Eth*, calling forth the *Ethera*—the soulmate bond. How can he protect his female when she can do so herself? What can she possibly need from him? What can he offer a female, not Etterian but human? Not that he can think clearly in her presence when she scents so good and makes him want to kiss all of her.

Maker help him.

Read it here:

https://books2read.com/u/bz1QGD

STAR FORGED

The Gifting Series #5

Macy is feeling a little left out, as usual. Who would have thought moving from one planet to another wouldn't change that loneliness? She is never alone these days since Etterians guard human women with an urgency she understands. But the lack of companionship is like a dark aching abyss inside her chest. On some days, it threatens to implode, and Macy Mitchell would cease to exist. Looming is her impending meeting with King Xeus of Etteria. How is she supposed to keep her shit together when presented to royalty? Not after she ran from the last king she met.

For Xeus, the void expands daily. Duty, honor, concern for his dying people, and endless loneliness fill his life. Having decided to search for pairings among other worlds, he is pleased his son found his soulmate among human women. It doesn't mean that Xeus's loneliness and longing haven't ended until he stumbles upon a crying female. Meaning only to soothe, he is spellbound when her presence brings him peace. Unable to resist, he forms an attachment to a female he can never have

Read it here:

https://books2read.com/u/3nXgp5

SHADOW FORGED

THE GIFTING SERIES #6

Forty-year-old Caroline is too old to start dating and too bored with her vibrator, but what other choices does she have. On the day she burns her shirt and breaks a fingernail, she meets Etterian warriors. As part of her job at E.S.A. (Earth Space Association,) she must 'entertain' the hot-as-apple-pie Chief Engineer she suspects isn't who he claims to be.

Operations Commander Malo, Head of Espionage, must act as an engineer and ambassador, hoping to invite human females to visit Etteria and save his dying race. From Princess Oriana, he has strict instructions to distrust humans. What he finds he cannot trust are his emotions and his body whenever in the presence of the human ambassador, Caroline. She does not believe in soulmates or in a forever with him. Convincing her to choose him is the greatest task ever set before him, one he cannot afford to fail.

Until she is stolen from him. He calls in favors, utilizes all his resources to find her. And *when* he does, he is never letting her off his battleship...or his bed.

Read it here:

https://books2read.com/u/bPNd8j

EARTH FORGED

THE GIFTING SERIES #7

Guilt hounds Izzy, who caused her sister's injury and subsequent blindness. But no matter how she cares for Simone or what she sacrifices, it doesn't ease the ache in her chest. With Simone and naive Caro, her best friend, Izzy's role as protector is fully realized. The cost? Hiding behind quirkiness, pseudo-joy, and giving up her hopes and dreams. What she needs is a knight in any armor. After all, beggars can't be fussy. She has no idea that armor, in her case, means black military and that a knight could come in any color, specifically bronze.

Oyaz wants to find his life force, his soulmate, and he'd like her to be human. Earth's females are soft, amusing, passionate, and their scents rival a garden of hahyt blossoms. His task is to guard their planet that promises so many salvations for his males. It's a duty he's pleased to perform, one he would die for. When Operations Commander Malo orders Oyaz to retrieve a human female, he's eager to oblige. That it would lead to his salvation is something he couldn't anticipate. What he hadn't planned for is an ambush that costs him more than his memory, the loss of his soulmate.

Now what? Nothing in their training prepared him for this.

And yet, despite not remembering kneeling for Izzy, he longs to claim her with every inch of his soul.

Read it here:

https://books2read.com/u/31V82D

www.ingramcontent.com/pod-product-compliance
Lightning Source LLC
Chambersburg PA
CBHW072202130726
47910CB00011B/1783